Miss Diagnosis

— A Novel —

Derek Dubois

filament
press

Copyright © 2022 by Derek Dubois

Published by Filament Press

Printed in the United States of America

ISBN 978-1-67800-550-4

MISS DIAGNOSIS is dedicated to Kathleen and Max, who always love a good story.

Prologue

The streetlamp had been flickering all night. Lien Chu was zoning out, nearly hypnotized by its staccato on–off, on–off Morse code patterning. She smiled, imagining it was as if the light were sending her a cryptic message: *Get out. Get out now!*

It had been nearly two hours already. She was waiting. Waiting, just as she was asked. But she didn't have much patience left. Lien had given up several nights a semester to sit in dark basement laboratories and cold lots and to deal with sketchy unnamed men. Very few instructions had gone along with the job. An address. A time. God knows why they needed her this late at night, in this part of town. All Lien knew was that she was waiting for the white van.

The radio was on, but all NPR was consumed with was news about a disgraced movie mogul who was also, apparently, a violent sexual predator. The way an entire industry seemed to know about his terrible crimes and yet chose to stay quiet for so long—it was something out of a cheap conspiracy thriller, the kind of books her friend Kate loved to read. Pundits on the radio were discussing the economics of consent and how influential people in privileged positions abuse their status and get away with it.

Lien wondered if this job with all its hush-hush secrecy held a deeper story. At first, it seemed completely normal that her own prestigious hospital lab—where she was now conducting her clinicals as a med student—would require 24/7 support. But the stipends for this work weren't coming from St. Christopher's. There was no benefit plan. No 401(k). It was all cash under the table, and she likely wouldn't be able to list this experience on her résumé. The radio crackled with static. Maybe this was some shit that would one day inspire an altogether different news story? She chuckled at the thought. *No way anything sinister could be this boring.*

Thinking more about what she was hearing on the radio, Lien concluded that she was lucky. Nothing grossly sexual had ever happened to her. No sad stories of abuse. The men with whom she interacted on these trips barely acknowledged her existence. They had one job, same as she. She drove. They loaded and unloaded.

In fact, men were not lining up like she imagined they would when she left for college. Nothing beyond the occasional overzealous frat guy at the bar on karaoke Fridays. Lien knew she was attractive. Okay, if she was honest with herself, maybe she was a little short and her lower front tooth sat a bit crooked, but in the aggregate (she loved that phrase, *in the aggregate*), Lien understood that she had desirable qualities. She should be in demand. But she was bookish, and coupled with this job, its weird secrecy, the late hours, everything hung on her like a bad odor. She needed to be more like her friends. More like Kate. She needed to be open to experience and fun. At least there was Sean Carraway. He was brilliant and cocky and beautiful. But he was engaged. That had stopped her, at first.

The argument on the radio was escalating. The pundits started to discuss the male gaze. Lien knew the penetrating fix of the male gaze. The way it could seize you in your tracks.

When you would start to hear your own mouth forming words you never thought possible, going along, acquiescing, just to avoid disappointment and rejection. Sean looked at her that way more and more lately, but with him it didn't feel gross, even if he was meant to be off-limits. Like this special assignment, the secrecy of his gaze infused her with power.

She worked hard to be a woman of substance, dimensional, worthy. As an undergrad, she double majored in biology and chemistry. Taught herself to invest money in the market, already having more in savings than her parents—Taiwanese immigrants—had made in their lifetimes. She read a new book each week, alternating between literature and nonfiction. Right now, she was halfway through *Mrs. Dalloway*. Short, but a difficult slog, as evidenced by the thin layer of dust settling on the book's cover. She awoke at five every morning to go to the gym. Her dream was bigger, bordering on the cliché, like the motivational poster of a tabby cat dangling from a branch framed on the wall above her desk. *HANG IN THERE.* But, in truth, she really did feel that she had the power to change the world. She just needed the right circumstances, the right opportunities. Only 34 percent of her graduating class had been female, and when she had been offered the internship by Dr. Louis Fenton—a man widely recognized as a titan in the field—in his research facility housed within St. Christopher's Hospital, she jumped.

So, what was she doing here? And where was this goddamn van?

Once it was strange being asked to coordinate a specimen transfer in the middle of the night. None of the other lab interns were given these tasks. She'd been accepted into the internship based on her grades and having passed a grueling eight-hour interview with Fenton and his team. Once she started, Lien was not allowed to discuss the details of her work with anyone else, including her friends. She honored it, no matter how often they asked. And ask, they did. That made it feel special. She was important. But it was clear this was off the books. It felt more akin to a drug deal, Lien supposed, though the closest experience she had on that front was two puffs off an older cousin's joint in a Baltimore cemetery at fourteen. This was the fourth mission of this sort in few months she'd been asked to run. They hadn't made her wait this long before.

She kept thinking about how all of this started. No one was to know about this work. That much had been made clear when Fenton pushed the eighteen-page NDA toward her over the desk. She'd grabbed for that ballpoint pen without hesitation. In many ways, it made sense. Fenton's lab trafficked in highly sensitive biological research, often funded by top tiers of government. Lien supposed it was only natural to take precautions to avoid corporate espionage and the risks of IP theft. She knew her role. She was a mushroom, fed shit and kept in the dark. That was okay, especially since Fenton took a shine to her. It made Lien feel like the only person who mattered. It wasn't sexual. It was power. It was intellect. It was the possibility of becoming someone who mattered by having proximity to someone who already did.

Getting here was an exercise in inefficiency. The GPS had been preprogrammed when it was handed over. She proceeded to follow its circuitous route through the blue-collar streets of the North Shore. The ride radiated away from St. Christopher's. Businesses became apartments, which became multistory tenements, which became abandoned factories, which finally gave way to the urban decay of pockmarked concrete and graffiti. All of it dissolving from one tableau to the next, down the ladder rungs of the American class system, until she hit bottom and there was nowhere left to go.

This place was hell. And she was freezing.

Lien was in the parking lot of an old brick textile mill where she'd sat parked for the past few hours. Tired of the news, she scanned the dial but there was absolutely nothing on. She found a station playing a Beatles marathon and listened to two-thirds of "A Hard Day's Night" before finally slamming the power button in frustration. Tonight, she prefered to marinate in smooth, angry silence.

Fuck this.

Nearing two-thirty in the morning, two hours after the agreed-upon pickup time, Lien turned the key in the ignition and was about to shift the car into drive. It was then that long amber cones of light swept around the side of the mill, lengthening the broken windows and empty doorways of its brick face into the roving shadows of a monstrous creature.

Lien stepped out of the car and held up her hand in a polite wave as if there were a crowd surrounding her. She didn't often think of Halloween since the days of her childhood but being outside, at night, in crisp October air always took her back. Trick-or-treating from house to house and the giddy glee of pretending to be someone else under the obfuscation of a rubber mask.

As the vehicle neared, it became clear that it was the white van she'd been waiting for. A sleek, polished Ford Econoline with no signage of any kind. It pulled up alongside her rusted Jeep. Fenton said she would be reimbursed for mileage, but that she had to use her own car for these trips, and if she was stopped by anyone, there was a phone number to call. "Just shut up and dial" were the only instructions.

A man in gray overalls and a blue Red Sox cap hopped out of the driver's seat. He was young, skinny, with the hint of a tattoo creeping up the side of his neck from beneath the collar of his shirt. He looked to Lien like he could have been an extra in *Law & Order*, the kind of guy who would find a body on his delivery route and wind up questioned by Detective Lennie Briscoe, complaining the entire time that he was falling behind on his work while the corpse under the sheet was bagged just a few feet away.

"You from the lab?" he asked. His voice was alert and crisp, just like the night air. He seemed skittish.

"Yeah," she said, her voice cracking as she cleared her throat. "You have the delivery?"

The man nodded as he went to the back of the van and yanked open the doors.

"You do a lot of nighttime drop-offs in the middle of abandoned mill parking lots?" she asked with a painted-on smile, trying to sound pleasant.

"You're going to want to open your trunk."

Lien stood there for a moment, the words hanging in the air and only slowly falling into place. Even with this being the fourth time, she still trembled out here alone. After a brief paralysis, she hopped to it. The sticker in her jeep's rear window that read *Silly Boys, Jeeps Are for Girls* disappeared as the back door peeled up.

The delivery man got behind her. Laid across his arms was an oblong load wrapped in a black nylon bag; the extra-strength zippers cinched closed with a small padlock.

Lien dove out of his way, but he just stood there, groaning under the weight of its heft, looking at her with baleful eyes. Only then did she realize—with some degree of embarrassment—that she still needed to clear the junk that littered the back of the SUV. She clambered in and tossed the stuff haphazardly into the back seat: the pants she had needed to return for two weeks, the slippers she kept forgetting to send to her father, the bag of old clothes meant for Goodwill. It all went sailing in pinwheels of colored fabrics. She backed out of the car, having finally cleared enough room. The nameless man carefully laid the bag into the back of her truck.

"What's in there?" Lien asked.

It was the first time in four deliveries that she had gotten up the courage to ask. In the past, she had spoken only when asked a question and kept her curiosity tamped down.

But the skinny, tattooed man in the blue Sox cap didn't say a word. He only nodded and climbed back into his van. He started the engine, then rolled down the passenger window.

"Do yourself a favor and keep your nose out of this. Trust me. The sedative doesn't last long. You should get a move on."

He rolled up the window while gunning the gas and peeled off into the night. A trail of dust kicked up by the van's tires on the dirty roads hung in the night air. It made a cloud, stained blood red in the glow of the van's taillights.

The sound of the van died away leaving her in eerie silence. Lien stood in place in the middle of the lot. It was nearly three in the morning. The waning moon cast everything in a pale-blue pallor. She debated whether to peek into the black bag and decided against it. Justin would be waiting for her back at the lab.

Yes, she would play by Fenton's rules. For now. Her magnificent future depended on it.

Chapter One
BEFORE THE STORM

Stumbling up the concrete stairs of the East Newton train station, Kate White emerged into the slate-gray morning light of South Boston. *Just three more blocks, dammit.* Hung over and head raging, she wanted to puke, even though she hadn't touched a drop of alcohol in three days. That feeling, utterly familiar, was just the antidepressants on an empty stomach. She shoved wordlessly through throngs of commuters, eyes down, the collar of her jacket chafing at the nape of her neck, her shoulders burning from the pull of her book bag.

Can't be late. Not again.

The wind picked up, carrying the faint smell of decaying leaves. It made the fine hairs on her arm stand on end. But she focused only on closing the distance to St. Christopher's Hospital. Dr. Vivian Lucas started rounds at eight in the morning. The minute hand on her watch—a gift from her mother for graduating pre-med—was creeping dangerously close to true north.

She bolted down the Chalkstone Avenue sidewalk, her footfalls a small, urgent drumbeat. She imagined Dr. Lucas calling out her name among her classmates, finding her unexpectedly absent. *The final straw? Expulsion?* She could picture it now: Dr. Lucas talking about her to the broader group of walleyed med students. Something like, "If you want to watch someone squander away a good thing, Kate White's your gal. Just ask anybody. They should sell tickets to that show."

The sky had darkened considerably. Thunderheads, bruised with purple streaks and swollen with rain, perched ready to flood the city. Her side cramped, and she clamped a hand over the pain. The night before, after showering, she'd taken a long look at her body in the bathroom mirror. She was quite thin. Her sunken skin pulled tautly over her ribs, replacing the soft curvature of femininity into the sharp, angular grille of a machine. Was it the pills? The booze? Stress? She'd been here before, four years ago, when all that shit had gone down in Boston at her aunt's condo. Then all over again when her dad died. Kate never worked out beyond lifting a large glass of cheap wine after a long day. Last night, she cried over her body for the first time in a long time. Then she felt stupid. She always wished she was in better shape. She wished for a lot of things.

It was difficult, coming back after a week off. Kate had emailed all her professors, using the subject line *"mental health time."* She even put the phrase in quotes. It was as if even she couldn't take herself seriously. A lot was piling on at once: the first anniversary of her father's death, midterm exams, her wedding. And while she did spend time studying, she had also found herself at the movies or sitting on the patio of Arturo's Bar, alone, until she felt she could face seeing Sean again.

The city glistened that queer, yellow pall that signaled an impending storm. Across the river, in the heart of Downtown, a seemingly endless line of cars crept in slow traffic. Horns blared. Pedestrians charged down the sidewalks, their earphones isolating them from any social interaction. It was fifteen after eight when she finally reached the side entrance of the hospital.

St. Christopher's had stood for much of Boston's history. Stamped into a keystone in the arch above the door was a date: *1817*. The hospital had expanded over time, addition by addition, wing by wing, into a sprawling campus of modern technical excellence. How she got in was still a bit of a mystery to her. Sweat beaded on her forehead, which she wiped away while snagging the ID card from her bag. Med students were issued new ones at the start of each year. She hated its picture: that wooden smile, those flyaway tufts of hair. The red LED flipped to green, and the door unlocked. Overhead, a gust of wind shook ancient trees, some of which had been standing firmly in place since before that old date above the door had been carved into stone.

Today, like every day, there was only one goal: make it through without any unpleasant Lucas run ins. The heavy door closed, sweeping her into the dark maw of the hospital as the first plump drops of rain released from the sky.

★★★★★

Kate joined her cohort as they left the rendezvous by the nurses' station. It didn't appear that anyone took notice as she slunk her way into the group, turning five into six. She hid in the back, sighing in relief.

It had been too late of a night. Too much yelling. Her throat was still sore, her voice raspy. And then there was the mechanical piston firing relentlessly into the backs of her eyes. Sean had left for work early in the morning without a kiss goodbye. Normally, he woke Kate at six-fifteen every morning, so she never set her alarm. But when she had awoken today to what she had initially assumed to be the unusually early sound of a garbage truck lifting bins into its bay, she clocked the time as ten past seven and nearly sprained an ankle falling out of bed. Why couldn't things ever go her way? She wondered. It was the universe that was against her.

Dr. Vivian Lucas led the pack from the front. A small-framed woman, five feet two at most. She walked briskly even with her slight limp, students in tow. The experienced engine pulling a fleet of shiny, new railcars.

Kate heard all about Lucas's accident on her first day of clinicals. As Lucas told it, she was eight years old, pedaling her new bicycle in the street outside of her house when her uncle—blitzed out of his mind on a case of Schlitz—drove his '52 DeSoto smack into her. She went flying, just missing whacking her head on the corner of the curb and woke up at St. Christopher's six hours later, her right leg fractured in three different places. It was her uncle who brought her in, downing another beer along the way, swerving all over the road, busted-up bicycle hanging out of the trunk. Lucas told this anecdote to all her new students. She said it was when she knew she wanted to work in medicine. Kate thought it reeked of a workshopped, reheated story. Probably now more fiction than truth. All the same, it made Kate feel inadequate. Kate didn't have a story of her own. No sort of literary epiphany for why she was here right now going through torturous med school studies.

Dr. Lucas led the six interns to an array of patient beds in the south wing of the ICU. Each bed was roped off with a privacy curtain. The sound of mechanized breathing and the beeping of monitors filled the air. Four months in, and it all still sounded as if she were cruising along on the bridge of a starship in some science fiction movie. More and more, the image in her mind when people asked about what she did came to be that of a coin balanced on its edge, one side life, the other death, spinning in some cosmic visual symbol.

The curtain around bed four peeled open, squealing along its metal track. An old man lay before them, maybe unconscious, maybe just asleep. His standard-issue hospital gown fell across knobby knees. His skin was a pale, vanilla soft serve. The old man's body was entirely motionless. Cables ran in all directions like the cover from some Michael Crichton pulp fantasy found in the bottom drawer of her father's old desk.

But there was something different about him. Kate glanced quickly at his slacken face and jaundiced skin and darted away. She still had so much trouble observing patients, especially when they weren't returning her gaze. It was like spying on them at their most vulnerable. It creeped her out. Thick-lensed glasses sat cockeyed across the bridge of the old man's nose, pushed askew from the lump of pillow behind his head. Now she knew just what was needling her. Kate couldn't factor how, in this hell of chaos and antiseptic, he appeared so serene.

The students crowded around the bed in a horseshoe, like small children at story time. Crisscross applesauce. Giddy nervousness was the default expression for all first-year med students in clinical practice. Each was adorned in matching white lab coats. Kate had slipped into hers, which she snagged along with her notebook and stethoscope from the staff locker room, as the group crested up the back stairs to the ICU, chugging air through tired lungs from busting her ass to make it on time.

Through the walls of the hospital, Kate could hear the thunder growing closer, growling like a subwoofer cranked up a bit too loud in the next room. If they had been anywhere near a window, she'd be counting the seconds between lightning strikes and thunder, trying to determine if the storm was moving closer or farther away. *One Mississippi, two Mississippi, three Mississippi...*

This ritual of med students making patient rounds together was performed every day of the week. The students were always visiting new departments and meeting various members of the clinical staff. The tours usually resulted in some test of sorts. Kate watched Lucas's wandering glare from her periphery, specifically attempting to avoid eye contact. Her nails dug into her palms, almost drawing blood. Kate witnessed the quick exchange of sympathetic glances between Daniel Parks and Lien Chu. Lien looked particularly haggard today. She sometimes ran off on these crazy missions at night for Davol Laboratory and couldn't ever talk about it. Daniel and Lien were the only other people in this cohort who Kate considered friends.

Kate was simultaneously afraid of Dr. Lucas and fascinated by her. She supposed it was like the way she loved scary stories. What was it that Jung had talked about? *Enantiodromia*? The pleasure of opposing forces. Even Kate knew the description of a tough-as-nails mentor was a cliché. Anytime she told a story that featured Lucas, she felt as if she were half remembering a forgotten fairy tale, casting herself as the put-upon damsel squaring off against a wicked witch. A short but fearsome woman born of scarves, thick-rimmed glasses, and an overpowering cloud of Jean Naté body splash.

The doctor's piercing, brown eyes, set deep above her knife-sharp cheekbones, lit on Kate. "Kate," she said, "I'd like you to please change the patient's drip."

Hearing her name spoken in Lucas's voice shook her. She felt the heat from the collective gazes of the other students and wished she could vaporize like steam.

"S-sure. Right now?" Kate stammered.

"Yes, Kate. Is there a problem?"

"No," she said. "No problem. It's just-"

Lucas had a reputation—the students had been warned—for riding one in every group. Even Dr. Lucas admitted as much on the first day, citing a peer-reviewed study commissioned by the AAMC that found something like 42 percent of med students never graduate. "Why not weed out the chaff early?" Lucas had said. "It's Darwinian, really."

For a while now, Kate had suspected that she was likely that sacrificial lamb.

Lucas eyed her intensely. "What's wrong, Kate? Not enough *mental health time*?" The words purred from Lucas's mouth to where Kate could hear the quotation marks from her email's subject line.

"No. I'm good," Kate assured her.

Dr. Lucas scanned the faces of her students. First Zach Saban, then Kieran McGlynnis, Greg Sugarman, Daniel Parks, Lien Chu, and back to Kate White. All of them kept their mouths tightly shut and their eyes vigilant. No one wanted to trade places with Kate at this moment.

"Let me ask you something, Kate." Lucas was projecting at a pitch. The others listened reverentially. "I assume you intend to be a doctor someday, correct?"

Kate nodded, blushing to the roots. She knew this was some sort of baited trap. She felt microscopic, even standing four inches taller than Dr. Lucas.

Dr. Lucas leaned closer until Kate could smell the doctor's warm breath. Kate trembled, her mouth and throat like wool.

The doctor glowered, "Grow some balls and act like one."

Kate wanted nothing more than to just run away. Through the double doors of the ICU, down the three flights of stairs, across the emergency room and out the gates by admissions. Down the walkway to Chalkstone Avenue, out of this life forever. Maybe she'd get lucky and be squashed by an ambulance. One quick *splat!* Out of her misery.

"Okay, everybody! Give Kate some space." Lucas shepherded the group over to the next patient's bed.

Turning back to address Kate one-on-one, Lucas softened considerably and spoke in a gentler tone. It was remarkable the way she could manage herself. "Just relax,"

Lucas cooed. "Relax. Breathe. Remember your training."
Opposing forces.

And suddenly, there was a shift, almost imperceptible.
But it couldn't be, Kate thought. Did she just register
encouragement?

"I've got this," Kate whispered.

Kate's hair fluttered as the privacy curtain closed. There
was a feeling of antigravity in the depth of her guts, like cresting
the hill in a roller coaster. Horror mixed with intense
anticipation. For a moment, she stood motionless, blinking
repeatedly, and adjusted to the shallow, claustrophobic moat of
space around the old man's bed. She spun around, taking in her
surroundings. Beside her was a steel tray, already prepped with
the tools needed for an IV changeover. It was a common
enough task, typically performed by a member of the nursing
staff. Still, it was regular practice for med students to acclimate
themselves to basic techniques before transitioning to
residency. Lucas, especially, expected nothing less than
perfection in her students regarding execution.

Kate inhaled sharply. She caught the faint aroma of Old
Spice aftershave, the kind from the white, buoy-shaped bottle.
It was her father's scent, and when she turned to the old man,
for a split second, that was what she saw: her father, lying there
in that sad hospital bed. Then her father disappeared. A single,
spliced frame in a film reel. It knocked the wind from her.

What the hell is happening to me?

She closed her eyes, thought of her father. A time when
she was still so very young, learning how to walk. His bear paw
of a hand wrapped around her own. The sun warm and radiant
on her face. The sharp blades of dew-stained grass prickling her
bare feet. "Good girl," he would whisper. "You've got this."
And then he would let her go, yet she still felt cradled.

The memory was almost warm to the touch. Kate
smiled, banishing any thoughts of surrender, and channeling all

the times she had practiced sticking grapefruits with needles. The training came rushing back: *Move the roller clamp about three centimeters below the drip chamber and close the clamp. Remove the protective cover on the IV solution port and keep it sterile. Remove the protective cover on the IV tubing spike...*

She grabbed for a long strip of rubber from the steel tray and tied off a tourniquet around the patient's bony arm. She forced herself to look, studied the craggy lines of his face like a map. His eyes, even closed, bulged in their sockets. Her movements were steady, compassionate. "You're going to feel just a small pinch," she said. "It'll be over before you know it."

No response.

She swabbed the crook of his arm with a cotton ball doused in alcohol, then grabbed for a .22-gauge needle, sealed like a new toothbrush, and peeled it open. Her fingers traced the arm, looking for the median cubital vein. She slapped the skin lightly. Since he was unconscious, she would have to ball his hand into a fist herself.

The rhythm of her breathing quickened. Her heart pounded fiercely, like an oil derrick in her rib cage, driving with enough force to crash through layers of earth and shale. The needle sank into the soft flesh of his left arm. Kate pushed against his capillaceous skin. Her wretch was automatic. She hoped above all else that he wouldn't awaken right at this moment and see her making that face of disgust while penetrating him. The old man didn't stir.

"Sorry," she whispered, realizing she had missed and would have to stick him all over again. Her fingers pulled the needle back. She went again. The needle plunged through his skin a second time. She shuddered a second time. She missed a second time.

"Gah." She was talking to herself again.

Blood pooled in the two puncture wounds she had left, but it coagulated rather quickly. Frankly, she was surprised there wasn't more of it. She closed her eyes, focused, and went back for the third attempt. If she missed this time, she'd have to give up and get Dr. Lucas or risk turning his arm into that of an addict's, full of track marks. Luckily, the needle slipped into place like a hot wire through butter.

"Yes!" she exclaimed.

She yanked the line out of the needle, and the blood came dribbling out of him in a stream of ruby red. Swaying, her hands flew backward to steady herself but knocked the tray of metal tools to the floor in a clatter, smearing his blood on her coat.

She connected his IV line as the curtain pulled open again. Dr. Lucas led the other five students back in. Kate was still picking up the tools from the floor and placing them back on the tray, damming a river of euphoria that was about to burst through her chest. She did it.

"How'd it go?" Dr. Lucas asked.

Kate ran the back of her tired hand over her forehead to wipe away the sweat. As she did, she felt the smear of the old man's blood run a brushstroke of scarlet over her skin. But still, in her victory, she smiled.

Lucas leaned in close to the old man. A solemn look washed over her, and she craned her neck to look up at Kate. Her eyes furrowed. "What'd you do, Kate?" she asked with concern.

"What do you mean? I changed his line. Just like you instructed."

"He's *dead*, Kate!" Lucas's eyes widened accusatorily.

Kate stammered, but no words came out. Hot panic crept into her face, and she felt her cheeks blooming crimson. Beads of sweat quickly gathered around her hairline. Her armpits moistened. Her stomach dropped out from her body, splattering to the floor in free fall.

Kate's eyes swept the room for the looks on the faces of her few friends. It was clear that the others—even Daniel and Lien, with their wide, doe eyes—were reading the gravity of the situation and backing up a few steps. It had suddenly become the single worst moment of Kate's life: deadly serious and deliriously confounding, and yet, somehow, it was dragging out forever in slow motion. Their collective gazes cast down on her. She fell against the wall.

Suddenly, Dr. Lucas broke into hysterical, cackling laughter. It pierced the room. All six medical students were reduced to kindergartners asked to solve complex differential equations. In Latin, to boot. Everyone remained still while Lucas nearly doubled over, tears forming in the creases of her eyes.

"Oh, Kate, I'm just fucking with you!" Lucas was trying to catch her breath. The damn woman was *gleeful*.

"Y-you mean he's *not* dead?" Kate stammered, unable to move, fear fixing her firmly in place.

Lucas lifted the old man's right arm and let it drop back to the bed, where it landed with a single, jaunty bounce. Her stethoscope hung around her neck, positioned like a sleeping serpent.

"Oh, he's dead all right," she said. "As a doornail. But it wasn't your fault, Kate. He died thirty minutes ago. Heart failure. And lucky for him, if you ask me, judging by how you handled that IV setup."

With the end of her pen, Lucas tapped the computer monitor beside the bed, which indicated the patient's lack of vitals. "Everyone," she called to the group of assembled students, "where Kate failed today was at the level of the diagnosis."

Kate was spiraling. Lucas wouldn't abate.

"The first—and most important—thing we can do for our patients," Lucas said, "is to correctly assess what the problem is. If I was to diagnose Kate's problem, it's that she failed to recognize that the condition to which this patient had ultimately succumbed was death itself."

Kate's vision went wild, telescoping in and out like that Hitchcock camera effect from *Vertigo*. Her pupils dilated until the lights became blinding, sending sharp, stabbing pain into the deepest reaches of her skull. It was only finally dawning on Kate that she, in fact, hadn't killed anyone today.

Dr. Lucas turned from lecturing the group and addressed Kate directly. But she did not lower her voice. This show was for all. "How you made it this far without learning to check the vitals first, I'll never know!" she exclaimed.

Kate's knees buckled. She slid down the wall to the floor, head in her trembling hands, her bloodied white coat fanning out beneath her. Lucas cut through the group of students, parting them down the middle like some biblical giant.

"Today's lesson," Lucas continued, "is that medicine requires a lot of you. *Everything*, really. And it starts with the application of common sense." This last line was delivered to Kate directly, like an uppercut to the chin. "Lesson number two, a bonus: you better get mighty used to seeing death if you want to work in a place like this."

And then Lucas left. With each limping step, the crash of a gunshot. Kate glanced up at the other students. Greg was giggling strangely, but it was clear, looking across each of them, that they were spooked.

Daniel leaned over to Lien and whispered, "Is that even legal? Like, can she really do that?"

"She just did," was all Lien could breathlessly muster.

"Well, this sucks balls!" Greg cried as he, Zach, and Kieran filed out. "Way to piss her off again, Kate." They headed toward the elevators, on their way to Del's Place for an early lunch. Somehow, they'd all already brushed off the trauma of the moment.

Three orderlies came in to collect the old man. They released the lines and cables and transferred his limp body onto a gurney. A crisp, white sheet was pulled over his head. *Just like in the movies,* Kate thought.

Lien and Daniel each reached for one of Kate's hands and pulled her up from the floor. Daniel tenderly grabbed her shoulder. "Hey, it could've been worse."

"How could that have possibly gone any worse?" Kate asked.

"She could've made you change his catheter."

Kate felt wasted, exhausted, like her week off had only set her further behind. It seemed as if the group had only grown closer in her absence. She was the outsider, not Dr. Lucas. Kate was a scapegoat they could all point to. *At least we're not Kate White bad.* She felt the once unlimited promise of this prestigious program dropping away.

"I need some air," she said to Daniel and Lien and ran out of the ICU.

And the great cosmic coin stopped spinning and landed on tails.

★★★★★

That was when the monster came for Kate.

It always started the same way, with a shape in the darkness. Low to the ground with hulking shoulders and piercing, yellow eyes. Its body rising and falling with ragged breaths. A coppery taste overcame Kate's mouth. Like blood. The smell of death was everywhere. Then the shape would shift, and the beast would stumble out of the dark. Every time it was different, but the same.

Her mind was reeling: *Please let me wake up; this is all just a bad dream.* She was alone. It only ever came when she was alone.

Everything had grown so quiet. Her vision went dim. She wanted to run but couldn't. Her feet were fixed in place. She could hear her own heartbeat going *thump, thump, thump* in her ears.

It shuffled closer, clinging to the shadows until she finally recognized the shape of the old, dead man from the hospital bed. His skin had rotted away from his mouth and eyes, baring sharp, yellow teeth set against blackened gums. A low, mewling sound erupted from his snout. The eyes—bright and yellow and distinctly inhuman—would haunt her for the rest of her days. They grew larger as it neared.

This place was somehow familiar. Kate thought she was in a nameless corridor of St. Christopher's—she recognized the taupe walls and spotted linoleum floor—but here there were no doors, no windows, nothing but an endless hallway.

She ran.

Then the walls were changing shape. The goddamn hallway was closing in. She ran faster, but no matter how hard she pushed, she could hear its shuffling behind her, gaining, inch by inch. Then there was an awful scratching sound, and it took her a moment to realize that it was dragging ragged claws over the walls, ripping pockets into the plasterboard beneath.

It spoke in a low and wretched voice: "Good girl! You've got this!" All snarl and hiss and venom.

She ran until her lungs were about to burst. She ran until the walls had narrowed together so tightly, she had to turn her body sideways just to keep going. Eventually, one wall pressed hard against her chest, the other holding her in place from behind. Then it was upon her.

★★★★★

When she awoke, she was in a different part of the hospital, in a place she had been before, though not often. *How did I get here?* she wondered. She was standing in the basement, at a T-junction where the only options were left or right or back up the stairs behind her. To the right was Davol Laboratory. It was guarded by a large, steel door locked with restricted access. To Kate's left was the morgue. Cold dread settled over her. The blackouts had returned.

★★★★★

Kate rubbed her eye sockets with the hams of her hands, igniting a kaleidoscope of geometric shapes and rainbow colors behind her eyelids. Tinnitus rang in her ear. The taste of copper flooded her mouth, carrying over from the nightmare? Hallucination? She hadn't had an episode like this in a long time, not since the day she had found out her father died. Even back then, she kept it to herself. She'd read books about panic attacks and other overwhelming psychological episodes: mania, fugue, dissociative states. But when it happened before, the world had normalized, albeit a little grayer and colder in her father's absence, and the attacks had eventually subsided.

She was already feeling better—marginally, anyway. Dreams had a sense of collapsing when waking, losing their power in the coherent light of day. That power had relinquished its grip, like morning mist receding back over the lake. She climbed the back stairs and entered the emergency room on the first floor. Here, the hospital chaos not only continued but escalated, unceasing. Paramedics tore through the halls, ushering several men on gurneys to where they were met by a team of nurses in bubble-gum scrubs. Kate was nearly bowled over. She jumped out of the way of the first gurney as it suddenly flew through and into the elevator. On the gurney was a man in his mid-twenties in a neck brace, unconscious.

The man in the second gurney trailing behind was very much awake. He writhed in pain, bloodied, and busted up. Three police officers swarmed closely behind him, their faces glistening. Their hair matted down from the deluge of rain. Uniforms soaked.

As the sound and the fury of the group sailed past, Kate couldn't help but notice this second man was handcuffed to the bed's rails. Through clenched teeth, he riled and roared. "Assholes!" he sneered. "I'll kill you for this. This is bullshit!"

Kate was forced against the wall. She held her arms up and out of the way, unable to keep from staring. The first of the three police officers launched on top of him.

"Shut the hell up!" The officer, a 260-pound hulking mass of flash, was yelling at the handcuffed man. The officer sailed a machine gun punch into the man's solar plexus. The gurney came to a halt in the middle of the floor.

"Hey!" St. Christopher's nurses erupted, flailing, breaking up the fight. One of them pulled a whistle from around her neck and started blowing shrill, bleating yelps that hushed everything to momentary silence. The ER grew still.

"That's enough!" Rosette, the head nurse, screamed. Her voice was harshly accented, but her tone was clear as crystal. "Stop it right now!"

The other two officers jumped in, grabbing their partner who was now nearly foaming at the mouth and held him back. One of them said: "Leave it, man. Guy must be tweaked out of his mind on meth or something." The officer gestured for the nurses to take over.

As the stretcher wheeled past Kate, the hysterical man in it began to laugh. He looked up at her. Something about him registered as familiar to Kate. It was as if she'd met him before. And even though she knew it was a preposterous notion, she was bewildered.

Finally, Kate collapsed on an empty seat in the waiting room to catch her breath. All around her was chaos, hurt, disease. One middle-aged man in dirt-stained jeans with a lime-green landscaper's T-shirt held a bloody rag over one eye, head tipped back. In another corner, a mother held an infant son with an unceasing bronchial cough. On the TV mounted to the ceiling, a conservative news outlet blasted cuckolded liberals for another fiscally irresponsible extension of the debt ceiling. This was a sad world, one she barely related to anymore. A festering cancer was rotting society. No one had the answers. Day by day, more drone strikes, deforestation, carbon in the atmosphere. More women like herself set to make a fraction on the dollar as compared to men. And to top it all off, she still couldn't get Sean to commit to a date for the wedding.

On the small table beside her chair was a copy of yesterday's newspaper, folded over. A headline from page twelve caught her eye. She picked it up and read:

BOSTON HERALD

7 Dogs Gone Missing in Possible Canine Theft Ring

Oct. 12, 2021

Pet owners in the Boston metro area are on high alert following the recent, strange disappearance of seven neighborhood dogs, many of them going missing during the past eight weeks.

The Suffolk County Sheriff's Department sent out a press release about the disappearances, stating: "Sheriff's Deputies would like to warn the public and seek their assistance after receiving multiple reports of missing dogs over the last few weeks. The Sheriff's Office and Dog Control Officer James McCready have received reports from the North End, Quincy, Back Bay, Somerville, Weymouth, and Millville of at least seven dogs reported missing. Anyone with any information is asked to contact the Sheriff's Office or McCready."

According to the recent reports, McCready said there was an attempted dog abduction on Monday night in Somerville. The owner of two dogs heard one of his pets barking, went to investigate and encountered an individual trying to put one of the dogs in a white transport van. The owner yelled at the person to stop, and the thief then dropped the animal, jumped into the vehicle, and drove off without the headlights on. Because of this incident and the number of canines missing, officials believe they could be dealing with a theft ring.

Currently, there are no significant leads regarding what is behind this recent group of disappearances. All dog owners in the area are encouraged to keep a close eye on their pets and report any suspicious behavior.

Gary Gamache, staff writer

Chapter Two
LENNON & McCARTNEY

The streets were left slick from the day's rain. City lights reflected in puddles studding the asphalt with soft halo rings. Kate, Sean, Daniel, and Lien had been sitting at their patio table for hours. The restaurant's patio—a term used generously to upsell the dining experience—was no more than a half dozen wrought-iron bistro tables, set one on top of the other, separated from the Witcham Street sidewalk by a low fence. Glowing propane heaters pushed manufactured warmth into the cool night. Arturo's Bar was slammed, like every other night of the week.

The street was lined with luxury sedans. Mercedes, Audis, BMWs, even a sleek, black Maserati. From within these beautiful automobiles, beautiful people emerged, flittering by in their best suits and dresses on their way to a show at the performing arts center or just to get a drink at Arturo's. Kate typically enjoyed the people-watching; she invented little backstories for these strangers as they passed. They being unaware of their place as the temporary lead in a Kate White drama. But not tonight. Tonight, the theater was shuttered.

They had finished their meal and talked at length about life at St. Christopher's. They vented about the stress, the sheer amount of work, and split two bottles of wine. Kate had mostly kept quiet aside from the occasional head nod, trying her best to seem present and engaged though she was a million miles away.

She grabbed for Sean's hand beneath the table and squeezed it. But he didn't seem to be connecting with her. She knew that Sean had been through it all before. Like them, he'd started by interning at St. Christopher's as a med student too. Now he was a superstar surgeon. Though they both spent most of their waking lives at the hospital, their very different responsibilities and the sheer labyrinthine maze of the place meant they rarely ran into each other during the day.

The wine washed away some of her embarrassment, but a nagging layer of anxiety was lurking. Blackened shale beneath the earth's crust. Kate didn't dare speak a word about her anxiety attack to Dr. Lucas, Sean, Lien, anyone. She was frightened. Figured people she held dear would lose any last bit of faith in her if they knew of her visions or her lost time. She would fake it till she made it. Seemed to serve that Theranos woman well for awhile.

But Kate knew well enough that she was on borrowed time. One more drink and Daniel would spew out the story, desperate for Sean's reaction. Daniel looked up to Sean. They all did. Now Kate wanted to get them out of there, and quickly. So why not now, when the edges of the evening had been sanded down by several bottles of red wine and the wounds were scabbing? She began the tale. Here it was, nearing eleven, late into the evening for a weeknight. Kate had gotten to the point of relating where Lucas had been chiding the group in a fit of cruel laughter when their waiter interrupted to collect their plates

"Can I get you all some dessert menus? Maybe something to go?" he asked.

They nodded and the waiter left.

"You were saying…" Sean encouraged her, genuinely interested. The warm, ocher candlelight on his face emphasized his good looks. His dark hair was neatly parted, and his navy blazer, tailored perfectly, framed his shoulders well over the crisp, white, oxford button-down. Everyone that Kate met would tell her how lucky she was when they learned that she was engaged to Sean. *That one's going places,* they would say. She tried not to think about what others said to Sean when they learned he was engaged to Kate.

"Never mind," she said, wishing that she had never started down the road of this story in the first place. "Today was just a very long day. I shouldn't be complaining." Her knife was in her hands, and she was testing the sharpness of its blade along the plump pad of her finger.

"Are you sure?" Sean asked. "You don't seem alright to me."

"No, really. I'm fine." She breathed the night air in deeply and smiled, but it was the painted smile of a plastic doll. "It's just hard to get back into the swing of things after time off. It's an adjustment."

A dead weight hung in the air. Kate believed she had cashed in her chips early and the house was collecting now. She knew they all saw her time off as her running away from problems. Career suicide. She'd regretted it immediately, especially because she barely made any progress on the things that weighed her down. Wedding plans had stalled. Her studies had stalled. The only thing she remained good at was knocking back alcohol on a regular basis.

Daniel jumped in. "That guy's arm looked like Swiss cheese." There was a wise-ass grin on his face as he slightly tipped back in his chair. His hair was short, sandy-colored, spiked with pomade. He wore the kind of clothing—like the obnoxious blue polo he had on now—that made it seem as if all his shopping was completed exclusively through a Zara catalog.

"Enough, Daniel!" Lien scolded. "That could have been any of us."

Kate glowered at Daniel with baleful eyes. "You know, you can be a real son of a bitch."

"I'm sure you're all overreacting," Sean said reassuringly as their waiter returned with some dessert menus and poured four new glasses from a third bottle of wine. Kate grabbed for hers before it could be set down. In a quick gulp, she drained half the glass and coughed.

The waiter left, and Sean leaned in close. "That's just who she is," he said. "Lucas needs to be the alpha dog in these situations. It's a power trip. Who cares? Let her be. This–" He paused, grabbing at the air with his fingers, searching for the correct wording. "This *control*, it's all she has. It's a total mind fuck."

There was another long pause. Sean cast his eyes downward as if within his glass was a window into another world. Then he added, "I dunno. At least, that's how I remember things from my time in the trenches."

Kate, Lien, Daniel. They loved having Sean as someone with all this sage wisdom. Someone who could prep them for what was next—the good and the bad—and give them insights into the realities of life as a new doctor. Kate knew that Sean, in return, loved their adulation.

Now Lien was staring at Sean with those deep, dark eyes. "Did you ever have these kinds of challenges?" Lien asked. Her evening dress shimmered in the moonlight, hiked high over her knees. Peeking out from behind its straps was the hint of a sea turtle tattoo on her shoulder blade. Kate realized she had something Lien wanted. Lien almost always got everything she wanted, it seemed. But not here, not now. Sean was going to marry Kate and Lien could deal with that while she was winning whatever overachiever award came next.

"Oh c'mon, Lien!" Daniel jumped in before Sean could get a word out. "Of course Sean didn't have to deal with it!

Lucas wanted to fuck his brains out! Don't you remember that night in the coat check after orientation?"

Sean choked on his wine. This set them all to laughing uncontrollably. It got to the point where other tables began to look up with spiteful glances.

"Can we just drop it, guys?" Kate asked. "Let's leave the bullshit in the hospital."

Sean raised his glass of wine as if the events of the last thirty seconds had never happened. "A toast," he said. "To us."

"To the four most badass doctors around," Daniel added. This sent them all off into a laughing fit again, except for Lien, who was eyeing Sean strangely.

Clink! Their glasses touched. They drank. Eventually, they fell into idle chatter. Dessert was brought to the table. Kate scraped up gooey strands of caramel, trying her best to drown in the hedonism of chocolate, sugar, and butter. Looking up, she watched as the low moon shone brilliantly.

★★★★★

Daniel and Lien shared an Uber uptown to the apartment complex where many of the residents lived. Sean and Kate had decided to walk and stumbled the four blocks to her apartment in Charlestown. Her name was on the lease, but really it was their apartment, as he was the one primarily paying for it. She wanted him to formally move in, to take the pressure off needing his money just to survive. But he refused to give up his own place. Said he felt better having a place that was uniquely his. Kate never went to him. He always came to her.

The brisk, night air went a long way toward sobering them up, and when they crossed the threshold, they were buzzed just enough to make the decision to keep things going for a little while longer. But she needed a shower to wash the day away and disrobed while standing on the cold tile of the bathroom floor. Steam emanated out of the tiny bathroom in a cloud of rich, silver vapor. It was the only time during the day she felt clean and new, and she stood under the water until her skin was turned the color of ripe raspberries.

Through the bathroom door, she could hear Sean on the couch. There was the crack of a beer opening and the play-by-play of the DVR'd Sox–Cardinals game. She didn't care much for sports, but she loved that he rooted for the local team. Kate had three Sox T-shirts that she would wear all through the summers. Ask her to name any of the players beyond Big Papi and she would freeze.

Ten minutes later, she cut the water and dried off. Kate wrapped a towel around her hair—but nothing else—and padded off to the bedroom, leaving ghostly, wet footprints on the floor which evaporated moments later like messages written in invisible ink. Her skin, taut and clean, chilled by the cool air in the apartment, left her with gooseflesh. She could hear Sean turning off the TV and following her nakedness. A bear with its snout caught in the honeypot. She loved this feeling of control. This was power. Command and control are what she lacked at St. Christopher's hospital.

From a pile of folded laundry on the floor, she snagged a pair of underwear and a tank top and squeezed into them. Then she quickly ran a comb through her snarl of wet hair and hopped into bed with a book. The sheets felt frigid on her legs, and she squealed, rubbing them back and forth. Two sticks trying to make fire.

When Sean entered her bedroom, he opened his wallet, took out six hundred-dollar bills, and placed them in an unmarked envelope on the dresser. That would cover this week. Watching the bills counted out and placed on her dresser, the feeling of power suddenly vanished. At first, Kate had leveraged herself to the max to afford off-campus housing, but now her undergraduate loans were coming out of deferment, and Boston was a costly city. When he had offered to help, she had protested. He'd been sweet, saying he remembered how hard it was at first when he moved here from Phoenix. For the past few months, the exchange had been wordless. He gave her money and then climbed on top of her. Usually, it was after too many drinks, like tonight, and it felt gross. Sexual currency. Exchange. Barter. But they had been engaged for a long time now. Still, no date was set. If she could force it along, she knew, that would make everything better.

After placing the money on the dresser, Sean left the bedroom again. Moments later, Kate heard the stream of his urine hitting the water in the bowl. She tried to press on in her book but was having trouble remembering the exact place she had left off. She kept thinking about Lien. Why did Lien look at Sean that way? Did Sean know there was a crush there? It was already nearly one in the morning, and they had to get up and start another strenuous day in about five hours. On nights like this, they really were stupid kids to think they could keep burning the candle at both ends.

In the corner of the bedroom's ceiling, there was a small *plip* as a droplet of water fell into a plastic bowl sitting on the floor. The pipes in the ceiling above had sprung a leak. A call had been placed to the landlord, who had said he would "get to it eventually." The plaster had taken on the permanent, high gloss of wet spaghetti. Black mold was spider-webbing out like the branches of a dead tree. Kate pulled the comforter up to her waist. It was one that Sean despised, with its brown-and-orange flowers that looked permanently dingy. He commented on that anytime they had a fight. He would throw in her face that her style was antiquated. But it reminded her of her parents from when she was little. Besides, her name was on the lease. She could decorate the place as she goddamn pleased.

The bedroom door squealed on its hinges. She tried to pay Sean no mind as he came back in and stripped. But Kate could feel his eyes on her, and so she laid the book into her lap and watched him. He was looking back at her, smiling, bleary-eyed, buzzed from the wine and beer chasers.

"You know," he said, "sometimes, with the right light and the right angle, you look like that actress."

"Who?" she asked.

"I don't know. She was in that messed-up movie with the guy in a bear suit who gets set on fire."

"Florence Pugh?"

"Yeah, that's it."

"Well she's beautiful, so thank you."

"You're welcome." He lifted the blankets and slid into bed beside her. "Shit, bed's cold!"

Thinking of the actress, Kate was reminded of her first date with Sean after they had met in the ER. She asked: "Do you remember we saw her years ago in that movie at the Landmark Twin?"

"Oh yeah." It was dawning slowly on his buzzed brain. "Wasn't that like our first date?" he asked warmly.

They'd gone to see *Lady Macbeth*. It was that same night, over chocolate cake and strawberry milkshakes in the diner across the street, that Kate looked into Sean's eyes and made the decision to go to bed with him.

He handed over his nearly full can of beer, which she placed on her bedside table without drinking.

"What're you reading?" he asked.

She changed her mind, grabbed the can, took a sip. "*It*," she said. On the over, a demonic clown smiled. But the book was so much more primal than how the movies made it seem. Kate could see King's familiar face on the back cover of the dust jacket, with his firm lips and reflective glare cast out over the turned-up collar of a black leather jacket.

"I don't know why you're always reading that trash," he said.

"It's my favorite," Kate said. "And it's definitely not trash."

She could see his face contorting into a look that communicated disapproval without conscious effort. "Okay, maybe it isn't trash. Fair enough. But if you have spare time for reading, shouldn't you be cramming textbooks or something?"

Kate was growing weary of his apparent condescension. "Let me ask you something: You know as well as anyone else how stressful med school can be. Are you saying I don't deserve to unwind with something that makes me happy once in a while? How's that any different than you falling down drunk watching the Sox?"

He smiled in that antagonizing way he so often did; there was something sensual when he crossed that threshold— a race car in the red, fired up, dangerous. It usually led to fighting or fucking. Tonight, it was too early to tell. He grabbed for the can of beer in her hands, gulped.

She pressed Sean further. "Sometimes, after a long day, it's just nice to pick up a good story with interesting characters. Okay?"

"Okay, okay. You're right. But Stephen King? Can't you do better than that?"

"You are an elitist dick," she scowled with arched brows. "And you talk to me like I'm stupid."

"I don't think you're stupid at all. Don't put words into my mouth. I just don't understand the appeal of books you buy at the grocery store. Just saying."

"Just saying," she mimed in her best Sean Carraway, her arms crossed rigidly against her chest. She paused, thought on it, and then added, "Are you done now?"

"Oh c'mon! You know I'm just kidding, right?"

Kate knew unquestioningly that Sean thought he was the smarter of the two. And he was, which made his attitude more infuriating. Now he was trying to navigate this conversation in such a way as to not quite say he was wrong and apologize, but to give enough to not close out the possibility of getting some action. Typical.

"You're wrong about a lot of things, buddy!" she said teasingly.

"Oh yeah? Like what?"

"I know one thing," she said, grinning the mischievous smile of a Cheshire cat.

"Don't you say it..." he warned. Now they were both smirking. Kate saw that Sean possessed the look of a friend—everyone has one—who can't keep secrets and has just picked up the juiciest nugget of forbidden gossip. "Paul was better." Bombs away.

"You lie!" Sean feigned a heart attack, clutching his chest. He fell over onto her. Beer sloshed out of his can and onto the comforter.

"Hey! Watch out!" Kate yelled. She smacked him on the shoulder with all the heft of an eleven-hundred-page epic.

"Sorry," he said about the beer on the comforter. "Guess we need to Goodwill this shit now, right?"

They were both laughing clumsily, feeling better. She sipped again from his beer, slurping at its foamy head, then put it down on the bedside table and rolled over onto her side to face him. His calm, blue eyes were deep, and in them, she could see the whole world.

"The proof is in the songs," Sean said. He sounded like an academic trying to plead the case for his dissertation to an uninterested advisory panel. "Just look at 'A Day in the Life.'" Compare John's part with Paul's. You're embarrassing yourself."

"I stand by it."

"You beautiful little fool," Sean quipped, but Kate didn't catch the Fitzgerald reference. He held her for a long moment in his gaze. It made her feel self-conscious and inadequate. All her recent failings came bubbling up. *Mental health time.* She knew how hard people worked to get where they were in life and how much she was trying, but it just wasn't clicking. Regardless, whether the intoxication came from the wine over dinner or the shape of his body beneath the sheets, she couldn't help always landing back in the same place: he was goddamn beautiful.

"Just do me a favor, and stop being afraid of shit that pleases people," Kate said. "It's annoying."

He met her eyes and swept the bangs back from them gently. "Hey, I like pleasing people," he said.

"Oh yeah?" she asked coyly.

His hand found its way beneath the brown-and-orange flowers that he found so unappealing, tunneling toward her warm, fleshy mound. Her sex was wet, and she wanted him. He pulled down her underwear, spread her legs, and curled one finger inside of her, drawing it forward in a "come here" motion. She whimpered.

"Does that hurt?" he asked, attentive to her sounds.

"No," she moaned and her book clattered to the floor with a thud. King would have to sit this one out.

Then Sean went down on her. His hands were strong and warm, and they rested on her lower abdomen right over her appendectomy scar. Mostly, Kate was terribly self-conscious of the scar, especially when it itched. She rarely wore any tops that revealed her midriff, even though with the years it had faded to but a faint, white line. Tonight, it didn't cross her mind at all. She liked his hands on her body. She felt safe and in his control.

Sean was good at this; she knew that much. And he was eager to do it. She could feel his tongue tracing the alphabet over her sex. Her fingers laced through his hair. Sounds of the real world melted away: the traffic noise outside her windows, the thrum of the bathroom fan she'd left on. Within her was a raging river of self-doubt, the fear of the unknown, but his hands on her kept that tamped down. In its place, faint, lush music enveloped her, erupting from some deep, dark chasm. There was a connection between them, almost harmonic, and it was never more secure than when they were physically together. Kate was giddy, like a young girl again, and she pushed his head deeper into her.

She felt a vast, deep wind rising within her, and then she was flying.

★★★★★

They nestled within the tangle of each other's arms. Outside, the air turned cold. The peaked roofs across the way had taken on the pale sheen of early frost. Kate always loved the disconnect between a crisp, cold night and a cozy room where the heat was turned up irresponsibly high. Sean was passed out. She felt close to Sean, which was less and less common these days. The metronomic sound of his hushed breathing soothed her.

She thought of her parents, missed the touch of her mother and father, the familiar smell of home. It had been a while since she called her mom. The last time, they'd argued. Her mother admitted she wanted to put the family house on the market. It was just too big to live in by herself. Kate hung up on her. Since then, she fantasized about her and Sean buying it. She thought it could create some sort of link from past to future. A through line to keep her sane. Why did she keep doing this? Having an ocean of thoughts, keeping them to herself? She kept everything to herself, even the feeling that she might not make it through this program.

But at least she had Sean. His slow, sleepy breathing fell on the back of her neck. His breath souring, but familiar. Kate let her eyes trace the organic spirals of ice on the window. Her lids were growing heavy.

Kate pulled Sean's heavy hand over her hips. Tomorrow, she would figure everything out. She wouldn't burden Sean. She wouldn't burden her mother. She wouldn't run away, scared, giving up like so many times before. Not again. She would kick this world's ass. One way or another.

Then she slept.

Chapter Three
BEDSIDE MANNERS

Kate's morning started with an array of classes. Then, a brief fifteen minutes for lunch, consumed on the walk between buildings, before clinicals at one. The patient wing on the second floor was quiet, but the atmosphere felt charged. It was as if tiny vibrations were pulsing out of the walls. One of the overhead bulbs was out. It created a break in the wash of even, florescent light, turning the hospital's hallway dim. Kate stood in the aberrant pool of darkness waiting for the lesson to begin.

Dr. Lucas led them to a door stamped with the number 217. Standing by the doorway was a uniformed police officer who nodded to the doctor with approval. He opened the door and gestured for the doctor and her students to head inside. He said, "Just stand clear of the yellow tape."

"This one will be different," Lucas said sternly, pausing in the doorway, addressing her students. "It's a police job. Patient's got cuffs on. Follow the officer's instructions. Stay away from the bed. He's medicated but, in these situations, you never know."

"Do attacks on hospital staff happen often," Kate asked.

"Rarely," said Dr. Lucas. "But we don't want to be the first."

Lucas pushed open the heavy door, and Kate and the others followed her into the darkened room.

In the bed, elevated at a steep incline, was the wild-eyed man who had locked eyes with Kate the day before. Here, he was a shadow of his former self. His labored breathing was harsh, irregular, like the sluggish sounds of an ox in heat. A three-foot perimeter had been drawn on the floor in yellow caution tape. Lucas's toes landed right on the edge.

From the glaze of his stupor, the patient's eyes loosely followed a history program on the television that hung from the ceiling. He barely turned to acknowledge the crowd of medical students gathering around him. On-screen, two men in hard hats were exploring an old, underground tunnel—something akin to a mine shaft—and marveling at the old industrial infrastructure.

The host of the program spoke: "It's unbelievable just how much of this hidden world has survived!"

"True," said the other, an expert in the field. "A lot of these interconnected tunnels are what served as the first sewer systems in America. You know, there's a whole forgotten world hidden beneath our feet."

Zap! Blackness engulfed the screen. Dr. Lucas had switched off the television. "TV rots your brain, Mr. Dallas," she quipped.

His mouth was nearly agape. "Well, what the hell else am I supposed to do in here?"

"How about working on your escape plan?"

"Don't worry 'bout me," Dallas said in a sluggish drawl. "I'm tunneling out of Shawshank tonight when y'all are sleepin'."

Kate laughed out loud at the starkness of this strange man's self-aware comment. Lucas shot her a glance to indicate it wasn't funny. From behind, Daniel leaned in and whispered into Kate's ear, "You hear about him in the news?"

Kate shook her head. She hadn't followed up, hadn't even realized he was still in the hospital. Outside of the day's weather, Kate barely acknowledged the news. But she knew now, just by looking at him, that he was trouble.

Daniel continued in a whisper: "Perp is Parker Dallas. He and his brother botched a heist of a jewelry store on Boylston. Cops shot him in the leg. His brother was DOA."

Kate sniggered. "Perp? What in the actual hell are you, Daniel?"

Kate could see that both of Parker's arms were restrained with heavy, leather straps. His torso was bandaged, and his tightly wrapped leg was elevated. She saw the lean, sinewy muscle that ran along his side where the hospital gown wasn't entirely tied down. He was in good shape, better than Sean even, and Sean took care of himself.

Dr. Lucas fingered the clipboard at the foot of Parker's bed, flipped through it rather quickly, and then beckoned for the students to gather near the far wall. Kieran and Zach hunkered by the window, locked in a whispered conversation about the specifics of gunshot wounds. Kieran was the oldest of their group and, at twenty-nine, even had premature flecks of gray in his beard.

Lucas brought them over to a fluorescent light box mounted on the opposite wall. From an extra-large manila envelope, she removed two X-rays and clipped them up. She flipped the switch on the side. The light flickered and came on. The X-ray images burst to life.

"What do you see, Kate?" Lucas asked. Kate knew she was being picked on again because of her laugh. "Look around. Home in on the right diagnosis."

Kate stepped closer to the light box. She studied the X-ray image with excruciating care. On film, the black-and-white peaks and valleys of Parker's imaged skeletal system resembled some sort of strange relief map. She turned to look over the man himself as if she could mentally overlay the X-ray image onto the actual patient in some sort of cinematic process shot.

"Seems pretty obvious to me," Kate said. "Patient was shot in the leg."

"No shit, Sherlock." Dr. Lucas quipped. She turned back to Parker in the bed. "Hey, Parker?" the doctor called. The manacled patient remained quiet, arms crossed, agitated. He was waiting for the opportunity to flip the television back on. To be left alone again. "Kate here says you've been shot in the leg. You satisfied with that?"

Parker Dallas smiled absently. He looked at Kate, really looked at her, for the first time since the group of students fell in his room.

"Well, ain't you the prettiest doc I ever saw," he said. His voice was slow, medicated, unfurling from him like a flag.

"Not yet," Kate said.

Kate continued, wind in her sails. "We need to look for penetrating injury. That was addressed upon patient's arrival when the scan for temporary cavitation issues was completed. After that, for gun shot wounds, it's ensuring the fragmentation of the bullet isn't poised to create longer term damage."

"Better," said Lucas, somewhat exasperated. "But look closer. Focus on the image, the data. Think back to what you learned across your human physiology courses last year."

Kate's mind mentally scanned her previous four years of pre-med education that had comprised a Rolodex of textbooks and lectures and videos and online practice modules but came up short. There was a terrifying blankness to it all. "I-I'm not sure," she stammered.

Parker looked from Lucas and then to Kate. In that moment, Kate saw the spark in his eye. He awoke from his stupor. She could see he was remembering her from yesterday. And Kate felt so goddamn inadequate in the moment.

The others in the cramped room were watching her. Kate closed her eyes. She saw the image of Parker's X-ray morphing into a series of hundreds—then thousands—of textbook pages. They fluttered by like a giant flipbook of human anatomy and disease states.

"What do you see?" Lucas prodded again, not unkindly.

Kate opened her eyes and took one step closer to the light box until the tip of her nose was not six inches away from the X-ray film. Her fingers lightly traced dark, jagged veins in the image. Kate was about to crumble and felt the symptoms of another anxiety attack lurking. She reeled with self-doubt. *Is this the last thing I'll think before I die? Will this be how others will remember me? Some useless idiot?*

Kate tried to banish the bad thoughts. She couldn't remember if she took her pills this morning with all the rushing around. *Focus on the image. Focus. Focus. Focus. Goddammit!*

"I see…" Kate began. "I see high-velocity gunshot tibial fractures. Fragments that need to be removed. The patient desperately needs to see an orthopaedic surgeon immediately."

Daniel clenched his fist in a small gesture of support.

"Okay. That's something," Lucas said. "But what else is going on here? Do you need to add to your diagnosis? Does the stress of the wound bring to light anything else?"

The pressure was mounting. Kate thought this might be a trick question. Maybe asserting confidence was the challenge here. "I stand by my diagnosis," she said. Her lilting inflection posed the response as a question belying her overall lack of certainty.

Lucas's expression changed. A plump balloon deflating into something soggy and empty. She waited, hoping more might emerge from Kate, but the well was tapped. "Anybody with a second opinion?" she asked. "Kieran?"

Kieran lowered his head, dejected. The other students avoided eye contact altogether.

Lucas began to admonish the group. "If you guys aren't the sorriest excuses for…" but stopped when Lien raised her hand like an apple-polishing third grader seeking extra credit. Lucas nodded for her to speak.

Lien looked at Kate sympathetically. "I think Kate's on the right track," she started, pausing briefly in a clear attempt to bolster her friend's spirit. "But there's more." She turned from Kate to Lucas.

"Which is?" Lucas asked with bated breath.

"It's that dark mass that Kate was looking at on the edge of the frame that has me worried. I'm thinking we may have signs of early, superficial infection."

Lucas nodded in pleasant agreement with Lien's remarks. Kate shrank, a wilted flower, and withdrew from the group into the corner of the room. Kate hated Lien in this moment. That traitorous bitch!

"Meaning...?" Lucas pressed Lien.

"Meaning that we'll need further testing. Go in with a scope. Potentially run a course of antibiotics to be safe."

Lucas patted Lien on the head like a small, toy dog. "Well done, grasshopper," she said. Then the doctor nodded to Parker. "Also, looking at an X-ray alone is never enough. Kate should've reviewed his chart and followed up with patient interviews to confirm."

The med students cleared out. By the door, Lucas grabbed Kate's shoulder and spun her around. She pulled up the chain around her neck and placed her glasses on the bridge of her nose. Lucas always wore a pair of somewhat trendy, round-frame glasses. She had them in all sorts of colors. Kate wondered about how it was that Lucas wore all these stylish, expensive clothes and accessories, yet she didn't wear them well. Always mismatched, out of sorts, looking kind of thrown together.

"Kate, you're a smart girl, but you're making dumb mistakes," she said in a matter-of-fact monotone. "You're capable, but you're not present. A lack of confidence and you'll be eaten alive your first time out of the nest."

"I didn't see anyone else jumping in with the right answer," Kate snarled. She wasn't sure how to take all of this. It was so damn defeating to be the recipient of someone's disappointment day after day.

"Lien had the right answer."

"I've gotta ask," Kate said, surprised to hear it come out of her mouth. "Why are you so hard on *me*?"

"Because medicine requires a certain precision."

"Ever since I first got here, you've ridden me harder than everyone else. I don't get that. What'd I ever do—"

"I wouldn't finish if I were you," Lucas's voice churned, low and guttural. Her eyes locked on Kate in a cold, steely glare. "I'm not a fan of this victim mentality bullshit that millennials spew." She imitated Kate in a whiny register: 'Oh, no one else knew the answer.' 'Oh, cancel my student debt, Mr. President. Life's too too hard.'" Lucas got angry. "Guess what, I don't give a shit."

The doctor shook her head in exhaustion. "And don't you dare take it out on me if you're not happy with my feedback." Each word driven home like a hammer to a nail. "When you're here, you're on *my* floor, in *my* hospital…got it? A lack of precision around here can be fatal. That's what all of you need to understand. If you don't get really serious, real fast, I'll see that you're out on your ass. Or you'll wind up killing someone."

Kate was pretty sure Lucas didn't blink once during the exchange. In her agitated state, the doctor stormed out of the hospital room.

Kate turned to see Parker, who had been watching them from his bed. "Hey, don't let her get you down," he said.

"Thanks." *God, he heard everything.*

"One more thing."

Kate looked upon the restrained man, his swoop of hair, his deep-set eyes. They were looking at her like no one else had before. "Yes?" she asked. Butterflies danced in her guts.

"Don't go."

She took two tentative steps toward the bed yet remained what felt to her like miles from the man. In truth, it was a small room, and if her arms were extended, she could have just touched the rails of his bed with the tips of her fingers. She didn't know why she was drawn to him. It was not based at all on logic. It wasn't even necessarily romantic. It was some primordial curiosity that had brought her here, something she admittedly didn't fully understand.

"You can come closer. If you like," he said, sensing her apprehension. "I'm restrained, you know." He lifted his arms the mere inches the restraints permitted. "Besides, I wouldn't hurt you. Everyone's out there saying things about me that just ain't true. I guess someone's gotta be the bad guy. Might as well be me."

"You don't look all that awful," Kate said.

"You know, you're very lovely," he said. "I bet you face a lot of obstacles in medicine because your beauty makes people think you have nothing else to offer."

She broke into a smile, pushed her hair behind her ears. She was now conscious of every action she took, and her movements began to feel performed. Each word, each gesture lagged with inherent delay as her brain searched for the perfect balance of femininity, strength, and conviction.

"That's sweet of you to say," she said. "But I don't think I have that problem."

"What problem do you have?"

"I keep making bad choices."

There was a bit more courage now, like settling into a hot bath. Kate inched nearer to the foot of Parker's bed and leafed through his chart. Maybe, at the very least, she could brush up on her skills while she was here making a fool of herself. But there was nothing but the typical vitals and one known allergy to ACE inhibitors.

"Are you in a lot of pain?"

"Not so bad. Actually, I feel like I'm floating."

She could hear the slight slur in his speech. "That's the codeine," she said.

"Honey, that's those deep-blue eyes of yours." He tried to adjust his position into something closer to sitting up, which was proving more difficult due to the heavy restraints and even heavier medication.

She grabbed a blood pressure cuff from a wire basket above his bed and wrapped it tightly around his left arm. With a press of a button, the mechanical device whirred to life and constricted on his bicep. It only took a moment. The machine beeped, and the indicators gave the readout.

"Good," Kate said, removing the cuff.

His attempts to adjust his position only aggravated his freshly sutured wounds. "Sssss," he hissed. "Shit!" His head hit the pillow.

Kate reached over him delicately for the switch in the line of his IV. "Whoa, whoa, calm down," she said. "See this?"

She grabbed the switch and depressed the single button. All the muscles in Parker's body went lax. He fell back into the bed in a drowsy haze.

"Don't play tough guy, okay? You're no match for my friend here."

He moaned; it was almost orgasmic. Kate had to stifle a laughing fit, giggling into the crook of her arm. "Try not to get too used to that," she warned. "It's when they cut you off that you're going to wish you were dead."

"That's some bedside manner, Doc."

"I've been told that I need to work on that."

"When I get out of here, I'm taking you to dinner," he said matter-of-factly.

Kate rolled her eyes. With the index finger of her right hand, she tapped her engagement ring, flashing it for emphasis. "I don't think so." When she glanced down, she noticed that she was well within the yellow tape perimeter.

From behind her, there was another voice, a familiar one, and it jolted her into a bolt upright position. "Kate?" the voice called.

She spun around, sucked out of her daze, as Sean entered the room. He was in a clean pair of green OR scrubs, his hair hidden beneath a cap.

"What are you doing here?" Sean asked.

"Just checking on the patient," Kate blurted out. She still had his chart in her hand and began flipping through it again, absentmindedly.

Sean stepped closer to her. Confusion was written all over his face. "Can I see you for a minute?" he asked. "Out in the hall?"

She followed him into the corridor. Two nurses headed in their direction accompanied by a middle-aged man, his wife, and two young children carrying balloons and flowers. The family stopped outside of the room right across the hall, knocked twice, and entered. Kate could hear their warm greetings as the door sealed behind them.

"Kate," Sean began, "you shouldn't be here alone. Why would Dr. Lucas send you up here unsupervised?"

"She didn't. I'm sorry. The group had been making the rounds, and I just kind of fell behind, I guess..." she trailed off.

"You need to go, please," Sean said.

She glanced down at the floor, embarrassed, as she left Parker's room. From the quiet corridor, in the pool of darkness beneath the broken light bulb, she could hear Parker addressing Sean back in his room as the door closed.

"That's some woman, doc" he said.

★★★★★

Lien was waiting for her in the hall, but when Kate saw her, she kept walking. Kate was smoldering, afraid that one more push, even unintentional, could detonate a well of dynamite that Kate herself was only just beginning to realize existed somewhere in the deepest reaches of her being. She'd never felt like this before.

"Kate?" Lien called. "Kate? Can I speak to you for a moment?"

Lien was only twenty-two. She skipped ninth and tenth grade and accelerated into college and then med school early. Maybe it was because of this or because she had spent her entire childhood nose down in textbooks, but Lien often seemed to lack a nuanced understanding of interpersonal relationships. Lien's inability to read the situation could frustrate the hell out of Kate.

Kate whipped around angrily to meet Lien in the middle of the hall. "You know, just because you have this *Asian thing* where you have to be number one doesn't mean you have to throw me under the bus to get there."

"Is it *Pick on Yellow People Day*?" Lien asked. Then she added, "Can you maybe say thank you? I'm trying to help because I don't like seeing my friends suffering, but if you're going to be nasty, then…then screw you, Kate."

"Screw me? Screw *you*!" Kate couldn't believe what she was hearing.

"Maybe if you put more work into studying rather than planning some stupid wedding, you wouldn't be at this point," Lien urged. She effortlessly retied her long, straight, black hair into a rigid ponytail. "Drowning people always bring you down with them."

Kate's fingers curled into small fists. She breathed a deep sigh and relaxed her hands until her fingers released and pointed down toward the floor. She was still in control. The real question was: how much longer would she keep it?

"Sorry," Lien said quietly. "That was too much."

"You know, it's not for lack of studying. When I'm alone, I feel powerful. Put me in a room with all your eyes on me—and Dr. Lucas—and I crumble," Kate said. "I'm sorry. It's not your fault. I'm just stupid."

"We'll figure it out together."

"I don't think so," Kate said. "At this point, I need a miracle."

Just down the hall, Dr. Lucas was boarding the elevator, limping into the car as the doors closed behind her. Lien and Kate watched her silently. Then Lien said, "Let's go out. Just you and me."

★★★★★

After their lectures concluded and they were dismissed, Lien urged Kate to join her back at Arturo's Bar for a drink and a chance to study outside of the bustling walls of the hospital. Even though the place was routinely slammed during the dinner rush, there was typically no wait in the middle of the afternoon. They were led out to the patio to the exact same table their foursome had occupied the night before.

It was difficult to find the same sense of magic in broad daylight. Daytime possessed none of that twilight romance, no soft reflecting pools of light, no smooth jazz music gently spilling from the open-close-open-close doorways of nightclubs up-and-down the street. The world in light was tamer. The people were different. Pedestrians walking by on the Witcham Street sidewalk were of another species. Soccer moms carrying large bags in the middle of an errand run. Elderly couples out for leisurely strolls. Even the waitstaff moved with a reduced spring in their steps. During the day, the tips were smaller.

Kate and Lien each sipped slowly from glasses of wine. The faint aroma of the Summer Red Maples, which had been planted in clean-lined rows along the Witcham Street median, filled the air. They'd just about shed all their leaves. Textbooks, notepads, and other study aids were strewn across the table. The flash cards were special ordered from the internet and had various images and facts regarding rare diseases. Kate and Lien had an intensive exam coming up in their Anatomic and Clinical Pathology course. They were both harboring a degree of nervousness about it.

Lien held up an image of a gruesome, microscopic parasite on a laminated index card: a sort of gray, segmented worm with serrated teeth blown up to a palm-size monstrosity for the flash card picture. It looked to be some hideous cross between HR Geiger art and a feral dog without legs. Lien's index finger intentionally obstructed the caption beneath the image.

"Parasite?" she asked.

"Trypanosoma cruzi," Kate said. She didn't even blink. They were going back and forth, testing each other, with the pitter-patter rhythm of an old, screwball comedy.

"Hosts?"

"Possum. Armadillo. Rodent. Human," Kate rattled off in a quick, dry manner.

"Location?"

"South and Central America."

"Transfer and treatment?"

"Transfer by feces. Entering by a mucous membrane or wound. Vertical transmission. Treatment: benzimidazole and nifurtimox."

Lien laid the card down, awestruck. "That's amazing, Kate! Not that my opinion matters, but I think you're the best I've seen with this stuff," she said.

"Yeah? Then why does every professor at St. Christopher's have my number? I'm hanging on by a thread."

"It's just nerves. Once you overcome that, you'll be fine. You're really smart."

Though it could have easily been interpreted as patronizing coming from Lien, Kate was genuinely pleased. "I don't know," she whimpered. "It would be so awesome if I could go into those patients' rooms armed with answers. All I want in life is to make Lucas eat her words and apologize."

Lien was looking at the next flash card. "Too bad you couldn't just sneak around infecting people with rare bugs. Do that the night before, you know. That way, during class, you'd know exactly what ails them," Lien said with a laugh. "Like paying a boxer to take a dive in the fifth. The inside track."

"You're terrible! Sounds like the log line to a shitty, direct-to-video horror flick," Kate replied.

At this, they laughed heartily. Then Kate said, "Okay, enough. Your turn."

She raised a card of her own and directed it at Lien. On it were two small pictures, each one containing a different view of color patterns for her wedding reception. "Which do you prefer?"

"Seriously?" Lien asked. She kept it jocular, but there was an undercurrent of concern. Lien sipped again, swallowed. "We have to stay focused!"

"I know, I know," Kate placated her. "But I'll focus better once I have this locked away. Sean's no help at all with this, and I think I've landed on which one I want. If you agree, I'll know I made the right choice."

Lien placed her now empty glass back down on the table very softly. She paused a space of a few seconds, then locked eyes with Kate. "Hey," she said, "I'm not trying to start anything, but do you really think that this is the right time in your life for this?" Lien was backtracking now, afraid of having gone too far. "The wedding, I mean."

"You mean 'stupid wedding', right? Like you said back at the hospital?"

"I didn't mean that," Lien admitted. "I was frustrated."

As far as Kate was concerned, settling this was all that mattered. To her, getting past the wedding and having that part of her life official, decided, tucked away in a neat, little box, would mean she could shift her attention to self-actualizing into a doctor.

"Do you guys even have a date set yet?" Lien pushed.

Kate's right hand instinctively cradled her engagement ring on her left hand. She had the proof, right there in the diamond. True, she had picked out the ring and specifically asked Sean to buy it for her. But he did it. He certainly didn't have to. She only had to ask half a dozen times. He always came through in the end. *Then why do I feel like I'm rushing through to close the deal before the buyer changes his mind?* She scooped up the cards and books before her and slammed them back into her bag.

"Hey, wait!" Lien cried. She watched Kate pack with plaintive eyes. "Don't go. I'm sorry. You know me. I don't know how to talk to people. That's why I'll spend the rest of my life in a basement laboratory."

Kate heard Lien, and in the moment, she realized the young girl sitting across from her was still just figuring out how to interact with other young adults like her.

"I think we need more alcohol," Kate said. She held her hand up trying to signal the waitress in the white shirt and black slacks on the other side of the patio making idle conversation with a busboy during the slow afternoon. The chirping birds were louder than the passing traffic.

"No, none for me, please. Fenton needs me in the lab," Lien said.

"When are you two finally going to get it on?"

"Ew!" Lien shrieked. "First off, he's like sixty-five. Second, he's creepy. Brilliant, but creepy."

"I know. I'm just playing."

"I only hope they finally let me contribute."

"Are you ever going to tell me about your secret agent job?" Kate asked, playfully.

Lien's glare said it all: enough already. "Nothing to tell. I've been running errands for them. And you know what I've not been doing? I've not been performing real research. If they don't let me start soon, I'm quitting."

"Okay, okay," Kate said. "Your turn now. For real." She picked up another flash card from the middle of the stack in the center of the table. On it was the graphic image of a woman's thigh with severely peeling skin, blistered to the point of rawness and lined with green pockets of slavering pus. "This is a sign of what infection?"

Their waitress returned carrying a tray full of gorgeously plated meals for the next table. Her eyes caught sight of the flash card, and its brutal image caused her to lose her balance. With a crash, broken dishes and Italian cuisine rained down upon the patio.

Chapter Four
THE OVERNIGHT SHIFT

A rolling fog had blown in, shrouding the hospital in a veil of gauze. From a cold front that had settled in, the air was destabilized creating an electric charge, the spark of possibility. After hours, Davol Laboratory really came alive with its true, intended purpose. At least, that's how it felt to Dr. Fenton.

The lab's usual bright surfaces were draped in elongated shadows drawn from warm pockets of track lighting. The day shifters clocked out hours ago. To anyone else, it would have appeared that the laboratory was asleep. Within the large, underground room, rows of dormant workstations filled the floorspace. Powerful computers, electron microscopes, one jerry-rigged mass spectrometer, and great bays of experimental equipment were arranged atop workbenches. Each station was covered over for the evening. In the back of the lab, Justin Ames, one of Fenton's most trusted researchers, hunkered by a vault door. He peered through its small window like a prison guard checking a cell.

Fenton greeted him. "Hey, what's the news?"

"Evening, sir," Justin said. His attention had been with the latest progress reports from the day's efforts. Justin was making his usual notes along the margins. Fenton was one of only a handful who could actually decipher the young man's scrawl, his open questions, his recommendations for next best actions. When the lab's interns returned in the morning, they would pass Justin's notes between them, looking for the Ames translator.

"Lien Chu is stopping by," Fenton said. "When she does, can you show her in, please?"

Fenton entered his office and dropped his bag on the desk. He collapsed into his pockmarked leather chair and let out the sigh common to all men of a certain age. These days, his body ached with pangs of arthritis. But there was no cure for old age, and he wasn't yet done with asking the bigger questions about life's secrets. So, he would press on.

Fenton still remembered when he had offered Lien the internship. She was immediately promising. Not just because of her intellect. St. Christopher's had no shortage of bright, young minds in its midst. No, Fenton had seen in Lien the qualities of someone who might one day join him in the work he held most dear: pioneering new applications of stem cell research and DNA reassignment. In Davol laboratory, they skated on the bleeding edge. These minds and this room held the potential to create miracles.

Back then, Lien sat across from him in this windowless office. The lab had been converted from a supply closet in the late 1970s when the hospital had given Fenton the keys. Slowly, it had expanded, manifest destiny, into the largely remodeled underground center of analytical excellence it had become. It took over the majority of St. Christopher's basement now.

For her interview, Lien had overdressed. Caked in poorly applied makeup, she rattled on about her background as if it had been a college entrance interview. As if he would care. Fenton tuned that stuff out. She was younger than her peers because she had skipped some grades. He remembered that. Their conversation had turned a corner when she referenced one of the lab's recent publications in *JAMA*.

"I'm impressed you're actively reading the latest research in the field," he commented.

"Actually, I hope you don't mind me saying, but I don't think your sample size was large enough to be conclusive." Her face betrayed no emotion when she delivered the criticism.

"You know that work passed rigorous peer-review, don't you?" he asked.

"Sure. But you're given leeway because of who you are. I don't think a less pedigreed researcher could get away with it."

"I don't think you know what you're talking about," Fenton said, with incredulity. "Submissions are blind."

For whatever reason, Lien was undeterred. "But everyone knows what you're working on. And you're the only one who writes like you. I don't think the boards are as blind as you think."

"I suppose I'll take that as a compliment."

"I mean it as a compliment. I'm sorry if I offended you. I love everything you do. I just think a larger control cluster to offset the COPD patient isolation could have added the right degree of confidence in the results."

She was right, of course. Even he'd wrestled with those choices at the time. However, the grunt work accomplished during the day was what funded his dream projects in the evenings. Publish or perish—a truer maxim had never been spoken. More importantly, that she had the fortitude to question accepted methods, that was something he hadn't expected out of any interview candidates. They were all so submissive, so sycophantic. Yes, she would do nicely here. The contrarian. That was important. Like with all interviews, he ended by saying that she would hear from him in a few weeks. However, as soon as she left, he had his secretary cancel the remaining interviews. Lien was going to be his protégé.

Trust-building was part of the equation. Fenton had Lien start slowly. Seeing how she went along with increasingly off-kilter assignments was critical. The real work they were doing might require breaking a few proverbial eggs. Watching how she handled midnight specimen pickups at ridiculous off-the-map locations were critical tests. It was the only way to know that she could go along for the ride.

Traditionally, designing controlled experiments requiring the administration of unproven technology to human beings could take decades of Institutional Review Board schmoozing. If it got off the ground at all. Fenton didn't have the time or the financial reserves. Doing it off the books, which was what he and Justin had been doing several nights a week after the lab closed, meant that he had to ensure there were no faults in his assessment of Lien. One whistleblower, everything would crumble.

Fenton kicked off his shoes and caught up on some emails while he waited. Lien wasn't on the inside yet. But tonight, he intended to change that. She'd been delivering the assets needed to continue the experiments for months now. Beyond that, as a general researcher supporting the daytime work, she was making incredible progress on a team running a series of trials evaluating mepolizumab, an anti-interleukin-5 antibody. It held promise in treating severe asthma. In another time, he'd have given it more attention. That work was far more conventional, laborious, but Lien proved to have the aptitude. She was a born researcher.

There was a knock at the door. Justin escorted Lien into Fenton's office. Fenton rose, politely, ever the gentleman, and indicated for Lien to take a seat. She sat in the chair across from his desk. He curled his toes along the sharp, plastic edges of the chair mat. He preferred being barefoot in his office. It was a gross violation of hygiene standards out on the lab floor, but, here, behind the desk in his office, his shoes were always piled up beside him.

His foibles never seemed to bother her. She sat with her notebook in hand, awaiting the next assignment. He could see the runners of fog behind her eyes that signaled it was time to take the next step or risk losing her. Lien was growing bored or impatient or both. Seemingly empty errands wouldn't fly any longer.

Compared to just a few months ago, she now looked much more confident. She had blossomed into herself. Fenton knew he played a major role in her development. It filled him with pride.

"So, you really want to make a difference?" Fenton asked playfully.

"Yes," she said. "But you know that."

"I want to bring you in on the project I'm working on. Are you okay with that?"

"You mean the anti-IL-5 cycles. Was there a development that I missed?"

"No," he said, leaning forward in his chair. She sat with such rigid formality it could be hard to read her. "Forget all that."

Her eyebrows arched. Hearing him reveal there was more happening at Davol Laboratory was something she clearly hadn't expected.

"Come with me," he said. "It'll be better if I show you."

★★★★★

Fenton walked Lien to the vault door at the rear of the lab. "Haven't you ever wondered what was back here?"

"I know only you and Justin have access. I just assumed it was a closet for controlled substances."

He laughed. "Maybe a little bit more than that."

Fenton swiped his key card over the badge reader. The mechanical slider bolt released. He pulled on the vault door and ushered Lien in. Justin was inside already. Fenton saw the wonder in Lien's eyes as she took it in. It was a whole hidden world, nearly half the size of the main lab she'd worked in every day for months. This hidden room had similar workbench setups with state-of-the-art equipment. Biohazard signs were littered across most doors and cabinets. And there was the room straight ahead, behind a wall of glass, that beckoned her. To think, until now, only Fenton and Justin ventured here.

Justin sat hunkered over a computer monitor. He did a double take when he saw Lien accompanying Dr. Fenton.

"It's all right," the doctor said. "The time has come. We need another set of hands."

Justin bolted upright, fidgeting. A ballpoint pen jutted out from between his lips. Being around a young, attractive woman threw him off his game even more. Fenton and Justin had grown close, and Fenton knew that Justin didn't make time for relationships. Neither had he, if he was honest with himself. But he'd had long-term relationships in the past. Vivian Lucas haunted him like a ghost. Justin's case was different. Their dynamic had solidified into that of a family. Fenton looked at the young man as a son. One who'd once demonstrated aptitude as a student in much the same way Lien did. Maybe now he'd gain a daughter? God, what a sap he'd become.

"We're still a go, right?" Justin asked.

"Yes. Proceed."

Justin was excited. A new and welcome thrust had been added to the evening. "Great to have you aboard, Lien," he said, brushing by her, "Excuse me. I need to suit up." Justin disappeared into the prep room.

Lien stood in the corner of this new-to-her lab. Fenton could see her glancing this way and that, taking in the surroundings, trying to stay out of the way. In the morning, he'd submit the security request to add her to the badge access list. Then, her ID card would get her in. She earned it.

Fenton handed Lien a fresh lab coat and safety glasses. She was familiar with the standard researcher uniform. The methods and approach in this backroom lab would be the same. No corner-cutting in the design or execution of their experiments. Science mattered. This work was too important and too dangerous to sabotage. The skin around Lien's temples had grown sticky with perspiration. Fenton saw just how nervous she was.

Justin returned donning a full hazmat suit, one piece of industrial rubber with a zip-on hood. It looked as if he were ready for a day of deep-sea diving. Davol lab was so segmented from St. Christopher's that it may as well have been 20,000 leagues underground. Slowly, he approached the antechamber.

Fenton asked Lien to connect the adapter for Justin's airline. She fumbled it into the port just above his tailbone. She had not worked with protective measures like these before. Fenton called to Lien, "You can stand with me outside of the chamber and watch. I'll talk you through it."

"Can I suit up? I'd love to climb inside and see firsthand."

Something inside Fenton told him it would be a bad idea. Too much about tonight's trial was unknown. Lien and Justin didn't yet have a working relationship. Sometimes, in close quarters doing highly technical work, one needed to ensure partners could come together like dancers. Harmony. Still, she wanted in. That was good. And he felt leveraged by what she already knew. Since she was eager, he'd give her some rope. It might braid into trust.

Fenton nodded in tacit agreement. Lien padded off to the back room to get into a new suit. When she returned a few minutes later, her walk was unsteady.

"You can enter the clean room," he said.

She unlatched the door from the antechamber and stepped inside. Through the window, Lien looked back at him. "Where's Justin?" she asked. Her voice came out muffled, but the microphone in the suit was patched through a small speaker on the control panel.

Fenton bent over the mic that sent his voice back to her. "He's going to grab the subject. He wanted to make sure you got in all right." Clean rooms required careful preparation. Researchers couldn't just hop in and out. They had to ensure everything they needed was brought in with them or abandon any hope of completing the day's work.

Fenton heard a low squeaking. He turned and saw Justin pushing a gurney. Justin's rubber suit crinkled as he stepped. Methodically, his hands on the rails to guide it, Justin pushed the gurney from behind, toward the antechamber of the clean room. On the bed was a large lump in a black bag, the size of a small child. After Justin was cleared for entry, he rolled the bed into the antechamber. Fenton watched from the outer room behind glass. He saw that Lien instantly recognized the black bag from her midnight transports.

Lien's legs were knocking together. Through the thick, plastic visor her eyes were losing focus. Fenton clocked her condition. She was suffocating, breathing her own recycled air. He motioned for Justin to connect her airline. When he did, there was the sudden whoosh of pressurized oxygen. She perked up immediately.

"Let's not kill ourselves just yet," Fenton quipped into the mic trying to diffuse the tension with a joke.

Lien smiled, embarrassed. He could read the blush in her cheeks even through the hazmat suit's visor. Strong overhead lighting illuminated the work surface in the clean room. The rails on the gurney sparkled with polish. "This," Justin said, "is subject Two-Four-Sierra."

"Noted," Fenton said into the mic. He recorded the details into his workstation computer program. Then he observed the conditions in the clean room from a bank of computer screens that monitored temperature, humidity, air pressure, and the biometrics of the researchers themselves taken from sensors in their suits. "It's time to go," he said. "Lien, you can stand back and observe. Just stay out of the way. If Justin needs any help, he'll ask."

"Understood," Lien said quickly. She stepped back until her rubber suit scraped the wall behind her.

Fenton kept a close eye on Lien, shrinking—yet curious—against the back wall of the laboratory workspace. Justin was collected, calm, as he laid out his tools on a tray-table in austere lines. Just as a surgeon would.

Fenton typed another line of notes into his program. He spoke into the microphone, "Assimilation test number four. Compound 112A."

Justin picked up a glass vial. Some sort of injectable. He read the label. "Compound 112-Alpha. Check."

"What's in the bag?" Lien asked Justin. Her voice cracked slightly.

"Shhh," Justin chided.

Fenton watched her closely. Even in the thick walls of the rubber hazmat suit, he could see her trembling. Her eyes were wide set, alarmed.

Fenton understood her nerves, but like any parent in a stressful situation, he tried to maintain his demeanor to exude the confidence of someone in charge, someone who had seen it all before. But it was merely a projection. His nerves jangled too. It was like the first day in a new school.

Fenton watched the scene unfold as if in the cinema. The action on-screen framed behind the glass window of the laboratory unfurled with a degree of anticipation and excitement. No matter what happened today, important milestones were being reached in their work. The latest compound, 112A, was another in a series designed to target DNA aberrations and facilitate a communication mechanism with an outside protocol. The potential applications were limitless. It could fix all sorts of chromosomal birth defects if introduced into the fetus during prenatal care. Or it could address brain damage caused by accidents or illness. This compound could be a way to supplement broken neural pathways, a neural joint filler, and complete the right sequencing. Even if 112A had no effect, it was only a matter of time before they found the right one. Then, there was what Father wanted.

Justin moved carefully, almost gliding, to a locked emergency cabinet on the wall. He punched in a quick key code, and a metal door slid open with a pneumatic sci-fi release. It looked like a gun cabinet. He reached in and returned with a long, black, metal pipe that came to a fork at the end. Fenton liked calling it *the trident*. A switch on the staff was flipped. Blue arcs of high-voltage electricity danced at the end of the prongs. Hot, white fire. Thin trails of smoke emerged from the vaulted room as a red light, like the light of a photographer's darkroom, cast everything in a phantasmagoric, blood moon glow.

He watched Lien who was watching Justin emerge with the cattle prod. In the red glow of the room, she tripped backward and fell against the rear wall. Justin approached her slowly.

"You alright?" he asked. "Don't worry. It's just a precaution."

"Yeah," she said, finding her footing again and standing up. "What the hell do you need that for?"

He thrust the device out, but Lien only looked at him. "Here," he said. "We'll be fine. Safety first."

She grabbed for the cattle prod. When Justin let go, Lien's arm dipped. She hadn't expected it to be so heavy.

Fenton felt compelled to reassure his charge. "Don't worry," he said, bowed over the console's microphone. "You won't need it."

"But if I do?" she asked, her voice high-pitched.

"Then push the scary end up against whatever you want to bring down."

Her grip tightened around the long carbon rod while Justin returned to the nylon bag on the gurney. Fenton turned to view their biometric markers. Lien's vitals were all over the map. Justin's were more in control, but still naturally elevated due to the circumstances. The markers for the subject in the nylon bag were stable.

Justin unzipped the bag. Lien took two steps closer until she was peering over his shoulder. Fenton knew this was a good sign: she was curious. It outweighed the weirdness of the situation. When Justin finished unzipping, he methodically pulled apart the flaps and slipped the bag off the subject. He handed the empty bag to Lien, which she seemed to take without noticing it. Her eyes were fixed on the gurney.

An adult dog, a German shepherd, lay before them, tongue lolling. It was alive, but heavily sedated, chest slowly rising and falling with shallow breaths. The dog strained to lift its head from the gurney and began to growl into the darkness.

"Wh–what the hell is this?" Lien stammered. She wasn't looking at Justin. She was addressing Fenton directly, through the glass. Her sharp brown eyes cut through her hazmat visor like two burning coals. "This is what you've had me transporting this whole time? *Dogs?*"

"Mostly," Fenton said into the microphone.

"We're testing on dogs? Testing what?" She was incredulous.

Maybe this was a bad idea after all. "Lien, I'll fill you in on everything, but right now, we need to administer the compound while the subject is still sedated." His tone was firm, direct. Lien shrank back.

Justin watched Lien as she ran a hand over the dog's haunches. Her rubber-coated fingers petted the animal. Her hand moved up to its neck, where she unclasped a collar with dog tags.

"This animal belonged to someone." She was losing focus on her hand with the cattle prod, and its end bobbed and dipped toward Justin.

"Careful with that," Justin warned. He opened a biohazard case on the supply table, withdrew a syringe, and picked up the glass vial labeled 112A. The clear contents looked no different from water, but Fenton was acutely aware of the molecular playground swimming within the saline solution. Justin pierced the vial topper with the syringe, pulled back the plunger, and filled it. He held it up to the bright, overhead light and pushed the air out.

"Back up, Lien," Justin said gently.

She did as she was told, and Justin administered the solution into the dog's hindquarters. Carefully and slowly, he began depressing the plunger. The dog looked up to the darkened ceiling and whimpered. Fenton watched with bated breath as Lien followed the dog's eyeline, but the suit wouldn't let her arch her neck enough to see. She was contorting herself into an arc, and as she did so, the tip of the cattle prod encountered the gurney's metal rails. A shower of sparks exploded, and her arm leaped back from the force of the thrust.

"Gah!" Justin said as his thumb jerked forward. "Oh shit," he murmured. On the small console speaker, Justin's voice was muffled but panicked.

Lien was on her knees trying to grab the cattle prod off the ground, but her hands were having trouble grasping at the carbon rod.

"What is it?" Fenton asked. "What's wrong?"

"I fucked up. I gave too much."

"How much?"

"I don't know, maybe a hundred and fifty mils? The whole syringe. God damn it. What's going to happen?"

Suddenly, the dog's legs began to kick. At first, it was as if the dog were dreaming, but soon, the kicking grew more violent.

"What do I do?" Justin asked in panic. "What do I do?"

Fenton stood at the glass pane in fright, unsure of what to say next. They had been testing in quantities exponentially smaller than this. Prior subjects had received no more than five milligrams. That was enough to synthesize the neural connections they needed. One hundred and fifty milligrams. It was many multiples above what they had ever thought possible.

The dog, still strapped on its side to the table, began kicking with all four legs into the air. Its tongue lolled in and out of its mouth, foam emanating from its jaws. Suddenly, the animal started to seizure, banging its head and limbs violently.

"Get out of there," Fenton said. He was attempting to reassert control. "Both of you get out of there now."

Justin reached behind his back, unclipped the air hose, and dashed for the antechamber. Within moments, he was unzipping his helmet and standing with Fenton on the other side of the glass.

"You could've helped her, Justin!" Fenton yelled. Then, into the mic on the console. "Lien, out, now!"

The dog whipsawed violently. Lien approached the table and put her hand on the animal's arched, rigid back to try and soothe it. The dog was sobering now. Its pupils finding focus. It started barking, slow and confused at first but increasingly ravenous. Howls of devastating pain. The animal thrashed against the thick, fabric straps to no avail.

"Shhh, it's okay," Lien whispered to the dog. Her voice as fragile as sugar glass. She reached up and unzipped her hazmat helmet.

"Lien do not do that. You are risking contamination. Get out! Get out now!"

But Fenton realized that the speaker was embedded in her helmet, and she could no longer hear him. She started petting the dog. She was crying, looking from the dog back to Fenton and Justin. Both men were cowering behind the bank of computers.

Justin grabbed for Fenton's arm. "I'll go back in and get her."

"No, you can't. Look. Something's happening."

Suddenly, the dog's body racked so intensely, with such grotesque violence, that its spinal column cracked. There was a whimper from the animal's jaws, and a trickle of blood began to ooze from its snout.

Lien was bawling uncontrollably now. Her muffled voice, no longer connected to the microphone, was a distant echo in another room. But Fenton knew what she was saying: "How could you?" Over and over.

"Let me go in!" Justin pleaded. "I need to get her out of there."

Fenton tried not to look at Justin. He knew if he met the young man's gaze, he would see the concern and empathy and crumble. Fenton forced himself to look at the computer monitors, where the dog's vitals flatlined to nothing.

Lien stood beside the dog, weeping for the animal. She rolled down her hazmat suit until she could extract her arm. With her bare hand, she caressed the dog with slow, langourous strokes. Her tears fell in a rain of despair, matting the dog's rough brown fur.

That was when it happened. First, it was a lone beep on the computer monitor. The distant ping of new life. Like mission control re-establishing contact with a ship emerging from the dark side of the moon. All of a sudden, the dog's abdomen split open, tearing from the inside, blood and tissue and viscera cascading forth on the gurney and splashing down on the lab floor. From the innermost depths of the animal, a long, fleshy tentacle unfurled and landed on Lien's bare hand. It pulsed like a fire hose receiving water from a massive, churning pump.

Lien screamed. Her voice came out lilting, feminine, as the tendril released, peeling away hunks of her raw flesh in its grip. Sinew and bone poked out from her decimated wrist and hand. Blood spewed in an arterial spray around the room, splashing across Lien's bare face and blinding her.

"What the fuck?" Justin screamed. He ran forward and started beating on the thick wall of glass. "Get out, Lien!"

Fenton ran over to Justin and grabbed him by the shoulders. He spun the young man around until they were eye to eye. Justin's eyes were welling with tears. Fenton saw the terror in them. The boy's heart was in the right place. But there were procedures to follow now.

"We have to get her out." Justin's whimper was a choked gurgle of fear and mucus.

"We can't," Fenton said matter-of-factly. "We don't know what that is. It must stay contained."

In the room, Lien fell to her knees. As she did, she fell face first on the cattle prod. There was a bloom of sparks across the room, and Fenton and Justin watched as the skin of Lien's face melted. Her long, black hair caught fire. The flurry of wild snarls gave way to a whirring mass of sound and fury. Wretched yelps. Then, another ropey tentacle spewed out of the dog's innards.

Lien stumbled to her feet, blinded, in wretched pain, losing blood. The two men outside of the glass room watched helplessly as she made her way back to the door and tried to find the red button to release it. But Fenton couldn't let her go. This crimson hell was it for her. The gloaming. Fenton entered the lockdown command into his console, and the security system took over. The sound of that metal bolt sliding home rang out like a twenty-one-gun salute.

Lien began pounding on the door, her back to the horror. "Help! Hey! Let me out! Please let me go!" She screamed until her vocal cords ruptured. Streams of blood and tears flooded her eyes as she wept.

Fenton saw the biometrics spasming on his computer screen. Blood pressure, pulse, perspiration. They were all going haywire.

"Please, I'm sorry! Please! Just let me out." Her voice was desperate. In it, she was searching for connection, for understanding. "I won't tell anyone. I promise. Please, I've gotta pee."

Fenton was unsure of what to do. Had he been hooked up to the same biometric markers, the computer would have been registering seismic activity for him as well. What the hell was that thing that had taken over the dog? So many questions. The adrenaline shut him down. He was useless.

This poor girl. All she wanted was to do a good job. To please him. He was the one who had shoved her into this. And he had framed it as if this were the launchpad to a successful career. No, this wasn't wrong place, wrong time. There was no excusing this. He selfishly kept her in the dark to protect his own research, and now this poor girl was dying. He couldn't stand to listen anymore, so he cut the feed to her mic.

Through the small, circular window, the eyes of the men watched her. She was fixed in their gaze. Fenton could hear her Lien's small fists raining blows upon the glass. They registered as barely audible behind its thickness. Still, he knew she was likely fracturing her hands into splinters. He threw up and collapsed.

★★★★★

He awoke on the floor. A panicked Justin shaking his shoulders. His vision swimming. The screaming had subsided. Fenton and Justin regrouped at the window, watching, wild-eyed, for any signs of life behind the glass. Lien was a heap of flesh on the floor, bleeding out by the second. The monstrous ropes that had unfurled from within the dog had since retracted back into it. The room was a tableau of gore. Stillness. Eerily peaceful.

Finally, Justin spoke first. "What do we do?"

Fenton was silent for a long moment. He considered all the possibilities. There might still be a way to save this. If so, Lien's death would not be in vain. He would see to that personally. Something magical had happened. Not magical in the perverted Hallmark sense. This was something altogether new. Science had never seen anything like this before. It was dangerous. It was deadly. It gestated incredibly fast. It had taken Lien in a fit of cosmic rage. Something about Compound 112A had synthesized—he didn't even know what to call it—a parasitic organism that rearranged the biological and chemical structure of its host.

But Justin wasn't thinking about the potential. The black half-moons under his bloodshot eyes were that of a soldier emerging unscathed from a sudden massacre. He had survived. Now he'd have to find a way to live with the guilt. Fenton saw nothingness. Justin was an empty vessel. He was in shock. Managing Justin and cleaning up this mess were the two most important things he had to handle right now. Screw these up, and it was all over.

Fenton put his hands on Justin's shoulders, looking him squarely in the eyes. "Here's what you do," he said. "Leave everything here to me. Leave the lab. Don't talk to anyone. Go straight home. Clean up. Eat something. Go to bed. Wait for me to call you."

"But what are you going to do? Are we going to the police?"

"To tell them what? Some crazy sci-fi monster inside a German shepherd exploded in a fit of rage and killed a young woman? Who'd believe that? God, they'd think we raped her and then mutilated her body to cover our tracks."

"I-I..." Justin stammered, his eyes falling to the room behind the glass. "It's still in there, isn't it?"

"Probably. Yes."

"What is it?"

"I don't know. Go home. I'll take care of everything here."

Tears fell down Justin's cheek. "It's my fault."

"What the hell are you talking about?"

"I gave too much. I killed Lien."

"You're in shock. You need to go. Can you make it?"

Justin nodded. It looked as if he was grateful for the opportunity just to escape. Fenton threw him a lifeline and, with it, might have just bought a second chance. Justin ran a hand through the wet mass of his stringy hair. He wiped his eyes on the back of his sleeve. Then he turned and exited. What else was there to say?

Since Davol Laboratory was empty at this time of night, Fenton listened to the echo of Justin's footfalls until they died away, returning him to a world of utter silence. He fished his cell phone from his pocket. For a moment, he thought about calling the CDC. This was certainly something to report. Then Lien really would have died for nothing. They'd immediately shut him down and cart him off to prison. He thought about dialing Vivian. God, they had once been so close, what happened? He was about to put his phone away when he remembered the government men who had set him up with this project. They had given him a number to call if the results yielded any findings. He would let them know and take his chances. But that would be after he cleaned up the mess. They didn't need to know about Lien.

A plan was mobilizing. Fenton would snag a hazmat suit, grab Lien's bag and car keys, and dash out the back. The hospital's cameras had an intentional blind spot at the rear entrance to the lab. That was by design, as he didn't need questions asked when vans showed up with overnight cargo. He could drive her Jeep out to the woods and run it off the road. It could be days before anyone found it. When it was discovered, there would be no trace of him. No DNA, no fingerprints, no hair follicles. It could buy him time. The fear churned in the pit of his stomach. All of this suddenly had the feeling of a straight-to-DVD horror flick. It made him sick that this was now his life.

Put out one fire at a time. Eyes down. Focus.

Fenton turned once again to the clean room. Whatever he had synthesized with his compound was likely still alive. He couldn't go in to retrieve Lien. That was why the room was built with contamination protocols. He typed some commands into the workstation. The program prompted him to swipe his badge. He did. It asked for confirmation. He provided it. The sequence was initiated.

Through the vault window, a hissing rush of smoke flooded the room, followed by a wall of red fire lapping at the windows. Fenton peered through the thick glass wall and gazed into the mouth of hell. The light hit at just the right angle so that his own reflection appeared to be looking back at him. The room was incinerated.

Chapter Five
DEVIL'S TOWER

Stacks of textbooks, old notepads, and folders brimming with medical school detritus had built up into a kind of monolith in the corner of Kate's living room. She often joked with Sean about it looking like the Devil's Tower in *Close Encounters*. She remembered not enjoying the film as a kid when her dad had taken her to some '70s sci-fi retrospective at the Landmark Twin. Recently, when catching it on television, she found herself pulled in for the first time. Something about a wayward adult magically escaping all his bullshit problems, traveling up to the heavens on a musical spaceship, was appealing to her in ways her childlike self could never have understood. This time, at the end, she'd cried. She kept that to herself. Whenever she brought up films like this with Sean, it would inevitably kick-start more fights on the artistic merits of mainstream pop culture.

Carrying her books, Kate bumped into the side table near the couch. A framed picture was sent tumbling. She picked it up, made sure the glass hadn't cracked (it hadn't), and studied it. In the photo, Kate stood wrapped in her father's embrace. It was high school graduation day. A moment preserved in amber, she in her cap and gown, her father's smile broad and genuine. She had loved him madly.

After resetting the frame, she took a seat at the dining room table. The table was a hand me down from her mother. She got it when she'd struck out on her own. In fact, her mother used Kate moving out as an opportunity to fill her own home with new furniture. Anything to distract from the loneliness. Empty-nest syndrome. Clearly, the spending spree hadn't worked to fill the void, as now she was looking to sell the home. Kate's table was the very same one upon which she'd eaten all her dinners growing up. Sprawled across it now was a sea of wedding magazines. *Brides. The Knot. Martha Stewart Weddings.* They layered every square inch of the table's surface.

She did not lazily flip through the pages to pass the time. Instead, she studied intensely; her brain cataloging every trend, every idea, every editorial suggestion into her mental Rolodex for that as-of-yet still unplanned date. She approached her wedding the same way she approached her studies. Methodically. There was the article celebrating the creative stories of couples who had eloped. The one on planning the ideal seating arrangement. This had become her routine on the nights Sean worked a double. His overnights had become more and more common recently. The television was on in the background, the volume turned down to a whisper. It made the small apartment feel a little less lonely. No, that wasn't true. It made her feel less afraid.

She looked up at the television as a bickering fight was erupting between two catty housewives. Kate cackled, licked her fingertip, and flipped the page. When her eyes started going fuzzy and she could no longer focus, she filled the washing machine and set the timer to turn it on in the morning. Then she dragged herself to her bedroom and climbed right into the cold, empty bed.

When reaching for the charge cord of her cell phone, she thought about how late it was and decided to call Sean anyway. After two rings, the phone went straight to his voice mail. The recorded message Kate had become so familiar with started to play: "Hi, you've reached Sean..."

She hung up. Her bedroom had taken on the musty odor of the mold spot spreading on the ceiling. The black spores continuing to bloom, a cancer inside the home. She cracked a window. The air was near frigid. She passed out on the bed.

★★★★★

When she awoke to the smell of freshly brewed coffee, she was thankful for a dreamless sleep. She stirred, made the half of the bed she had slept in, and remembered that she'd spent the night alone. In the kitchen, to her surprise, Sean was standing by the sink, sipping black coffee from his St. Christopher's mug. Kate grabbed a bowl from the drying rack over the sink, poured herself some cereal, and popped two of her Xanax.

"Surprised to see you here," she quipped. Inside, she was filled with a deep well of emotions, but she wanted to play this cool. Ice him out for his absences lately.

"Got in late. Figured it'd be best if I crashed on the couch."

Kate glanced over at the sectional in the living room where a throw and a pillow were still laid out. "What time did you get in?" she asked.

"Maybe three. Three-thirty."

"You didn't come to bed?"

"Didn't want to wake you."

"Oh shit," she said. "Almost forgot the wash."

Kate disappeared into the laundry room to shift the wet bundle of clothes into the dryer. The chugging of the dryer's basin roared to life like a truck's engine. The laundry room closet was dark and warm. She closed her eyes, breathed deep. Something strange was in the air. Why hadn't Sean come to bed?

She stepped quickly into the bathroom, checked her appearance, and swallowed a gulp of Listerine. It burned like fire in her throat. She loosely piled her hair atop her head, leaving her neck exposed. The knifelike blade of her collarbone poked from her T-shirt's neckline. She knew that it drew Sean crazy.

"Sorry," she said, returning. "Didn't want wet clothes growing musty all day."

"It's fine."

"What's your day look like? Wanna do lunch?" she asked, hopeful, as she splashed some skim milk on the corn flakes and dug in.

"Would love to," Sean said. "But can't. I'm scrubbing in within the hour." He sipped from the last of his coffee and then started brushing his teeth right at the kitchen sink. He ladled a handful of tap water from the faucet into his mouth and spit.

Kate had always been mystified by surgeons who cut and rooted and healed people from the inside. She wanted to be mad at him, to screw with him, but couldn't.

"God, what you do, the power you have. It's so amazing." Hearing herself be so sycophantic in his presence made her sick to her stomach. She dumped the half-eaten bowl of cereal into the sink.

"You'll be out on the floor in a few more years," he said. "Besides, you're doing good work now already."

"But I'll never do what you do." It was a rare truth. "In fact, I've been thinking a lot lately."

"About what?" he asked. He appeared genuinely interested in what she had to say. Maybe that was because she had played to his ego with all her godlike talk of saving lives.

"I don't even know if this whole thing is for me after all. Maybe I should just go back to school. Find something else?"

Sean smiled tenderly. "We all hit the wall at some point. Just hang in there."

Just hang in there. She envisioned the tabby cat clinging to the clothesline in Lien's poster.

Glancing at the time on the clock on the microwave, Sean said, "I'm late."

"You just got off two overnights. Why do you have to head back in so soon? You need a proper night's sleep."

"I'll sleep when I'm dead," he muttered. "This one's important. Remember Parker Dallas? Gunshot wound?"

"You mean the guy you bitched at me for visiting? I don't think I'll forget him any time soon."

"He must have a guardian angel. Getting put in the hospital was the best thing for him. When X-raying his leg for bullet fragments, the imaging team found a hole."

"A hole?" Kate asked. She thought of the black mass Lucas had been challenging her on. She thought of Lien saying more testing was needed. "No shit," Kate whispered. "There was something there."

"In his thigh bone. Usually, a mass like that showing up on an X-Ray indicates a tumor. Confirmed by oncology yesterday. Dude had no idea. We're going after it today."

"Is he going to be all right?" Kate asked.

"Should be. He's lucky. Would have been months before the pain brought him into the hospital, if ever. Guy like that, he may have tried to tough it out. By then, cancer would have spread. I think we're getting to it early enough."

"Huh," she said. "So, you'll patch him up, make him right as rain. Then he can sit in a jail cell for the rest of his life."

Sean washed his hands in the kitchen sink with a squirt of dish soap and dried them on paper towels. "Guess so. I'll see you around."

He kissed Kate on the cheek and left out the front door, walking to where his black Audi A8 was crookedly parked in the apartment's lone space.

Kate held in the doorway, a mother sending her baby off to the first day of school. Her stomach was still upset. She didn't know if it was the Xanax dissolving into her bloodstream or anxiety over Sean. Kate couldn't shake the feeling that he was up to something. She had a sudden urge to call after him, just to get him to turn around so she could look him in the eyes one more time.

"Don't forget about tonight!" Kate called after him.

With his hand on the Audi's door, Sean stopped, spun around. His rich, blue eyes were slits. The early-morning sun had just cleared the horizon and cut into his eyeline, forcing his hand to block the sharp light from his eyes. A faint breeze ruffled Kate's extra-long Clash T-shirt that she'd worn to bed, the one with the *London Calling* album cover on it. Her arms broke out in gooseflesh as a chill went down her spine.

"Tonight?"

"We have that appointment. To order our wedding invitations. You promised. Seven o'clock," Kate said, perturbed. Then, going off Sean's look, she added pre-emptively, "Remember?"

"Oh shit," he said. "Of course. Yeah, okay." He had the sputtering voice of a high school senior who had forgotten his homework yet again.

"But we can't order invites without a date. So come prepared. One way or the other, it's getting done. Got it?"

He waved her away with a flash of his hand, nodding, the way he did when he just wanted her to go away. Then he was in his car, revving the engine and speeding off down the quiet, private road of the apartment complex.

★★★★★

The very tall man in the white lab coat was Dr. Childers. His patient was supine on the gurney before him. The doctor ran the transducer of an ultrasound machine over his patient's chest.

His demeanor was dry as a bucket of sawdust. The patient, a middle-aged man, lay still and silent in the center of the classroom. Patient/Doctor class was structured around demonstration. A bastardized version of art schools where everyone sat in a circle sketching rank nude models. Kate looked around. She was not the only student seconds away from crashing forehead first onto the tabletop before her. In her chart, it would read: *Confirmed cause of death: extreme boredom.*

The patient's gown was pinned open. Childer's probe ran over saggy skin that layered over his rib cage like a wet pelt. His black socks poked out of the hem of the gown; toes pointed up toward the bright stage lighting. The ultrasound machine was hooked up to the state-of-the-art projector which broadcast the image to the entire class. The mechanical pumping of his heartbeat echoed through the auditorium's expensive speaker system.

"Patient is Shusett, Roger. Number KL504048. Lateral wall view," Childers said in a voice that was barely above a hushed whisper. When projected through the marble-sized microphone pinned to his coat's lapel, it sailed cleanly to the back rows where Kate and Daniel perched. Childers had his hand on the patient's shoulder in a calming gesture while he spoke.

"Here's a quick test you can do," Childers said, addressing his class. "We have them sniff, and then you watch their IVC collapse, and if it collapses easily, that tells you whether the patient has normal lung pressure."

The doctor had his patient mimic this movement and dragged the probe forward a few inches, circling his chest, pointing out the indicators on the massive screen. Even through the boredom, the material was clicking with Kate. What would have sounded to most other folks as technical jargon was coalescing into a story, like learning a second language.

Behind her, Daniel typed rapidly with a clickety-clack into his Mac PowerBook. Kate picked up her cheap, plastic ballpoint and burned a hole into a Moleskine notebook. It seemed they were the only two in the small sea of med students trying to get something out of this.

The hall door opened, flooding the room with a splash of white light. The nocturnal spell momentarily broke Kate glanced back. She'd been waiting for Lien to arrive. It wasn't her.

"Hey," Daniel said, noticeably above a whisper.

"Shhh," Kate hissed.

Childers continued his demonstration. His wary eyes fixed on the commotion in his audience. With one hand guiding the probe, his other typed key commands into the machine. On the big screen, the image paused, the pumping heart frozen.

"Any irregularity," Childers said, indicating the screenshot, "can be an indication of a deeper problem like ascariasis or other parasitic infections."

Daniel leaned in closer. "Have you seen Lien today?" he asked.

Kate craned her neck back to him. His breath smelled like the everything bagel he ate every morning. "Did you call her?" she asked. But it was of no use. Kate had tried calling three separate times.

"No," Daniel said. The other students were starting to look perturbed at the conversation.

Kate took out her phone to double-check if Lien had left a message. Nothing. She started typing out a text as Daniel said, "You're right. It's weird. She never misses class."

Childers's voice bellowed from the round, "You with the phone, what's your name?"

Kate felt hot panic seizing her. "Kate.

"Kate what?"

"Kate White, professor."

"Miss White, am I boring you?" He was exasperated, held his class in nothing short of total and utter contempt.

"N–no," she stammered. Daniel kept his head down, completely unwilling to jump in and take the bullet. "I'm sorry, I'm just turning it off."

"It's very disrespectful, you know." He tapped his temple with a cadaverous index finger. "I remember things like this."

Childers returned to his lesson. Daniel placed a supportive hand on Kate's shoulder. "Sorry," he said with a mischievous grin.

"Fuck me," Kate whispered as she and Daniel sank lower into their seats.

★★★★★

The door to Davol Laboratory didn't look like other doors in the hospital. It was formed of solid metal and was adorned with biohazard warning symbols. Standing before it, the door looked like an armored train car stopped on the tracks. Entirely immovable. An array of lights, indicators, and sirens—all docile, waited for the magic key card to either grant access or sound the alarm.

For their Advanced Methods class, Lucas had arranged for a tour of the laboratory. Kate was excited to finally see where Lien was spending all her time. No one in the cohort but Lien had ever been down here. It was like an elite country club, and those with access never spoke about what occurred behind closed doors. Kate was curious if Lien was already in the lab, having been sidelined with some project. Maybe that was why no one had seen her? That was the only thing, Kate imagined, that would have kept Lien from attending class.

The metal door was so polished it served as a mirror. Kate's body was starting to feel like a cadaver recently delivered from the morgue. She looked even worse. Her gaunt mouth pulled down now in a nearly permanent frown.

They had been waiting for Dr. Lucas. This was unusual. But finally, the old Doberman tore around the corner in a huff. When Lucas spoke, her class shut up. "Sorry I'm late, but I've just heard news that there was a situation in the lab overnight. A fire. I'm not sure today's the best day for a tour, but, selfishly, I want to know what's going on here. So, we're going to try anyway."

Dr. Lucas swiped her key card at the reader by the door where they were gathered. The badge reader flashed red; the door remained locked. Lucas looked down at her card as if it could be nothing but a mechanical error. Then, on its own, the heavy door slid open with a hydraulic release. A timid researcher intern waved the group through.

Lucas held her card up to intern's face. "Really? I'm out? We're going to have to talk about this."

Lucas pushed into the chamber. Her students filed in behind. Once the five of them entered, the large door locked back into place.

"Everyone ready?" Lucas called, counting her students. "Where's Lien?"

Kieran called out from the back, "Haven't seen her all day."

Lucas shrugged it off. Davol Laboratory was awash in activity. Entire stations were cordoned off with yellow caution tape, and gruff men in suits hurried about like ants on a picnic blanket. Kate had never seen these men before in the hospital.

"All this for a fire?" Kieran asked.

"I'm really not sure what this is about," Lucas said.

"Who are these people?" Greg asked.

"They look like G-men," Lucas said. The anachronism struck Kate as odd. It wasn't a term she'd heard. Lucas and the students gathered at the yellow caution tape like onlookers at a parade. They watched the men scurrying, taking in the sheer impressiveness of the spectacle. The laboratory was incredible. Kate was wild-eyed. A hidden city, hiding underground beneath her feet.

A strange-looking older man standing with a packet of manila folders tucked under one arm clocked Dr. Lucas and the students from the other side of the room. He gestured with a finger to indicate he would only be a minute and wrapped up a crucial-looking conversation with one of the serious-looking men in suits.

"That's Dr. Louis Fenton, head of Davol Laboratory," Lucas said. There was a barely perceptible upturn in the corners of her mouth. As the old man approached, Lucas's body became girlish, loose.

"Hey, Lou. What the hell happened?" she called out to him.

Fenton approached. From his stance, it was apparent that he had at one point been expecting them and then forgotten. The old man possessed an aura of insouciance, signaled mainly by his untucked, button-down shirt covered in pineapples, and the barely tamed shock of hair. Everything about the old man contrasted sharply with the rigid formality of his staff and the men in their suits.

"You in trouble?" Lucas cackled as Fenton neared. They shook hands briefly. To Kate, the look in their eyes said more; that there was some sort of a relationship buried there. They were wallpapering over intimacy with strict professionalism.

"Ah, nothing for you to worry about." He winked. "Surprise audit. That's all."

"I was going to say, didn't look like a fire broke out here." Lucas quipped.

"We'll need to reschedule the tour for another time. I hope you don't mind."

"I do mind, Lou," Lucas said lightly. "What am I supposed to do with this lot?" she added, sweeping a hand outward to indicate her students.

"How about teaching them all of your tricks for good bedside manners?"

"How about I teach you to shut the hell up?" she said with a riotous cackle. Kate winced. Like Pavlov's salivating dogs, Kate had been trained to expect horror on the other side of Lucas's laugh.

Lucas resigned herself to needing to turn back. "It's fine. We'll manage. This place gives me the creeps anyway."

"You're breaking my heart." Fenton smiled. "What's not to love?"

"Let's just say I prefer it upstairs in the world of the living."

Fenton's face was peppered with a few days of growth. Kate only now realized why something kept nagging her about his appearance, why things just didn't seem right. He was barefoot.

"Lou, would you at least say something to the students who have been looking oh-so-forward to this visit?"

"Hi, class," he said. Then he brought both fists up a few inches above his head. A demented cheer. "Go science!"

"Well, it was short, anyway." Lucas smiled, placing a warm hand on Fenton's back.

Kate stepped forward. "Dr. Fenton, have you seen Lien Chu? She works for you, right?"

Lucas jumped in, "Yes, she's normally a part of our cohort. I was surprised when she didn't turn up this morning. You got her burning the candle at both ends?"

Fenton scratched his head. Kate saw the man's hands shake momentarily and then dip in and out of his pockets like he was trying to stage his body. "You know," Fenton said, "I haven't seen her. She was here briefly last evening, but said she was heading home around ten, ten-thirty."

Something about this man, this room, the activity of the men in suits, and Lien suddenly missing gave Kate the creeps. Fenton met Kate's gaze and immediately glanced at the floor as if ashamed of something. Then, resetting, he looked back up at Lucas and gave a polite smile. "I really should at least give your class a quick intro."

Fenton turned to the students. When he spoke, he did so in a measured drawl. "Good morning," he said, extending his arms in a wide-open, welcoming gesture. They were still separated on opposite sides of a length of yellow caution tape. "Welcome to Davol Laboratory. Apologies that we haven't the time for the full tour today. At the very least, I can give you the thirty-thousand-foot view."

Kate drew her fingers across the black countertops of the nearest workstation, admiring its rich, polished luster. She didn't know what most of the specialized equipment was for, but the room was indeed something to behold.

"Here, we're leading the way in stem cell research," Fenton said. "We've taken very primitive human stem cells and learned how to direct them to form the different types of cells that we want with memetic gene enhancement."

Kieran, Zach, and Greg were listening astutely. Kate knew that Kieran, especially, had been considering moving into research when it was time to concentrate in the program in another year. He had told Kate once, a long time ago, that he coveted Lien's reputation. And her youth. He asked Kate if Lien was single. Of course, Kate had told Lien immediately, and the two had laughed, for hours, over a box of wine.

"We're also making progress in viral, parasitic, and disease control," Fenton said. His bare feet rested on the spotless, shimmering VCT flooring. He pointed the group toward a sizeable industrial freezer marked with biohazard stickers. The lid was locked with an electronic, numbered keypad.

"What do you keep in there?" Greg asked. He was gripping the yellow caution tape in both hands like a child holding the bars and trying to peek just a little farther into the lion's den at the zoo.

"That's where we keep samples of all our various biologics.

"What do you have? Anything dangerous? Ebola?"

"There are a few nasty viruses that we're looking at."

"Doesn't every James Bond film have some terrorist stealing a lab virus with the intention of holding the world ransom?"

"Oh, and zombies," Zach chimed in. "Don't forget the zombies. Always zombies."

"Uh, yeah, sure," Fenton said, dismissing the dynamic duo with barely a wave of his hand.

The air shifted in the room. Kate felt the strangeness of everything all at once. It was like someone had turned the air-conditioning on. Her neck erupted in a shiver of gooseflesh. Apparently, they all felt it, because when Kate looked from Zach to Greg to Kieran, they were all on edge. Kate looked upon the freezer with great awe, her mind spinning, cataloging, labeling. Exactly what, she didn't know.

"Dr. Fenton, can you comment on specifically where your disease-based research is going?" Kieran asked with utmost sincerity. Without Lien, he moved into the role of apple polisher. *At least he's trying to bring some maturity back to the conversation*, Kate thought.

"As I'm sure you can imagine," Fenton said, "much of our work is in strict confidence. It would require you to have need-to-know status and sign an NDA. But I would encourage you to follow our publications on the hospital's website to stay on top of whatever latest breakthrough we yield."

"What is it that drew you to this particular kind of work?" Kate asked. Over her shoulder, Lucas smiled at the engaged question. She clearly wanted her students to impress Fenton.

"The thing about viruses," Fenton said, "is that they're such perfectly engineered creatures." The intonation of his voice had changed. There was a vitality in the movements of his hands as they gestured. "We go on the offensive, but they-they learn. They adapt."

On the large screen above the nearest researchers' station were sepia-tinted images of patients, children, ravaged with unnamed diseases, their faces flooded with permanent sadness. "Mankind has come so far. But, when pitted against what's in that freezer…well, we're still in the dark ages."

One of the men in his off-the-rack, gray suit stalked over to Fenton, cupped his hand, and whispered into the doctor's ear.

Fenton turned to Lucas and the students. "I think that's all for today, folks!"

"Is everything all right, Lou?" Lucas asked. "Seriously?"

He nodded but said no more, turning and disappearing around the bend, leaving the students and their mentor alone at the yellow caution tape.

"C'mon, all," Lucas said. "Class dismissed."

They exited: Greg, Zach, Kieran, Kate, and Daniel. Lucas stood in the doorway until they all cleared out, their faces cast in solemn stone.

★★★★★

The large, laminated photo album plonked on the countertop. The woman behind the counter opened it randomly. Sample upon sample of different kinds of invitations. Tabs for weddings, showers, anniversaries, birthdays. The plastic pages crinkled, covered in the fingerprints of everyone who ever handled the book. It was like looking through frosted glass.

Kate pointed to one relatively tasteful design, navy blue, with foil-pressed printing in an art deco style. The gilded edges and intricate border pattern struck a good balance between the feminine and masculine. She imagined the invitation's sample names replaced with *White* and *Carraway*. The delicate filament of the serif font caught the light and glinted.
She thought Sean would like it. He still wasn't here though.

She repeatedly whispered, "Kate Carraway, Kate Carraway, Kate Carraway"—emphasizing the alliteration and letting the repeated velar sounds lull her. She wanted his last name. *Does that mean I'm not a proper feminist? Am I setting my entire gender back?*

"This one," Kate said.

She flashed on a vision of the two of them raking leaves in front of her childhood home. Kate hadn't mentioned anything about her mother selling the place. It would be yet one more thing on the pile, and surely, their Jenga tower could only take so much wobbling before it crashed. He might balk at the cost or the fact that Kate herself had no savings at all right now. But the fantasy wouldn't stop playing on repeat in her mind's eye: Morning coffee on the patio. Summer birds. Children.

Kate had been hanging around the print shop for nearly an hour now, flipping endlessly through the same few plastic pages. Her body was sweating. She was still in her jacket, the trench with the soft fleece lining, but was too embarrassed to remove it now. It would be admitting she was settling in for the long haul.

"He's a doctor, you know." Kate said. "Sometimes, he has to work late unexpectedly."

The woman behind the counter slipped the mock-up out from the plastic sleeve and handed it to Kate. If the woman behind the counter had a problem with Kate loitering, she didn't once express derision. For that, Kate was thankful.

Kate checked her watch.

The woman behind the counter saw this. "I don't think he's gonna make it, honey."

"Maybe not," Kate said, defeated.

"Have you two agreed to a date yet?"

"No."

"I've seen lots of couples stall here. It's not just you. You need to sit him down and have a chat."

Kate closed her eyes, inhaled, and handed the sample invitation back. "Maybe you're right," Kate said.

Her mind was spinning in the dark. The woman behind the counter slipped the mock-up back into its place within the book and fit the album back onto the metal shelving behind her.

★★★★★

Kate's apartment was stifling. She had a habit of leaving the thermostat cranked to seventy-five day-and-night from the moment the first frost started appearing on the ground. The apartment air was thick and stale. It felt as if she were walking through a sea of foam cushions.

After tearing through the place—all three postage stamp sized rooms of it—she flung open all the windows, dropped her bags to the floor, and collapsed on the well-worn couch. She pulled out her cell phone, nearly dead from her compulsively checking it all day, and tried both Sean and Lien. Each went straight to voicemail. The unsettling feeling that had been lurking in her stomach solidified into an image in her mind: maybe they were together right now?

Two of the most important people in her life were off the map. The past few days had been full of pent-up emotion: still being unable to nail a diagnosis, getting called out in

Childers's class, Sean clearly avoiding her. Kate felt unmoored. This wave of anxiety was cresting. Tears spilled down her cheeks. She curled up on the couch in that very hot room and wept.

After a while she got up. Her eyes were puffy and raw. Her throat sore. She padded over to the refrigerator. On the top shelf was a large, white pastry box. *SAMPLES* was written in black magic marker, cutting across the printed logo of Zaccagnini's Bakery. When they'd first started dating, Kate and Sean would venture there almost every Sunday morning for coffee and muffins. They hardly made the trip these days.

The bakery had sent Kate home with wedding cake samples five days ago after Sean had bailed at the last minute to pull a double. Now the cake was sitting stale in her fridge, and they hadn't had a moment together that wasn't fraught with awkwardness.

Kate grabbed a flimsy paper plate and used her thumbnail to slice through the tape that sealed the box's edges. Inside, six small squares of cake and frosting combinations. She tipped the box over. Layers of yellow and chocolate cake, daubs of buttercream frosting, pools of ganache, sliced strawberries, and fondant all ran down into one big mess onto the plate.

She skipped dinner and went straight to bed with the plate. She gorged on sweets and reality television. Her mind constantly bouncing back to the last time she had talked to Lien, at Arturo Bar's, when Lien had worked to bolster her confidence. Kate replayed the conversation over and over. Was there any clue that would explain why she was missing? Nothing came. Kate just kept circling the drain, remembering Lien's playful suggestion to start infecting patients to master her diagnoses. Then, delirium overcame her. She fell asleep, face down in the paper plate of cake crumbs.

★★★★★

Her dreams were nightmares. Her mind wove a tangled tapestry of the day's events. She remembered a psychology professor once saying that dreams were made from the day's residue.

In one of them, Sean and Lien had eloped and were halfway to Las Vegas. Then storm clouds rolled through, and the mental channel changed. Suddenly, Kate was back in the hospital. This time, she was in a gown, strapped to a gurney like Parker Dallas. The horrible, old, dead man was shuffling toward her with his yellow eyes and feral, vampiric teeth. He spoke to her in a ghastly, hectoring screech, and when he finally did catch her, he sank his teeth into the soft flesh of her neck.

★★★★★

When Kate came to, it was the middle of the night, and she was back at St. Christopher's, confused and cold, with no idea how she had gotten there. Everything was sputtering, in and out. Was it even really happening? Or was she dreaming?

No, she was here, fully dressed in yesterday's rumpled clothing, standing in the middle of the patient wing of the hospital. The door standing before her had a familiar number on it: 217. She licked her lips where powdered sugar frosting had congealed.

The blackouts had never been this bad before.

Chapter Six
INFECTION

In the early-morning hours, just before the sun rose, the east patient wing of St. Christopher's hospital was an altogether different place. Nurses stepped quietly. Half of the lighting grid was turned down low. When people spoke, barring emergencies, it was in whispers. It was like the hush that overtakes the cabin of a red-eye flight.

What the hell happened? Kate thought. Why was she here? Why, when unconscious, did her body move her through the city, into the hospital, and to this place? To room 217? Was it some divine gravitational pull? Some kind of somnambulant video game with God directing her here in this red eye gloaming. Maybe there would be an answer inside?

She needed answers and so Kate slipped quietly into Parker's room shutting the door behind her. She peered out the door's small, square window looking back out on the east wing to ensure that no one had seen her enter. For now, at least, the corridor was empty.

Parker's room was dark save for the flickering glow of the television. On it, the History channel was airing a late-night documentary special about the Tuskegee experiments. Its volume had been turned down so low that the only sound Kate heard was Parker's buzz-saw snore. It rose and fell in violent yawps.

Kate stood motionless, her back against the door, for what felt like an eternity as her eyes adjusted to the darkness.

Finally, when she could see well enough, and she had mustered the courage, Kate glided over to Parker's bedside.

Her arms and legs were trembling. They had been ever since she'd woken up here in the hospital. Of course, there was the immediate panic about lost time. This fugue state. She felt certain now that, yes, she *was* going crazy. If she had any hope at all, it was that this shit was stress induced. She would need to take drastic measures to reduce it. Above all, she needed to start doing well in her courses and get this program back on track. Then, maybe – just maybe – Kate would regain agency over her life. And for that, then, maybe an answer lied in room 217. Why else would her subconscious bring her to this place?

She grabbed Parker's chart from the foot of his bed. Her shadow obstructed the glow of the television. An eclipse, turning Parker's chiseled face into the dark side of the moon. She held her breath and prayed he wouldn't wake. She knew she shouldn't be here, unsupervised, in a patient's room after hours. Especially this one. In fact, where was the police officer who was meant to be guarding the door?

Kate flipped through his chart, page by page. At first, nothing jumped out. His symptoms, pain levels, date of admission, last recording of vitals. All were etched in pen by the nursing staff. All aligned with everything Lucas had said when the class visited earlier. Kate flipped. Flipped again. On the Chart Audit Review, she finally found something.

Under the notes for the Any Known Allergies, the attending physician had written, *ACE inhibitors*. That had struck Kate previously, but she hadn't known why. Now, reflecting on it, the primal part of the brain, the lizard brain, was already striking the match to the wick of some distant plan. But what? Its rough-hewn edges were still too sharp to fix in her mind.

ACE   inhibitors   were   common   in   fighting cardiovascular issues. She knew that much. That would be strange for someone with Parker's build and physique if he wasn't in the process of detoxifying his system of the hard drugs he'd been abusing. What else did she know about drug allergies? Typically, this kind of allergy was far from life-threatening. It simply led to a few unpleasant side effects. Mild swelling. Discomfort. Who was ever really comfortable in a hospital anyway? Was there something here? There was. The boxer going down in the fifth. She had an inside line.

The sound of a hacking cough rattled her, peeled back her skin. Parker stirred. Kate held her breath, still as a statue. She could hear the thrum of her blood rushing through her temples. The squirm of her guts. Her adrenaline went into overdrive. His snore returned. Comforted, she replaced his chart and slipped out of his room as quietly as she'd entered.

Kate went scurrying down the hall to the nearest nurses' station. Her footfalls splashed gently on the linoleum. She couldn't conceive of a way to trek down to the hospital pharmacy and procure an IV of enalapril without too much risk: paper trails, forged prescriptions, witnesses. Didn't matter. This was not a medication with addictive properties. It would be readily available in the emergency kits kept at each nurses' station. When she arrived, there was only one nurse on duty. Kate crept along the wall, waiting behind a supply cart. On the cart was a balled-up lab coat. Kate slung it on covering the heap of wrinkled clothes she was wearing. She waited until the nurse moved off down the hall in the opposite direction. When the nurse finally entered the nearest patient room, Kate pounced.

The pharmaceutical kit looked like any generic toolbox from a home improvement center. The lid lifted back. Inside, an array of smaller compartments, each holding the most commonly dispensed medications. Beneath the top grid was a series of drawers. In the drawer for IV/cardiovascular meds, Kate found enalapril right away. She grabbed an IV bag, slipped it into the deep pocket of her white coat, and crept stealthily back down the hall.

As she made her way, Kate stopped midflight. Her back stretched against the wall as she waited for the night nurse to move down into the next room. The bulletin board in the hallway was full of St. Christopher's brochures. The hospital promoted itself within its marketing literature with corny corporate copy like *"bastion of healthcare excellence"* and *"nestled in picturesque Southern New England."* Kate knew that she likely would never have been accepted into the program had it not been for a bit of a miracle with her MCATs and Sean pulling some crucial strings for her. It was always a kick in the teeth. Why did these acutely depressing thunderheads crowd her brain at the worst times?

When she finally re-entered Parker's room, she paused and let her eyes readjust once again. Parker was still out cold. The wall clock marched forward with a steady tick, tick, tick. On the muted television, an infomercial flashed for some new, can't-miss kitchen helper.

She took the existing bag of saline from the hook above Parker's bed and switched it out with the enalapril, adjusting the computer to administer only one-eighth of the traditional dosage rate. This would ensure Parker wouldn't flare up immediately.

After shoving the empty saline bag and all the assorted debris into her coat's pockets, Kate retreated to the door and left the room as silently as she'd entered.

Between Parker's room on the second floor and the side entrance at ground level, she only passed three people, none of whom she knew, and two of whom—cleaning staff—she didn't believe even spoke any English. Here, in the middle of the long, lonely corridor, was a door to the incinerator chute.

She looked left, looked right. God, it was all so quiet. She turned the coat's pockets inside out and dumped every scrap of evidence down into the fire.

★★★★★

By four in the morning, nothing was open aside from St. Christopher's emergency room. The metro wouldn't make its first run for another two hours. Though the city slumbered, Kate was much too wired to head home. She sat on the Witcham Street sidewalk, like a drunk, her back against the iron fence of Arturo's Bar. The restaurant staff had closed, shut the lights, and locked the doors a lifetime ago. Her last time at Arturo's had been the last time she'd seen Lien. Everything about this week had since become a flaming train wreck: nightmares, sleepwalking, a missing friend, an absent fiancé. It felt as if her very life was hanging by a thread.

The night sky was cloudy. No ounce of glow from moon or stars. The blank, black void above felt immensely oppressive, reinforcing the empty dread that there was nothing, no one, looking out for her.

Kate checked her cell phone again. Still nothing from Sean. Or Lien. The memories of what she'd just done – deliberately taking action to harm a patient - were refracting, distorting, disconnected pieces. It still didn't feel real. She trembled. It wasn't like her to want to harm anyone. But this was a man who intentionally tried to hurt others. Would she really be judged harshly for this?

She got to her feet and lodged her earbuds into place. Anything to blast away the nagging worries. Barely enough battery life left in her cell phone, she scrolled to a playlist she'd been building for her and Sean's wedding reception. Thundering into her ears was a rock and roll song from her father's favorite record. She wanted this to be the song to which she and Sean were first introduced to the world as a married couple, in honor of the father–daughter dance that would never come.

The rollicking tom fill. The arpeggiated A–major chord. The driving bass line. Kate's father had loved The Heartbreakers, and he and Kate had sung all their songs throughout her childhood, woefully tone deaf, until they would collapse into each other's arms, laughing.

The music was giving her a second wind, keeping the bad thoughts at bay. She supposed there would be time to feel sorry or shame or guilt or *whatever* later. But for now, she marched.

Halfway between the hospital and her apartment was a small bridge that crossed a section of the Charles River. Kate stopped in the middle, allowing herself the opportunity to gaze out across the city in a picturesque, pre–dawn tableau. Not even the sound of another car disturbed the moment. She looked around and then scaled up the barricade until she was standing on the thin banister. A gymnast on the balance beam with shaky knees. The strong, cool wind off the river sent a shiver down her back. One wrong step would send her plummeting seventy feet to certain death. She closed her eyes. The Heartbreakers launched into their resounding chorus, and she melted in apostasy.

She screamed the lyrics over the Charles. Her voice drowned in the crisp gales of wind pushing back at her: *"She's gonna listen to her heart. It's gonna tell her what to do! Well, she might need a lotta lovin', but she don't need you!"*

Kate began to giggle, churlish and innocent. She hugged an iron support beam like a trusty friend. In the distance, dogs barked. She could barely hear them over the music in her ears. A smile overtook her face. It was hard to explain, just a feeling she had. Back in Parker's room, she acted on instinct. That was how she rationalized it to herself now.

But maybe, in the end, there was hope for her yet. She felt that things could still work out.

When Kate closed her eyes, she saw a spreading patch of black mold spiderwebbing inside her body. Running through her veins, controlling her fingers, piercing her brain. It was changing her. She felt transformed. She felt stronger.

Above her, pale-blue streaks began to speckle the skyline, giving rise to a brand-new day. All that hopeful Hallmark card bullshit. Kate had a feeling of omnipotence, of being so kinetically, so urgently, alive while the rest of the city slumbered.

Today would be a good day.

★★★★★

There was no time for rest or relaxation. Not now. Not in this mania. Not with everything piling on. When the alarm sounded, she was up. She dragged herself back to St. Christophers. How long had it been? Three hours? Four? The prior night's activities had taken on the sheen of a bad dream, nothing more. She met her class for morning rounds and together they returned to Parker's room. Everyone was too polite to call out Kate's bloodshot eyes and a mouth still stained with sugar frosting.

Zach, Kieran, and Greg were waiting in awkward silence. Finally, when Dr. Lucas arrived, the class got down to it. Daniel scrambled in late, tying on his lab coat in a huff as he joined the team. Kate couldn't help noticing that Dr. Lucas didn't comment on his lateness the same way she would Kate's own.

"Morning, all," Lucas said. Her voice was chipper.

Daniel approached Kate, leaned in, whispering: "You alright?"

"Never better," Kate said, masking a manic glee. "Any news on Lien?"

"No. I'm getting nervous. Really nervous. That's why I was late." He handed her a small business card. It read: *Oscar Ramirez, Detective, Boston Police Department.*

"A cop is asking about Lien. Why?"

"Who knows? Said he's talked to her family. They don't know where she is."

"But why'd he want to talk to you, Daniel?"

"Lien's family reported her missing. They told this guy that she spent all her time at the hospital. I guess they found me first. Think about it, we're all she has."

"I assume they'll want to talk to me too?"

Lucas was crossing by as Kate said this. "And what are you two on about?"

"Sorry, Dr. Lucas, we're talking about Lien and how no one has seen her in days."

"I'm sure she'll turn up."

"Do you think we should be here right now?"

"Where else would we be?" Lucas asked.

"I don't know. Out there?" Kate pointed out Parker's window, which looked over the industrialized Boston landscape. "Trying to find her?"

Dr. Lucas rested a comforting hand on Kate's shoulder. For a moment, to Kate, it was like putting her tongue to a 9-volt battery. A sudden, but not unpleasant electrical charge.

"The best thing we can do for Lien," Dr. Lucas said, "is to let the police do their jobs. Lien's a smart girl. I'm sure there is a reasonable explanation."

Then, Dr. Lucas began addressing the full class. "All right folks, I know it feels a bit odd without one of our own here. I'll pass along any updates as I hear them, I promise. For now, let's continue with the rounds."

Kate stood on tiptoes, peering over Zach's broad shoulders. To Kate, looking for symptoms of an allergic reaction was like looking for seedlings sprouting in a garden.

Luckily, she didn't have to till too deeply into this soil. Parker Dallas already looked worse for wear. His head sunk deep into a pillow soaked with sweat. The heavy lids of his eyes remained at half-mast. His slender, chiseled face smeared with blotches of red. Everything about him was deflated. He had shallow and unsteady breathing, reminiscent of a horse's whinny. This man, a once great building, was now reduced to rubble, condemned.

Kate never expected it to happen so quickly. Or intensely. God, what had she done?

Dr. Lucas turned to Parker. "And how are you feeling today, Mr. Dallas?" she asked.

He stuck his tongue out, wagging it, trying hard to swallow. "Pretty god damn terrible," he said. "I feel like I've been run over by a van."

"Well, many would suggest you deserve that very fate." She grabbed his manacled hand in her own in an attempt at patronizing compassion.

Dr. Lucas turned to address the group of students. "If you'll remember," Dr. Lucas said, "after we last met, it was determined that some tests needed to be performed on the patient." She opened a manila folder. From within, the doctor found a stapled packet of test results.

"What you'll be interested to learn is that a dramatic turn of events has transpired since our last visit." There was pride in the older doctor. Pride that her group of roving medical students had caught what others did not.

"The patient was diagnosed with a cancerous, abnormal growth amassing in his left leg. Oncological imaging caught it when surveying the area impacted by the separate, unrelated trajectory of the bullet that shattered his tibia. Surgeons rooted it out yesterday."

Lucas scanned the face of her students. "So now, tell me what you see in terms of his progress recouping."

It was time. Kate knew it. She stepped forward to seize her chance. "Excuse me," she said, gently placing her hands on Parker's throat. "May I?"

Kate massaged his glands with swirling movements. They were enlarged, just as she expected. She snagged a penlight from her lab coat pocket and said to Parker, "Open wide."

He did as he was told. He even added the patented "*AHHHH*" along with it.

Kate clicked the light off. "Have you been feeling tired? More than usual?"

Parker stopped, scratched his arm, thought on it. Even his thinking was sluggish. "Yup."

Kate fingered through his chart and drew her eyes from left to right across the pages, pretending to read. By this point, she had the damn thing memorized.

"Dr. Lucas," she said, without looking up. "I'd suggest the patient is suffering from an acute allergic reaction."

The doctor was taken aback. "And on what grounds are you making this diagnosis, Kate? The tests ordered were carried out. We've already confirmed the issue. Treatment will commence."

"I think this man is having a reaction" Kate said. "I see in his chart that he's allergic to ACE inhibitors."

"But there's nothing in his chart about an ACE inhibitor having been administered. What on earth are you talking about?" Lucas asked, genuinely perplexed.

Kate pointed out the IV bag hanging above Paker. She watched as Lucas followed her finger and ultimately clocked the enalapril. Lucas tilted her head slightly to one side like a dog who has been asked a question. She looked at Parker and for the first time really saw that he looked terrible. The instant thermometer beeped: 102 degrees.

Her face fell when she clocked the readout. Kate stood with her arms crossed, smug.

"Well, I'll be," Dr. Lucas exclaimed.

★★★★★

The students were dismissed. Lucas called after Kate from her position near Parker's door out in the hall. "Kate, one moment please!"

Kate sidled up to her mentor, trying to tamp down the frenetic mixture of pleasure infusing her like an injection of morphine. She had scored a big win while straddling the knife-edge risk of getting caught.

Lucas removed her glasses and let them dangle on the chain. She stood emotionless. "I just wanted to say…" She trailed off.

"Yeah?" Kate asked. The twist of her mouth was severe as she tried to read the cues of Lucas's storied face for an answer.

"Good catch today."

Kate smiled. The dark circles under Lucas's eyes meant that Kate wasn't the only one having trouble sleeping these days. She proceeded carefully.

"It's embarrassing to admit, being one of the faces of physician training, but all of us fuck up at some point. Sometimes we get away with it. Sometimes, we don't. Luckily for someone, you caught this mistake early. That man should have never been on that medication. I have no idea how it was missed."

"I'm just glad I could help."

"We'll be lucky if we aren't sued." Lucas's response was a cold canteen in a desert. Apparently, there was no suspicion on her part.

"I hope he gets better soon," Kate said.

"Not me," Lucas quipped. "But I don't want that to be because we screwed up." She made to walk away, stopped, and turned back at the last moment. "Hey, Kate, let me ask you a question?"

"Sure."

"A few days ago, I put you on the spot in front of everyone. That was wrong. I'm sorry about that. Back then I asked if you really wanted to be a doctor. It was a patronizing question. But I always like to check in with my students to see what's really driving them. So let me ask you – and you don't have to answer if you don't want. What really made you want to be a doctor?"

Kate looked away, fixed on the AED mounted to the wall. Lucas's words were stronger than current to the heart.

Lucas continued. "Forget it. Just don't think I'm grilling you. I'm trying to better understand you."

After all the weeks of needling, Kate was thrown off balance by Lucas seeming to take an interest in her life. She didn't trust it. Her response came out defensive. "Do you not think I'm doctor material?"

"I didn't say that" Lucas replied, laughing. "But I could see how you'd think it." The doctor brushed her hair back from her eyes. "I've been too harsh."

The confessional made Kate uncomfortable. "You don't need to-"

"No, I've been a bitch. Really. But I'm trying here. Give me a break. I really want to know."

Kate thought for a long time. This was a question often posed to her, and Kate usually offered the story of a plucky, young woman wanting nothing more than to eat her father's cancer instead of letting it ravage him before her very eyes. A story where the tragedy had instilled in her a driving ambition to save as many lives as possible and make up for the one that had slipped away.

"I thought I could be good at it," Kate said. "Lately, I have never felt less sure of anything." Kate straightened her white coat. "I haven't been the best student."

"And, if I'm being honest," Lucas said, "I'll admit that I tend to be really difficult with students who remind me of myself." Lucas reached out and adjusted the collar on Kate's coat until it was folded just right. "I don't think any of us knows what truly drives us. It's hard work and some days just don't seem worth even getting up in the morning."

"I have those days a lot."

"I know. I can see it in your tired eyes," Dr. Lucas said.

"So, what do we do?"

"Whatever you did today. In there." She pointed to Parker's room. "Keep doing that."

Lucas turned and, with slow, plodding steps, marched down the hall. Kate stood in awe of the moment. Lucas didn't once turn back.

Chapter Seven
FLATLINERS

The cafeteria off the main lobby of St. Christopher's was frequented by a mix of hospital employees—when they weren't filling up Del's Place, the all-night diner across the street—and patients' family members. Sean Carraway wasn't really eating, just picking over the depressing chicken Caesar salad plopped in s sickly green heap on his plate. The kitchen churned out standard-issue cafeteria fare. There were stations for pre-made sandwiches, salads, burgers, hot dogs, chicken tenders, and grease-laden pizza slices. The food was so unappetizing that Sean had resorted to people-watching instead, having affixed his gaze on the young and frightened man at the table in the middle of the floor scarfing down a quick bite. From what Sean could gather, the nervous man's wife was probably in the early stages of labor. When the maternity ward nurses fret over the mom-to-be, boyfriends and husbands got pushed out of the room, resorting to stuffing their faces down here. *Poor bastard.*

Sean and Daniel often sat in the back by the windows that overlooked the employee parking lot. If their schedules allowed, they'd grab a bite with some of Sean's OR staff. Above them, on the wall, a television was tuned to a twenty-four-hour conservative cable news channel. Jeremy Ryerson raised his arm to the side of the mounted flat-screen TV and toggled the channel button until it landed on ESPN Classic. On screen, it was suddenly 1990 again. Fourth quarter, a high-stakes college football game between the Texas Longhorns and the Houston Cougars. There was a particular desaturation to the color in the image on the screen, coupled with a certain grain in television programming from the era that made it instantly recognizable.

"No way! I remember this game!" Jeremy said. "This is the one where Krieger, no, Klinger, threw fifteen touchdown passes."

"Bullshit!" Daniel spoke around a mouthful of bacon cheeseburger. "No one has ever thrown fifteen touchdown passes in one game. That's impossible."

"Okay, maybe not fifteen, but it was a lot. And this guy Krieger definitely has the record. This was that game!" Jeremy yelled, really animated. "I swear, I was like five years old at the time. But I remember it like it was yesterday. My father threw a full beer can at the television and busted the screen."

Sean and Jeremy both sat in their matching green OR scrubs. Daniel sat across from them munching on a chicken patty sandwich. He was a kid among men. The little brother who always seemed to latch on. Funny, Sean realized he wasn't actually friends with either one of these guys but spent so much time with them that they'd come to feel like family. All three came from different worlds. Fate and circumstance had thrust them together into this environment of stress and adrenaline. People on the outside never understood it. They thought it was like on TV, *ER* or *Chicago Med* or something. All the friends Sean had growing up had fallen off along the way, even though he felt that he had more in common with a box turtle than with Daniel. Just now, Jeremy and Daniel were bickering across him.

"Can't we just keep the news on, guys?" Sean asked. He was worried about Lien. It had been a few days since he had heard from her. He couldn't talk to Kate about it. Something in his guts suggested there was a problem with Lien being off the map for so long. Things like that never happened in life. And when it did, the guy who was secretly sleeping with the victim was almost always the suspect. God, he didn't need this shit right now. He and Lien normally didn't go a day without some sort of interaction. Dragging his fork across the brown-edged lettuce, he realized that he hadn't eaten in two days.

"The hell's your problem, man?" Jeremy asked.

Daniel laughed a mirthless laugh. Both were still the same annoying frat boys at heart that they'd always been.

"Sorry, guys. I'm just a little off today. Too many overnights, you know?"

"Oh yeah," Jeremy joked with a dig of his elbow into Sean's ribs. "Forgot that Sean here was a born with a pussy."

Laughing, Daniel crammed a fistful of potato chips into his mouth.

"Screw, guys," Sean said. "Not today."

Sean pierced the congealed half of a deviled egg with his fork and forced it down. He had met Lien a couple years back when she and Kate started in the program together. Lien and Kate always studied together. At the beginning, Sean would drop by Kate's apartment and Lien would always be there. They'd stay up all night, surrounded by a sea of textbooks and notebooks, deeply debating the merits of some new technology or just gossiping about others in the program. They'd always turn to Sean, pull him into their conversation, solicit his opinion. It felt good.

It seemed—to Sean, anyway—that Kate had noticed his puppy-love crush on Lien and began inviting Daniel into their study group as a way of balancing things out. It's not that Daniel was worthy of abject hatred. He had a good heart. It just so happened to be wrapped up in narcissism and the veneer of someone who'd never experienced a real challenge in his life. A silver spoon trust-fund kid who relied on parental wealth and connections to get by.

Kate was only the second woman Sean had ever slept with. In high school, he'd dated a classmate named Christine LeBay for three years. It ended amicably when they separated for college. Sean and Christine never had designs on a future together. He fully intended to travel east to Boston to pursue medicine. She was going west for musical theater. A few months back, he had a friend request come through Facebook from Christine. He rarely ever ventured online. The request had been sitting there, waiting for him to accept for over six months. He clicked on her profile. She was now a waitress at a Denny's with four young boys. He denied the request. In another life, it could have been him.

Sean had not consciously pursued a relationship with Lien. It was difficult for him to remember how it happened. They'd always flirted. Attraction had been in the air.

But one day, the group had gotten wasted on too many bottles of wine at Arturo's Bar. Winter was settling in; the sky had been dark for a lifetime. Everyone headed back to Kate's, and Kate passed out on her bed. Sean remembered taking off her shoes and pulling the blanket over her. Daniel left and Lien was putting her coat on. At the door, Lien leaned in and kissed him. Her lips were sweet and bitter, a deep-burgundy merlot. Her tongue gently sought out his own. Sean thought about pushing her away but didn't. Couldn't. He remembered the feeling of his heartbeat throbbing in his temples. They went no further that night, but for weeks, Sean saw Lien every time he closed his eyes, even when he was with Kate. It made him sick to his stomach how much he wanted her.

Cut to Lien missing.

There was so little Sean knew about her. He knew she came from a strict, close-knit family. Her parents emigrated from Taiwan. Lien was only an infant when they had arrived. He hadn't met them. Would never meet them. He and Lien never went anywhere but his place. The only way he could make it work was to compartmentalize their dalliances. Now he wanted to talk about it. He wanted to stop every stranger on the street and ask, "Have you seen Lien Chu?" But he couldn't. No, he couldn't break Kate's heart.

Then, suddenly, over the hospital's PA system, a blank voice announced: "Will Sean Carraway please report to room 192? Sean Carraway, room 192."

Before the announcement concluded, he was already standing and inhaling mouthfuls of salad. He had to eat, or he wouldn't make it through the afternoon. "Shit, I've got to go," he choked out. A smear of Caesar dressing dotted his lips.

"What do they want with you? You're entitled to a lunch break just like everyone else," Jeremy said.

Sean shrugged. "Hell, if I know. What's room 192 anyway?"

None of them knew that room by number. Sean tossed the remaining half of his salad, launching it like a pro baller in a perfect arc, where it fell gracefully into the open mouth of the garbage can seven feet away. His hands stayed in the air in an overextended follow-through. Then he directed a high middle finger at both men.

"Oh man!" Daniel said. "Kobe Carraway es en fuego"

Sean scurried back from the cafeteria into the hospital's main lobby. He turned left, raced down the corridor, broke left again, charged down two more hallways, and finally stopped at a closed door. The number plate to room 192 read *CHAPEL*.

It must have been a mistake, Sean thought. *Or maybe I misheard the room number?* But then the announcement was repeated over the PA system, and he was sure as shit it was saying, "One-nine-two."

Sean had never been here before. He had no idea what the room looked like or who in the hell would be requesting his presence here. His hand on the knob, he pushed inside.

★★★★★

In Sean's mind, hospital chapels were perpetually dark wood-paneled rooms, shards of red and gold-stained glass, low lighting, a few rows of back-breaking pews, and maybe a large cross with Jesus wearing the weary expression of some dude having a really bad day. In his mind, all churches were Catholic churches. Rooms of unimaginable sadness. And the hospital chapel would be the saddest of all. A place where doctors without answers encouraged families without options to seek some inner peace.

Room 192 was not that. Sean looked around. This place was nothing like he'd imagined. Yes, it was small, but the light was radiant, the room sunny. One entire wall was lined with floor-to-ceiling windows. There was a lectern, but no altar and no world-weary Jesus. Behind the lectern, an archway built of glorious green-and-yellow stained glass depicted a sunrise over a field. Instead of hard, wooden pews, there were three rows of four mahogany chairs with plush blue-and-gray upholstery. Sean stepped inside, and the din of the hospital faded away.

She was there. Sitting in the second row. The back of her head was to him, but when she heard the door close, she turned and smiled.

"Kate?" he said. "What're you doing here?

"I'm waiting for you."

"Did you have me paged?"

It was taking his eyes a moment to adjust to the radiant light. He shuffled his way up the small aisle between the rows of chairs and sat one row behind her. He was close enough to smell her almond-berry shampoo.

Kate had changed into a gray lace midi dress of lined, woven chiffon that emphasized her figure. It was the kind of dress a woman might wear to a spring wedding. He wondered why the hell Kate was wearing that dress now instead of her scrubs. Through the wall of windows, obscured slightly by gauzy curtains, Sean watched trees depositing the last of their fire and ocher leaves on the ground. The sky bright, but crisp. Winter was around the corner.

"I had a wild idea!" she said.

Kate grabbed for his hand and held it in her own. Her eyes were ablaze, the corners of her mouth pointed up. She was downright giddy. For the first time in how long?

He was looking around the room, taking everything in. "Come here a lot, do you?"

"You don't like it? I think it's nice."

"Not saying that. It's just, in four years with you, we've never gone to church once. I didn't even think you believed in God." He paused and looked her right in the eyes. "Do you?"

"No," she said. "Not some bearded man in the sky anyway."

After a moment, Sean pulled his hand away from hers. "Honey," he said, "I'm a little busy right now. Can't we talk about whatever this is later? I've got to get back to work."

"I had your calendar cleared."

At this he was genuinely confused. "How did you-? Never mind."

Kate stood, walked across to the front of the chapel, and rested a hand on the lectern. "You know how you've always said you didn't want a big ceremony?"

Behind them came a soft knock on the door. A smile crept over Kate's face. Whatever surprise resided behind the chapel door; she was expecting it.

"Kate, what's happening?" he asked cautiously.

She walked up the aisle and opened the door. In came a small balding man in a simple, black, wool suit. Kate led him toward the front of the room. He puttered on aged legs, with folds of skin collecting at his eyes and jowls.

Now Sean was on his feet, unsure of what to say. Although it was just the three of them in the room, it was starting to feel hot and crowded. Kate moved closer to him, drew both of his hands into her own.

"Like I was saying, I had this idea" she said. "I just know you're going to love it! I'm sure of it."

"Well out with it!" Sean exclaimed.

"I want us to forget about the wedding. Screw it all." She turned to the small old man, chuckling nervously. "Sorry." Then she turned back to Sean and said: "Let's just get married. Right here, right now."

"Umm, what?" he stepped back. His hands dropped to his side. The collar of his scrubs was chafing his neck. She couldn't possibly be serious, right? Had she gone off the deep end?

"Kate, who is this man?"

"Why, the minister, of course" she said proudly.

There was a long beat of silence. The minister laughed politely and stepped forward, introducing himself and shaking Sean's dead-fish hand.

"What a happy occasion, and so fitting for you two!" he said under a shiny dome of a head, wisps of white hair in his ears.

Kate pulled Sean off to the side while the minister laid a book on the lectern and readied himself. "I know the wedding has been coming between us. We're fighting more. I'm not as focused on my clinicals. So, I had one of those epiphanies."

"Epiphanies?"

"Yes. We should just forget it all. All the pomp and circumstance. No giant expense, no fighting in-laws, no invitations or cake samples or music. Just you and me. Now. Then we can both just focus on what's next."

Sean stuttered, looking for the right words to say. "N–now?" Inside, Sean was spiraling. Mild tachycardia. He closed his eyes. In that moment, he envisioned Lien's face overlaying Kate's in some kind of cosmic superimposition. Eyes full of bright panic. She was screaming.

Sean opened his eyes. His mouth had run dry. He fiercely grabbed Kate by the hand and dragged her up the aisle to the doorway. His voice held a desperate urgency. "Kate, this isn't something that you spring on someone!"

Kate's eyes were welling, but she didn't lose it the way Sean would have expected. He expected histrionics, so this was some sort of emotional growth.

She tried to speak. Only air came out, so she cleared her throat and tried again. "You're saying that you don't want to do this?"

Sean looked away. The minister was waiting for them. This would be the culmination of everything. There was no temporary bridge through this scene in the movie of his life. There was no landing on the other side where everything would be as it should. This ending was a long time coming.

"No. I don't think we should," he said.

There was a long pause. Kate steadied herself. Her eyes were red, but not angry. A puppy with unconditional love that had just been kicked.

"Is it because of Lien?" she asked.

"What do you mean?" he replied, trying his best to dress up the shaky voice coming out of his mouth in a genuine tone of wonderment.

"You've been seeing her, right?"

The minister was eyeing Kate suspiciously. There was no way he could hear what they were saying, but he could read their body language. This forced Sean to straighten up and relax his arms by his sides. Now he feared he looked aloof and awkward and that this would only make Kate further indict him. If a soft wind had blown through the walls of the hospital, he would have floated off like a dandelion gone to seed.

"Don't you think it's weird that she's missing? Like, is this the best time to be pretending everything's all right and getting married?"

"Pretending?" She started to cry all over again. Tears cascaded from her eyes as if melting icicles. "You refuse to set a date with me. I've been stringing along the print shop for months now, trying to force invitations out of you. I ate an entire cake's worth of samples the other night. I'm not stupid. I knew you didn't want to be involved in planning a wedding."

"You know I love you." It sounded weak and pathetic coming out of his mouth and he immediately regretted it.

"But when will be the right time? I can't keep spinning my wheels. Have you not seen that I've been barely keeping it all together?"

"I don't think you're hearing me," he said. Then he took a deep breath. "I don't think we should get married. Ever." There was a finality to the last word that resonated in the air like a deep, sustained note wrung from a grand piano.

"Hell, Sean, you're the one who asked *me*, remember? You got down on one knee and said, 'Be my bride.' Do you remember that?"

"Of course, I do," he said. And he did. But what was once this far off rite was suddenly so much more constrictive. The wedding. Children. Home. When he pictured his future, did he really picture it with Kate? He wasn't sure.

"I've wanted to talk to you for a while now," he added. "But you've been so busy, and the timing just never seemed right."

"Wait, what?" She was gasping for breath. "You're admitting you haven't loved me for a while, and you blame the *god damn* timing? I wanted us to settle down. Get a home together. Make a nice life for ourselves."

"Sorry, I did love you—I *do* love you," he was stumbling. His eyes wandered the room. He couldn't look at her for this. "I think it's over." He leaned in and kissed her softly on the cheek.

She just stood there, paralyzed. That's what bothered him the most. Sean didn't know what else to do or say, so he immediately left. He felt bad for the old man brought here for nothing. It was embarrassing. He needed to get out. Amid this turmoil, Sean couldn't help but notice the rays of warm sunlight dancing through the green and yellow stained glass. The warmth hit him as he raced out of room 192. Why did everything beautiful always turn to shit?

★★★★★

After Kate's attempt to corner him, Sean headed home to his little apartment and crept into bed. He lay there staring at the ceiling in silence for nearly an hour, on the verge of sputtering into sleep, when he heard a knock at his door.

First, he held his breath. *It must be Kate,* he assumed. Coming to ask him why and how and what now, but he didn't have the energy or the answers, so he didn't get up. But then Daniel's voice, muffled and low, called from the other side of the door. God, if there was anyone he wanted to see less than Kate right now, it was Daniel.

There was a low, rustling sound near the door, and then Sean heard Daniel departing. His footfalls grew softer and softer until they disappeared into silence. When Sean got to the door, he opened it and saw a folded-up copy of the *Boston Herald* lying there. He reached down, picked it up, and saw her picture.

BOSTON HERALD

Medical Student Still Missing

Oct. 15, 2021.

A frantic search continues for a missing woman who vanished three days ago without a trace.

Lien Chu, a 22-year-old medical student from the Boston metro area, was last seen late Monday evening after leaving work, where she interns as a lab assistant at St. Christopher's Hospital. Police are being extremely tight-lipped about their investigation, and so are friends and family members who say police have asked them to not talk to reporters.

"This disappearance has affected all of us—her classmates, her teachers, everyone." St. Christopher's spokesperson Charlotte Valente told reporters.

Chu had been enrolled at St. Christopher's medical program for the past year and a half. Prior to this, she received her pre-med certification from Johns Hopkins University in Baltimore, where her family resides.

Friends say Chu is generally well regarded for her overall excellence and self-minded determination. "Lien is a beautiful, bright, intelligent young lady. She's one of our accelerated students, destined to do amazing things. She has been interning to become a laboratory specialist," said Dr. Vivian Lucas, one of the student teaching professors at St. Christopher's Hospital.

Chu's family told reporters that they feel in the dark about the matter. Chu's father, Chen Chu, who had been back in his home country of Taiwan visiting relatives, is now enroute to Boston after learning about her disappearance.

Police say they scanned the hospital's security video, which captured Chu's Jeep Patriot driving off the night she was last seen, and that of nearby businesses, but saw nothing helpful. Then yesterday, Chu's car was found in an embankment beneath a layer of brush off Salem's Court, a half mile from the hospital. Investigators have tried tracking Chu's cell phone, but again, police say the information has not been helpful.

In the meantime, St. Christopher's Hospital has notified students and staff to be vigilant, just in case. "They know to try to keep a buddy system when possible and, especially now, to ask for security if they are leaving a building, particularly at night," Vallante said.

"It's been really crazy because you just don't know what happened. It could be really good news, or it could be really bad news. We don't know. It's hard not to assume the worst, but we're trying," Chu's friend and fellow medical student Daniel Parks said.

Chu is 5 feet, 4 inches tall. She was last seen wearing her white hospital scrubs. Her family is offering a $20,000 reward for information leading to her safe return.

Gary Gamache, staff writer

Chapter Eight
ROOM 217

Kate was afraid that the lock on the bathroom stall would fail, so she made a habit of sitting forward on the toilet and holding the door closed. Today was no different, though her mind was a million miles away. Her body assumed the position as a kind of muscle memory. Her free hand clutched her cell phone to her ear. She had mostly finished sobbing, wiped her eyes and nose with bunched wads of toilet paper, and urinated. She noticed a small dot of blood on the tissue paper. Just great, spotting already.

Her voice echoed within the tile box of the staff restroom. She'd made sure before entering that she was alone, even bent to check for legs in the stalls. No signs of life. Her mother's voice warbled through the cell phone and, though Kate still didn't feel great, she was marginally less miserable now.

"I just don't know what to do, Mom," Kate said. She wiped away more tears. When she swallowed, she could taste buttery ropes of mucus.

On the line, her mother retained her usual calm solemnity. It wasn't the first time in Kate's life that she called her mother in hysterics. Lord knew it wouldn't be the last.

"I know, honey," she responded. "Breakups are hard. But you need to try and find the good in everything."

"What's so good about this?"

"When breakups hurt, it meant that the relationship was worth having." There was a long pause. Kate's mother regrouped. "Maybe now you can focus more on med school?"

"Have you been talking to Lien? You sound just like my friend."

"No, but she sounds pretty smart to me if that's the advice they're giving. There'll be time for meeting new people later. Just get through school. You know all of us are so proud of you."

"I know," Kate said. It was something mothers had to say. But her mom had a way of couching sentiments in genuineness, so they didn't sound like they came from the mom-playbook.

"I won't pretend it's easy to get over someone, but you don't need to be attached. You need to study."

"Yeah," Kate said. "But I'm not sure if I'm cut out for this."

"You were always so dramatic."

The last time they'd spoken was when her mother revealed that she was thinking of selling the house. Now Kate's fantasy about buying it with Sean and making a new start had vanished. How quickly everything changes.

"Thanks," Kate said. "I'll be okay."

"I know you will. Honey, are you sure that you're feeling okay?" her mother purred through warm, syrupy tones. Her voice coated Kate sweetly.

"Forget it," Kate said. "Listen to me blathering. How're you doing, Mom? Any news on the house?"

"Oh," she said, "nothing with the house. Your cousin Paul came over to take measurements for the realtor, but I haven't heard from anyone in weeks. You know how it is back home. Same old, same old."

Kate smiled to herself, knowing this was usually how her mother began outrageous stories: as if nothing out of the ordinary ever happened.

"Actually, I just had an interesting experience getting my nails done. I was sitting next to this woman, and the more we got to talking, we realized we were neighbors back thirty years ago! Do you remember Dot McGill?"

Kate leaned back on the toilet tank and let go of her hold on the stall door. She stared up at the ceiling and, noticing peeling chips of paint, wondered if there was still lead paint anywhere in the old walls of this ancient hospital. There was silence on the line, and Kate realized her mother had asked a question and was waiting for an answer. "Not really. Can't say I remember her."

"Eh, maybe that was before your time," her mother said. "Before we moved to the house on Minerva Street. Anyway, we started talking about the business."

The business, as Kate's mother referred to it, was a sex toy franchise that her mother bought into the year Kate left for college. She'd used the money from Kate's father's life insurance. Now, her sixty-four year old mother hosted parties—for women of a certain age—and showcased all the latest items in her arsenal. To think her mother now kept a Rubbermaid tote filled with standard-issue vibrators, plugs, and pheromone-laced body lotions. Yuck. The day Kate heard about this latest endeavor; she nearly died. This sounded so unlike the woman she remembered from brown bag lunches, PTO meetings, and pecan pies at Christmas. And yet, at the same time, the unpredictability of it all was exactly like her mother. Kate often thought it was so amazing how people were built of contradictions.

"I can't believe how comfortable you are selling dildos to old ladies," Kate whined.

"Adult novelties, darling." She said *darling* in an affected regal accent, so it came out closer to *dah-ling*. "And I was under the impression that if you owned a business, getting the word out was a good thing?"

"Yeah, yeah, yeah. I'm just teasing you." And she was. Kate had never felt closer to her mother than she did right now, even though for the first time in their lives they were living apart. "I think it's really cool."

Kate flushed the toilet and stood up, buttoning her pants.

"Wait, have you been on the toilet this whole time we've been talking?" her mother asked.

"Only place in the hospital with privacy," Kate said. Then she heard the flush of a toilet through the phone.

"Me too!" her mother said with an excited bent. "I was just too embarrassed to say so. I was going to sit here until we hung up. Now I have a giant red ring around my ass."

"Maybe there's an ointment in your Rubbermaid tote for that."

"Anyway, these three women—you know, the nail techs from some faraway country—they were listening to Dot and me. Eavesdropping, really, but that doesn't matter. Then Dot left, and I was the last customer in the place. They locked the door and started asking me all these questions."

"Questions?" Kate asked. "Like what?"

"Well, apparently, in their culture, these women are never taught about sex. One said that she had been brought up to feel ashamed of it. It broke my heart."

"That's so sad," Kate said. She was standing in the stall with one hand on the lock, waiting for the conversation to end so she could return to the floor.

"Right? And it made me think about how much better I could have been when you were growing up."

"Don't worry, Mom. I learned what I needed to."

"I guess."

"Did it get all awkward after that? With the nail techs?"

"Of course not! I sent them home with Pink Rabbits. Those things will change their lives."

"Your life is so weird now."

"Oh, Kate, it's just so quiet in the house these days."

"I miss you too."

There was a long beat of silence as Kate's very real problems came flooding back all at once. "Well, who knows?" she said. "Maybe I'll be back sooner than you think."

They said their goodbyes, and Kate slipped the cell phone back into her pocket. She tore one more piece of toilet paper off the roll, wiped her eyes, then crumbled it into a wad and dropped it into the open bowl.

Kate opened the stall door. Then her heart leaped into her throat. Dr. Lucas was standing right there at the sink, watching her emerge from the stall through the mirror.

How long has she been in here? Kate worried. She hadn't heard anyone come in. Looking past Lucas, she saw her own reflection. Her eyes were swollen and puffy. It was clear that she'd been crying.

"Allergies," Kate muttered.

It took an extra effort to make that first step and start moving again. Kate washed her hands at the sink right beside the doctor. While drying them, Kate fantasized about getting in her car, driving clear across the country, and cutting all ties. It was a feeling she'd been experiencing a lot lately, wondering how to disappear completely. At this rate, she would be slinging pink rabbits door to door with her mother by Christmas.

Her fingers closed around the handle of the bathroom door. Lucas called out from behind, "Try a cool washcloth on your face, dear," she said with a knowing glance. "Good as new."

There was a crackle over the hospital loudspeaker. "Kate White to nurses' station 2A."

"Sounds like you're needed," Dr. Lucas said.

Kate eyed the squat gray speaker box on the wall and wondered who the hell could be asking for her. Then she nodded with appreciation to Dr. Lucas, ran a hand through her hair, and took off.

★★★★★

All the years of nightly cleanings—tens of thousands of spent spray bottles, aerosol cans, burnishers, buffers, and carpet washers—had created a distinct atmosphere. That smell, sharp and acrid, left a mark on the intensive care unit. It had been baked into the taupe walls and checkered linoleum floor.

She could tolerate the smell. It was the constant chaos that bothered Kate most about her time in the ICU. Doctors and nurses always scurrying back and forth, running by with heads bent over clipboards. Pushing carts of supplies to rooms desperate for goods. But beyond that was the forlorn look in every family member visiting a loved one. Overtired mothers or fathers. Their constant searching, careening through the halls on the prowl for vending machines for small children who ran amok in fits of boredom.

At the nurse's station, a small group were laughing cheerily. Kate could hear them before she even rounded the corner. When she finally did arrive, two nurses—one male, one female—stopped mid-conversation and simply looked at Kate with familiar disdain, waiting for her to open her mouth and speak first. The contempt was for Kate and all the other med students, the lowest wrung on the ladder. They looked at Kate as if she were there to deliver a singing telegram.

They stood behind the desk in their matching blue scrubs, picking at salads made of mostly croutons doused in oily dressing. The bulletin board behind them was covered in a mess of tacked-up pages, SOPs, and phone extensions. A third older nurse was sat with her back to Kate, arguing on the phone. Something about a patient's Medicaid eligibility not coming through.

Finally, Kate broke the silence and spoke. "Excuse me," Kate said, clearing her throat.

The male nurse responded, "Yeah?"

"Yes, I was paged here," Kate said. The lack of confidence in her voice turned the inflection upward at the end of the sentence, framing it more like a question. Uptalk. She remembered Lien describing this trait after one of those women's studies seminars she always raved about. She felt her standing sinking even lower. Quicksand.

"Sorry, we were picking up our lunches. Maybe you should check the front desk?"

"Isn't there anyone?" Kate said, perplexed. Then the nurse who had been arguing on the phone cupped a hand over the receiver and looked at Kate through the smidgen of space between the other two.

"Janice," the phone woman said to the female nurse who was now chomping noisily, "that was me." Then, directly addressing Kate, she said, "Kate White?"

"Yes, ma'am."

"You're wanted by that prick in 217."

The floor fell out from beneath her. She was sure that it was Parker Dallas's room. *Why would he be asking for me?* Kate thought.

"217? Really? Are you sure?"

"Honey, he asked for you by name." The third nurse turned her back on them and was already raising her voice to the unfortunate customer service rep on the other line.

Janice wiped her mouth clean with her napkin. "Down the hall, you'll wanna make a left. Just look for my sexy friend in uniform," she said, laughing. "That's officer Jim. He has a great sense of humor. Doesn't he, Carter?"

The male nurse, half-listening. "You betcha. A real riot."

Kate wasn't amused. "I know where it is. Thanks."

She spun around, couldn't get away from this asinine place fast enough. Away from Janice with the big green leaf of lettuce in her teeth.

★★★★★

It was a pair of legs dangling from the ceiling. That was what Kate initially noticed when she rounded the corner. A maintenance man in gray overalls was halfway up an eight-foot A-frame ladder. His top half had been swallowed by the open mouth of the ceiling where the ceiling tile had been shifted clear out of its track. He was replacing a dead light bulb.

Kate sidestepped to avoid the ladder. She didn't need to invite any more bad luck into her life. By now, bad luck had a spare key.

The maintenance man was whistling a Rolling Stones tune, but she wasn't sure which one. "Ruby Tuesday," maybe? They all sounded the same to her. What was it that she remembered McCartney once saying—that they were just a blues cover band that had randomly made it big?

That regular ol' stand up comedian, Officer Jim, was posted outside of Parker's door just as the nurses had said. He stood tall with a familiar, husky build and neatly pressed uniform. Kate's gaze narrowed in on angular shape of the gun on his hip.

"Can I go in?" she asked, her hand already on the door handle.

"Stay behind the tape." He was barely paying attention, instead minding the maintenance man's rickety ladder.

The momentary distraction had almost made her forget. Almost. There was something off about her being paged to room 217. There was literally no business for her to be heading up for Parker Dallas. And standing here once again, the heavy door between them, she wondered why she'd been summoned. Ultimately, her curiosity outweighed the rational part of her brain that was screaming for her to alert Dr. Lucas and seek advice. But as Kate was wont to do, she tamped down reason.

She opened the door slowly and slinked inside. As she did, the hall light was reconnected, and the flickering, white light bulb burned hot for a moment, snapping on with a harsh, flashbulb-like spear that turned her vision spotty. For a few seconds, she stood in Parker's presence, acutely aware of his eyes on her but unable to see him. Her vision returned, a developing Polaroid picture. There, in the lone bed, Parker lay with a devilish grin on his face, still tightly constricted with the leather straps. He appeared to be much more coherent than Kate's last visit. The puffiness was gone, returned were the sharp angles of his jawline. A few days of healing had made one hell of a difference.

"Morning," Kate said. If she'd held out her hand, Parker would have been able to register her trembling from across the room.

"I didn't think you'd come," he said.

She could kid herself that it was in the altruistic vein of medicine that she'd answered his call. A form of working on her bedside manner, even if the patient at the bed was a monstrous creep. But in the wake of her life with Sean crumbling, it honestly buoyed her spirits to have a man ask after her. Maybe that was too reductive, it was just a chemical impulse. She heard her name. She followed.

Even if triggering an allergic reaction was relatively risk-free, it went against everything a doctor's code of ethics stood for. At first, Kate had chased the high of scoring points off the devilish plan she'd concocted. But the immorality of it all had since settled into her bones with a cancerous ache. If her father was alive today and heard that she'd deliberately infected someone—even a criminal who made it his life's work to hurt others—he would have been so terribly disappointed in her. It was enough to melt her into a puddle of shameful goo just thinking about it.

Now, Kate was here at Parker's request. But it was an opportunity to start making amends, she guessed. To check on him. To ensure he was on the mend. To repent.

The room had one large wall of windows, beneath which was the HVAC system that was set to a warm seventy-four degrees. The view wasn't all that great. Room 217 looked out over an employee parking lot and a cluster of much taller buildings that enclosed St. Christopher's in a claustrophobic cage, blocking the sunlight. If it had been a hotel getaway, she would have asked for a refund.

Beside Parker's bed, there was a tray of food with congealed scrambled eggs, a few pulpy slices of orange, and two cups of lime-green JELL-O. He had arranged his napkins and plastic utensils into two place settings.

She moved closer to his bed by the back wall and addressed him.

"Remember the other day?" he asked, pointing to his tray of food.

"What's this?"

"I promised you dinner. Sorry, I could only get dessert."

"I bet you can't even spell dessert."

"Two s's. Because you always want more."

Beside Parker's bed was a tall-backed, vinyl, reclining chair. Many desperate people had spent painful nights trying to catch a few hours of sleep on that uncomfortable piece of shit.

She took a seat on the edge of the chair, unwilling to let her body settle in.

He caught her eyeing the handcuffs. "Can you even eat with those things?" she asked.

"Funny you should ask. No, I can't," he said. "Not really, anyway. They're supposed to send a nurse in, but I asked for you instead."

She looked at the tray of food. "Your eggs have gone cold."

"Come on. Dig in. It's on me."

She grabbed the cup closest to her and a spoon from his tray. Then she peeled away the lid and started to eat. She hadn't had this gelatin sugar water in years. It was good. "How'd you manage this?"

"I've been a really good boy," he said with a grin. "I think they like me. Those pretty nurses. Ain't it the Florence Nightingale effect?"

"You certainly think highly of yourself. Maybe they just pity the broken man who can't feed himself?"

"Ouch," he said but didn't seem all that bothered. "Leave me with some dignity, will you?"

Kate put the cup down and looked Parker straight in the eyes. "Armed robbery," she began. "That's dignified? The cop you shot—that was dignified?"

"What do you want me to say?"

"Hey, you're the lucky one," she said. "Your brother, not so much."

He cast his gaze down into his upturned palms that lay limp his lap. In this light, wearing this expression, he looked more like a lost, little boy.

"We knew the risks," he said at a near whisper.

"All you guys these days thinking you're in some movie. *Reservoir Dogs* or whatever. I just don't get it."

"Are you telling me you never wanted to break the rules a little?" he asked. "You know, shake things up?"

"You asking if I ever wanted to shoot someone? Outside of rush hour, no, of course not. I like to think I'm a decent human being. Besides, that's not what I'd call breaking the rules." She grabbed his bed rail for leverage and erupted from her seat. "And I gotta tell you, this stunt you've pulled doesn't impress me in the slightest either."

There was just enough slack in Parker's restraints for his index finger to brush up against Kate's hand. She pulled it back, but not immediately.

"Then why'd you even bother coming?" Parker asked. "You know, I can see it in your eyes." They were staring at each other intently now. "There's something mysterious in there. You're not such a goody-goody."

Standing over him, Kate was infected with a sense of some power that made her confident. She popped the spoonful of Jell-O in her mouth and twirled it around in a way she calculated would be read as seductive.

"My turn," he said.

"I'm not going to feed you like a child."

"What, ain't you never seen *9 1/2 Weeks*? Just pretend I'm Kim Basinger. You can be Mickey Rooney." He pulled up on his arms, which moved less than an inch with the tightening of the leather in the rigid buckles.

"Rourke" she sneered. "And you're not gonna win points comparing me to that lunkhead."

"My gun wasn't even loaded. It was my brother. He just kind of snapped. You know? I never saw anything like it." His eyes went glassy. "Was he in any pain?"

"Who?"

"That cop. Was it quick? I hope it was quick."

"I'm sure they did everything they could."

"What was his name? No one here tells me anything."

"I'm not sure."

"Trust me, I know I should rot for this. Really. I just wish you'd all left that cancer in me."

Kate sensed a deep current of remorse within Parker. An untapped well of emotion. Was that even possible? Or was he manipulating her? He certainly appeared genuine, and it softened her like butter left in the sun. She looked left, looked right, and leaned in. "Here," she said. Her slender fingers unbuckled the strap on his closest hand. "Two minutes, that's it. Just eat your dessert."

"You're an angel, darling." The strap released, and Parker clenched and unclenched his hand as if testing out a brand-new limb. Bruises and cuts marred the wrist where he'd been shackled.

She took her seat again, smiled, peeled opened his cup of JELL-O, and pushed it closer on his tray. His hand reached out but was a few inches shy. Seeing this, Kate placed the cup directly into his hand.

"Thank you," he said. And in that instant, his grip tightened like a vice wrapping around Kate's pliant wrist. He was so strong, a mechanical vice, and he pulled her toward him like a rag doll in a Rottweiler's jaws.

Her scream was autonomic, but her voice muffled when he pulled her into his chest. Then her mouth was full of fleece blanket and the fabric from his hospital gown. She bit her tongue and tasted the salty blood as it pooled in her mouth.

"Shut the hell up," he said at a low volume through a rough growl that nearly scared her into paralysis. *How is he so calm?*

"Don't hurt me!" she cried. The iron grip of his fingers dug into the soft flesh of her neck, squeezing off the pathway for air. "Please." The sounds strained through her larynx slowly being juiced like a lemon.

"Shhh," he said.

He was so strong. His eyes, no longer glassy, were red and focused. His large catcher's mitt of a hand covered her mouth. She quieted. Her eyes danced with fight-or-flight surges of adrenaline. Panic gripped her. She gasped for air as he held her face against him so hard that she felt like she was drowning here on the second floor of St. Christopher's Hospital.

"Keep it together, Kate," he said. "Just another few seconds. Now, focus. Go ahead. Unbuckle this second strap for me."

By now, she was choking for air and unable to see from the whipsawing flailing of limbs and blanket. Tendrils of mucus fell from her nostrils. "What?" she asked, genuinely confused.

"My other fucking arm!" he screamed. "Untie it. *Now!*"

She leaned over him and set to work on the buckle with her shaking hands, her chest heaving on Parker's face.

"Normally, I wouldn't complain about a pair of tits on my face, but could you hurry it up, please?"

Her fingers shook so much she couldn't get the strap from the buckle loose. Just then, from the corner of her eye, she noticed the Call Nurse button on the side of the bed and pressed it with all her might. The button glowed orange. If he noticed, he would slit her throat. Of that she was certain. But the indicator light was just behind his arm, and she kept him focused by writhing and pushing against the mass of his body.

She continued to press her body deeper into his, trying to keep him down and obstruct his view. She fumbled with the buckle. After another few seconds, she leaned again on the button.

"First, you're going to untie me, then we're going to wait for the officer here to head back down to his fan club at the nurses' station. He's always leaving his post."

The door to room 217 swept open. Parker and Kate both froze. The voice entered the room before the speaker did. "You need something, sugar?" The open question hung there.

It was Janice, one of the floor's nurses, and she stood in the doorway with a look of complete confusion. It wouldn't have been unreasonable for her first thought to be that she had walked in on Kate and Parker about to perform the naked pretzel. Only then did Janice clock the knife at Kate's throat.

"Help me," Kate said. Her voice leeched out. With all her strength, Kate laid across Parker's free hand. But he was immeasurably stronger and seemed able to lift her entire body a few inches off the bed with the power of his forearm alone.

"G-get the cop," Kate stammered, choking.

"He's not here!" Janice yelled.

Janice took off running. Kate continued to wrestle with Parker. Her hands grasped at anything and everything. She remembered Parker's leg, fresh from surgery, and she rammed her fist into the bandaged appendage with two forceful blows. She didn't have time to question how he thought he would get anywhere on only one working leg.

Parker screamed in pain. The shriek cut right into her ear, which was only inches from his mouth. There was a high-pitched ringing sound that she might have diagnosed as tinnitus in a different moment. The pain made him more forceful, and he pulled at her hair and skin, scratching, and clawing. He was a tiger in a trap.

"You know," he said, seething with all his energy to hang on to her and keep the position of power. "I saw you creeping in here the other night. I saw you switch out the bag. I've got your fucking number, Kate."

Her stomach dropped out, and she vomited on Parker's lap and bed. His grip on her loosened and his face turned down sickly; it was a purely chemical response of disgust.

She was so angry, she didn't want to give him the satisfaction of taking her down. Not this asshole. Not now. She found the switch above his bed that administered Parker's morphine. She knew it was now or never and that she would have to lift herself off him. When she did, he would have a good chance of plunging that knife into her neck.

Time slowed. She counted to three, closed her eyes, and leaped for it. Her left arm pushed off his stapled thigh. She could hear him bellowing in excruciating pain as his hand momentarily loosened its grip on the knife. With her free, outstretched hand, she grabbed the device and clicked the button as if she were launching a rocket into space. *Three. Two. One. Blast-off!*

Parker's body went limp. The plastic knife clattered on the floor. She freed herself from his ropey arms. In a panic, with shaking hands, she managed to reclasp his free hand in the leather strap. She tied it off so tightly that his hand turned blood red. The leather dug into his flesh.

Through a hacking cough, she sputtered. "Goody-goody, my ass. You son of a bitch," she seethed.

Kate grabbed at her throat. When she pulled her hand away, there was a palmful of blood. She collapsed to the floor, gasping. Janice and Officer Jim, gun drawn, blasted back into the room.

Officer Jim took sight of the war zone. "What the-?"

But there was nothing left to say.

Chapter Nine
DOGS

Prior to medical school, *shock* was a word Kate White had always associated with the movies. Today the experience was made real. When the ER attendants scooped her from the floor of room 217, placed her on a gurney, and brought her down to trauma for evaluation, it was as if she had checked out of her mental hotel, gone on holiday, and only returned hours later to this strange room. There was a black void, no memory of how she got here. Another blackout.

Blinding lights shone into her eyes. The cold, silver dollar head of a stethoscope was pressed intermittently on her chest and back as she breathed deep, shaky breaths. The vice around her arm constricted so tightly that she could hear the drumbeat of her heart in her ears.

At the foot of the bed was a man she'd never seen before, but she could tell immediately that he was police. He looked craggy, a bit like that actor, Roy Scheider, with his crew cut and a brown off-the-rack suit a size too large, roomy in the shoulders. He was in the middle of speaking to her in long monotonous tones. When she came to, she was unsure of how long he'd been talking. Had she been replying? What kinds of things did she say when in the middle of a blackout? Kate's world came into view like someone turning on the lights in a dark, windowless room. First nothing, then everything, everywhere, all at once, in an overwhelming wave.

Dr. Lucas flanked her side at the hospital bed. The older woman's voice was the voice that had brought Kate back. "Oh, here she is," was the first thing Kate consciously heard Dr. Lucas say. "Kate? Kate, can you hear me?"

Kate's vision swam into focus. She turned, nodding her head. Dr. Lucas's face was stolid, reserved, betraying no sense of emotion.

The man in the brown suit interrupted, "So Miss White, as I was saying, I hope you don't mind, but I just need to ask you a few questions."

Kate turned back to the detective. "Wait. Who are you?" she asked as her eyes narrowed. She wasn't much in the mood for this right now.

He held out a meaty right hand. Kate shook it. Her own hands were clammy, though she was shivering. She flushed, embarrassed, when he took his hand away. She envisioned him wiping off the moisture on a handkerchief, but it didn't seem to bother him.

"My name is Oscar Ramirez," he said. "Detective with the city's police department." His hand reached into the inside pocket of his jacket. As he did so, the sweep of his coat revealed a shoulder-holstered pistol. When his hand returned, it was brandishing a card. The very same one Daniel had showed her earlier. "I just wanted to clarify a few of the details from today's events."

"I know you," Kate said. Her voice was lethargic and druggy.

"You do?" he asked.

"Well, I don't *know you*, know you. But you talked to Daniel Parks about Lien."

"That's right, Miss White. I've been trying to get in touch with you too over the past few days. Funny how the universe brings people together sometimes."

At that, a trigger was pulled, and the whole thing came whooshing back into view like a magic picture where the angle had to be just right to see the dancing bear. The shame (or was it anger? Confusion?) that had been festering swallowed her whole. She wanted to flee, anything but lay in a hospital bed answering inane questions.

Ramirez didn't bother waiting for a response. He was still, his voice calm, yet authoritarian. "We'll talk about Lien in a moment. First, we need to address the situation at hand. To clarify things for the record, you untied Parker Dallas, is that correct?"

Her memory of everything was crystal clear. She could call it up like a film in her mind and replay it again and again in real time. She knew she was in a spot now. The delay in her response to the detective's questions came from finding the right way to answer. Some way to save herself embarrassment— more importantly, to save herself from admitting yet another screwup right in front of Dr. Lucas.

"Yes," she said. "But just one hand." At this, she turned to Lucas. "So, he could eat," she clarified. "I wasn't going to feed him like a baby. That would have played into exactly what he wanted."

Lucas maintained her composure, and she nodded at Kate's response. They both turned back to Ramirez, awaiting the next question. He scribbled something in a small notepad.

"And you knew that was a violation of law enforcement protocol? To untie a violent suspect's restraints without the presence and/or direct order of the overseeing authorities?" There was no emotion in his voice. *Just the facts, ma'am.*

"I wasn't thinking about protocol," she said, not untruthfully. "The patient asked me to do it, and I did. So, he could, you know, ingest food."

"And you were aware that he was under police supervision and intended to be under restraint at all times?"

"Yes, but in the prior week he'd been through a large physical trauma. I didn't assess him as posing any sort of threat. I mean, even if he'd succeeded in getting me to untie him, I don't see how he would have made it out before--"

Ramirez interrupted her. "--I don't want to sound harsh. I *am* sorry for what you've just gone through, but I want you to refrain from editorializing. Just answer the questions directly, all right?" There was a simmering heat behind his eyes. She could see he was a man capable of great rage if provoked.

Before Kate could respond, Lucas jumped in. "Okay, okay, Mr. Ramirez-"

"-Detective Ramirez."

"Detective Ramirez, of course. Anyway, I think that's enough for today."

The look in Lucas's eyes finished the conversation. Whatever virile strength Ramirez possessed; it was no match for Dr. Vivian Lucas. *Hell hath no fury*. Kate had never been more thankful for the looks that the old doctor could command, especially because this time—for once—it wasn't aimed at herself.

Lucas added: "These men and women are doctors. They take an oath. They are trained to think about offering the best possible patient care. You wanna blame someone, blame me."

Kate had never been called a doctor before. Technically, it wasn't true yet, but she accepted the description silently, as a badge of honor.

Kate jumped in: "Detective, where was your officer at the time of the attack? Why wasn't anyone posted outside the door? Why are all the nurses so smitten with Officer Jim?"

Ramirez pulled lightly at his collar. Even Kate felt that it was starting to get a bit warm in the room. "We're, uh, we're looking into that," he said.

"I suggest you do," Dr. Lucas said, rising quickly. "Now please leave."

Ramirez flipped the cover of his notebook down, returned it to the inside pocket of his brown wool suit jacket, and promptly left the room with a small nod.

Kate pulled back the starched sheets, shifted into a sitting position, and dangled her feet over the side of the bed. There were a few scratches along her shins and the start of a deep-purple bruise around her right knee. When she looked across the room, her eyes landed on the first thing she could find—the red fire alarm—and focused intently on it. Her head was dizzy. She steadied herself and hopped to her feet. Lucas swooped in to guide her, one hand on Kate's own hand, the other on her lower back.

"Whoa, take it easy there, Kate."

Kate realized that someone had changed her into a hospital gown. She could see her black slacks, pale-blue collared shirt, and lab coat neatly folded on the seat beside the bed. She walked around the foot of the bed and over to the window. It was raining again outside. The flat, gray light cast the world in somber tones.

"I'm so sorry. For everything," Kate said.

Dr. Lucas met her solemn gaze, the hospital bed now between them. The left side of Lucas's face was lit by the bright fluorescents along the near wall, carving her into two halves: the light and the dark.

"Kate, I'm not going to pretend that what you did wasn't dangerous," she said. "But it's not your fault that he attacked you. He's a monster and he should be put away."

Kate instinctively glanced to her feet. There was more to the problem, and Lucas could sense it. She came around the side of the bed, put her hand gently on Kate's chin, and pulled on her jaw until Kate looked her mentor directly in the eyes.

"I don't think you should be alone right now. Someone should be here with you. I'm going to page Sean and have him come see you."

"No! Please don't!" Kate said, her voice strained and full of emotion. She hated herself for the display. She felt like a teenager who had just been embarrassed in front of the varsity football team. "We're, uh, we're not on good terms right now."

"Hey," Dr. Lucas said, "I'm sorry if this is too personal, but--"

Kate was on the verge of tears. She swallowed hard.

"Have you ever--" There was a pause. Lucas was searching for the right words. "In your history, has there been an assault?"

"What? Really?"

"I only ask because your behavior lately is consistent with other trauma cases I've seen."

"I wasn't raped, if that's what you mean," Kate shot back, lightning fast. "But-" Her lip began to quiver.

"Physical aggression—sexual or otherwise—can be a major trigger for emotional distress. One in four women, on average, report experiencing misconduct, Kate. This shit is ugly. It carries on. And it can manifest itself in as PTSD. Headaches, inability to focus or sleep."

"What about panic attacks?" Kate asked. "Blackouts?"

Dr. Lucas stopped the questioning and drew her in for a big embrace. Immediately, Kate began to cry into the soft arc of Lucas's shoulder.

The older doctor ran her thin fingers behind Kate's head, stroking her hair. "It's not your fault," she kept repeating.

Kate pulled back, sniffled, and wiped her eyes. "I was stupid. Just like today. I can be so fucking stupid." She closed her eyes and saw herself back in her Aunt Linda's apartment, four years ago.

★★★★★

Twenty-year-old Kate White awoke in a bed much larger than her own, feathered in late-morning sunlight. It wasn't every day that she found herself in the sprawling master bedroom of a Back Bay loft apartment that overlooked the river. A stiff, cool breeze tore through the open windows, carrying with it the hushed murmur of soft, lapping currents. She extended her arms up straight, reaching for the crystal light fixture above, feeling a million miles away, and smirked. She pictured her Aunt Linda hiring men in matching jumpsuits, carrying long ladders to change out all the bulbs.

"Molly!" she called. Nothing.

All week long, the routine had been constant: just before daybreak, Molly's cold, wet nose would burrow into the nape of Kate's neck, and the dog wouldn't leave Kate's side until kibble hit the bowl. She put on sweats and, on a whim, tried on a pair of Linda's gold earrings which shone in the reflection like two miniature suns orbiting her head.

Being away from home had shed weight from her shoulders. The sentiment manifested in a girlish gait as she galloped from room to room. She popped some bread into the toaster and then went to relieve herself in the bathroom, the latest issue of *Vogue* poking out from a magazine rack right by her feet. Her toes were painted with one of Aunt Linda's many expensive polishes: Tom Ford's Sugar Dune. As she sat there, she wondered just how her aunt had managed to claw her way out from under the family curse that was their lower-middle-class existence. When she got to feeling this way—call it jealousy, though it was more complex than that—Kate would fill with self-loathing.

A housefly landed on Kate's shoulder. She blew on it, watching as it danced out of the bathroom. Her eyes followed until they clocked the distant and quite unnatural lump on the floor of the kitchen. She hoisted up her pants and took off running for the dog.

"Molly! Please wake up!"

Her fingers poked and prodded the animal. She tried to lift it, but its body had stiffened, and so she let the dog drop back to the floor with a resounding thud. Two charred slices of toast sprang up from the toaster. Wisps of black smoke curled into the air. The dog's veiny, leprous tongue hung over the side of its jaw, collecting in folds on the floor.

The violent shrieking of the apartment's fire alarms stopped her heart. The noise was overwhelming. She grabbed the slices of bread, burning her fingers. They fell to the floor with a soft crackle, spewing crumbs. She dragged a stool across the tile floor with a jagged sputter, climbed atop, and furiously fanned a dish towel at the alarm in the ceiling, her chest pounding, until it finally quieted.

The air was tinged with the acrid odor of burnt toast. Overwhelming panic seized her, and the next few minutes whirled by in a flurry of manic pacing and verbal stuttering. She would have to tell Aunt Linda that Molly had died. There were no right words, not for Aunt Linda. How could Kate ever hope to do anything with her life, rise like her aunt, if she couldn't even keep the damn dog alive?

She dialed. The phone rang twice. An assured voice answered. "Yes?"

Kate bawled. It was not her original plan of attack, but it was a strategy of sorts. Tears ushered forth like a volcanic eruption, the words a plume of melodramatic emotion.

"Aunt Linda, it's horrible!"

Her aunt's voice gave rise to mild panic. Still, she remained restrained and professional in tone. "Katie? What is it? What happened?"

"I...uh...I..." She pulled the receiver from her ear to better focus herself. "It's Molly."

"Did something happen?"

"Yes, she's, uh, Molly's dead."

"*Dead?* What the *fuck* are you talking about?" Aunt Linda's voice bent into furious, pugilistic jabs.

Kate's aunt traveled routinely. Her role as a consultant for Boston-based financial companies necessitated it. Kate envisioned her now, standing at the head of an enormous conference room table in a perfectly tailored, pinstripe suit and Manolo Blahnik heels, various gray-haired C-suite executives looking on, mouths agape. This wouldn't have been in the slide deck.

"I'm sorry." Kate didn't know what to say next. Then she listened, and for quite a while, ten seconds or so, there was nothing but the sound of Aunt Linda's breath as the realization hit home.

"Oh," she uttered in a sedated drawl. "Shit."

"She was an older dog, right? It seemed peaceful."

"You must get her to the veterinarian. Maybe there is something they can do?"

"I'm pretty sure there's noth—"

"You're not a fucking doctor, Kate! And if she *is* dead, you'd have to take her anyway. The tenant association doesn't grant permits to dig graves in the front yard." Linda was always going on about *the association* and what they would and wouldn't allow. "Goddamn it. I've really gotta go. I'll call you tonight. Take care of this."

The line went dead.

The carry-on suitcase's plastic wheels droned a lulling rhythm as they popped over the cracks in the sidewalks as she pushed her way deeper into the city. Her petty cash had already gone to food and shopping leaving her a couple of stray bills in her wallet. The dog had barely fit in the case, but at least she could roll the damn thing. Kate yanked it out of the apartment, down the street, and underground into the Quincy Center station T-train. One hand squeezed the plastic handle on the case. The other clutched the prepaid metro card her aunt had left for her. Rushes of people flooded by.

Kate's eyes adjusted to the fluorescents. The air was thick and stale. She stood on the subway platform, her toes teasing the yellow caution line, as her hands wrapped around the handle of the case.

She turned and saw through the crowd that a young man was eyeing her. When his brown, focused eyes found hers, they suddenly darted away. He appeared to be around her age, surely a local college student. He wore horn-rimmed glasses. A day's scruff on his face. She found him immensely attractive. When he looked her way again, she offered a momentary smile before snapping her head forward so as not to seem overly interested. They were engaged in a game of glances, a game she knew how to play well, and for a moment, she forgot all about the dead dog by her feet.

With a thunderous roar, the train exploded into view, causing Kate to jump involuntarily. She glanced back and caught him smirking. Now she was losing their unspoken game, and her face radiated deep scarlet to the roots.

The train slowed to a stop. The gathered crowd swept her aboard. It was a handful of stops to Downtown Crossing, which would put her a few blocks' walking distance from the dog's vet. She grabbed a support pole by the sliding doors, the suitcase resting at her feet, and scanned the car, wild-eyed, uneasy.

"Hi there." His voice startled her, surprisingly assured for someone with his almost skittish appearance.

"Hi," she said.

She didn't believe in love at first sight. She had read all the books and seen all the films that girls were meant to experience, of course, and she even knew what it was like to feel thunderstruck in a boy's presence. But she reserved the concept of love for something else, something greater.

"I'm Cal."

He extended his hand. She shook it, noticing it was slightly moist but firm. She took her hand off the subway's pole but not the suitcase handle, never the suitcase's handle, and nearly lost her balance.

"Kate," she said.

"Nice to make your acquaintance," he said in a rather anachronistic way. His breath was sweetly sour. Not enough to be off-putting. "You from around here?"

"No, uh, yeah—I guess." She was stumbling, trying to land on how much truth to impart. She quickly decided to wrap herself in fiction and adopt her aunt's lifestyle. "I'm over in Back Bay."

"Got it," he said. "Saw the luggage. Figured you were from out of town."

Kate clutched the suitcase tighter. He certainly didn't carry himself as if he routinely flirted with women on subway trains. Besides, it wasn't as if he were proposing to her. All in all, he seemed rather harmless. He smiled warmly. They stood together amid a crowd of other passengers. He shifted his weight from one leg to the other.

"What about you?" she asked.

"Me?"

"Yeah, you from here?"

"Not originally. I'm really from the Midwest. Madison. Moved here three years ago for college."

"Ah, I figured. What're you studying?"

"I'm in a creative writing program. I just make shit up for a grade." He smiled, at least he was humble if he was going to be poor.

They continued speaking in that get-to-know-you back-and-forth for a few more minutes. Kate told Cal she was a sophomore pre-med major. He talked about his band. They both effused a love for The Beatles and a shared affinity for "Dear Prudence," in particular. Inside, she felt light, like she was constructed of delicate, flaky pastry dough and could crack with the slightest prodding.

Kate shifted on her feet and bit her lower lip. Cal was not like any of the men she knew growing up. He reached further back into her core DNA, reminding her of the primacy of pre-adolescent fervor that could suddenly grab hold and consume you. He was *Tiger Beat* love. He was Beatlemania.

Kate continued. "What kind of stuff do you write?"

"Nothing worth talking about. Yet, that is."

"Glad you have such a strong belief in your abilities," she sarcastically joked.

The train slowed to its first stop. The car vibrated, and the suitcase toppled forward. She lunged after it, knocking straight into the young man. He kept his balance with one hand and reached out with his other to help her right herself.

"Whoa, careful." His sharp eyes seemed to see everything: the suitcase, then her deep-blue eyes. "Looks like you're guarding that thing tight. Must have something really special in there."

"What?" She steadied the suitcase upright. Luckily, the zippers had remained closed.

"Just that you all but impaled me for that thing."

Her small hands cinched tighter around the handle. She would have to lie. It was a bit late into the conversation to admit she was ferrying the corpse of a slowly rotting dog through Boston. Actually, was there any good time to bring that up?

"No, no, it's my aunt's. She travels on business and left her suitcase behind. You know, work computer, a couple of important drives that she really needs. She called me to overnight it to her."

Kate fingered the curvature of Aunt Linda's gold earrings, which she had forgotten to remove.

Cal moved closer to Kate and sandwiched the suitcase between them so it wouldn't fall over.

"There," he said. "Now it's not going anywhere."

"Thanks," she said.

He glanced to the floor and smiled sheepishly. They both fidgeted and squirmed, and the fluorescent lights of the underground tunnel filtered past like shimmering bats in the night.

The train slowed for another stop. The passengers shifted. Cal reached for the pole as inertia worked to fling him forward, and his hand landed on hers. She smiled, only to herself, and Cal left his hand on hers a little longer than necessary. The doors closed with a pneumatic gust, and just outside of the window, the overhead cables sparked like small fireworks.

"So do you maybe want to grab a late lunch or something?" he asked. "I really don't have anywhere to be for another few hours. I'd hate to see us part so soon."

She glanced down at her suitcase. Streaks of blood had formed in soft pools on the floor. "I'd love to, but I need to take care of this case first. Wanna meet up after that? In an hour?"

They agreed to a date.

Kate was elated. It'd be her first since coming to Boston. Cal scrawled his number on a scrap of paper and folded it. It would be another three stops before she could get off, get rid of Molly, and move on with her life. The subway slowed as the station platform entered her view. The white-tiled walls through the scratched, plastic windows were cast in a dull and pallid gray.

Cal pointed outside to the approaching platform. "Well, I guess this is mine," he said.

The doors opened. Cal took the folded paper and pressed it into Kate's palm. While doing so, he leaned in as if to kiss her gently on the high blade of her cheek.

"Sorry," he whispered into her ear.

It didn't immediately click. But the sound of wedding bells gave way when, in a flash, his balled-up fist connected in a solid left hook with the side of her face. The skin was still tinged with a blush of embarrassment when cracks of heat lightning lit up behind her eyes. She stumbled back, falling onto the open seat behind her. The handful of other passengers within the car yelled chaotically and ran toward her. Blood trickled down over her chin, warm and sticky.

Cal grabbed the suitcase and tore out of the subway car. The doors closed softly behind him, and he sprinted into the distance of the darkened station and out of Kate's life forever.

The other passengers crowded in a semicircle around Kate, all their eyes searching her, penetrating her. She wanted to scream or, at the very least, cower under the thick mass of blankets back on Aunt Linda's bed. No, she wanted to be home, in her own bedroom next door to her mother.

Kate closed her eyes and steadied herself. Her face was swelling in concentric bruising that extended in deep-purple caverns below her eyes. Her fingers trembled uncontrollably, and she struggled to sit up. The pain came all at once in a radiating wave.

An old man who had been working on a crossword puzzle got up and parted the crowd. He stunk of cigarettes. He reached for an emergency call box on the wall behind them. "I'm going to call the police, miss. Did you know that man? His name? Anything?"

"Cal, I think," she mumbled as she opened her first revealing the scrap of paper he'd given her. Her fingers fumbled nervously. She turned it over in her hands, but it only contained a single word: *SUCKER*.

"No. I didn't know him."

An hour later, she was sitting on a gurney in the ER of St. Christopher's hospital. Her face was throbbing. Her arm going numb from having to compress the towel over her eyes where the nasty cut had opened. Her clothes were covered in her own blood. All she wanted was sleep.

The curtain was pulled back, and two men entered. The older man spoke first.

"Hi, Miss White. I'm Dr. Byrd."

He exuded patience under a quaff of pearly white hair. Behind him was a young man, not much older than herself, in green scrubs with a stethoscope slung around his neck.

"And this here is Sean Carraway. He's completing his clinicals right now. Do you mind if I have Sean take over the procedure? I'll be around to make sure everything goes according to plan."

Kate looked into the young man's warm eyes. Normally, she would have preferred the doctor with more experience, but in this case, something deep inside her was giving permission.

"It's fine."

"I won't hurt," Sean said, smiling.

"Great," the doctor said. "I'm sorry you've had to wait for so long. We're a bit backed up tonight, as you can see. I know Sean can handle this."

Kate nodded. Dr. Byrd left, immediately breaking his promise to look over Sean's work. But it didn't matter. Kate felt oddly secure. The doctor closed the curtain behind him. Now it was just her and this man named Sean.

"Rough night?" Sean asked.

He prepped and administered a local anesthesia via a small needle into three points around her brow and temple. It hurt so incredibly much. Kate screwed her jaw together to keep from screaming. The pain from that little needle was so intense, so unexpected, that Kate couldn't help but bust out laughing. She couldn't stop laughing, in fact, and tears started streaming down her cheeks.

"I guess you could say that."

"I saw the police report," Sean said.

He moved Kate's hand down, relaxing the compress so that he could get a good look at the cut.

"Ouch," he said. "Good news is that I'll have you right as rain. Should only be three or four stitches to clean that up. There won't be any long-term scarring."

They talked for nearly forty-five minutes, but what Kate remembered most was the warm sureness of Sean's hands on her face and shoulders while he worked. The determination of his focus. Yes, it hurt, but she pretended it didn't and when he was done, he spoke first.

"You know," he said. "This is expressly against protocol. But can I maybe take you to dinner some time? Or a movie? Only if you're interested, no pressure of course."

She smiled, which brought pain above her eye where the ridge of stitches was very tender. She winced. "Not now. God, I must look a mess."

"I didn't actually mean right now," he laughed. "Besides, I get off at two in the morning."

"Rough hours."

"Happens when you're on the bottom of the totem pole. Gosh, you're beautiful. The contusions really bring out your eyes."

They laughed heartily. His eyes, they could see the whole world in her. She wanted to tumble into them, to wake every morning to those eyes looking at her from across the pillow.

He continued. "How about this weekend? Maybe we can see a movie and grab some milkshakes or something?"

She nodded. It was a date.

Chapter Ten
CRASH CART

The attack left her feeling grimy, violated. So much had changed over the past four years. Now, after Parker's assault, a shower sounded too good to pass up. It'd help her feel better. Kate signed herself out of St. Christopher's care, but she didn't bother going home. She didn't want to be alone, not after all of this, so she found herself in the shower stall of the employee locker room.

It did feel good. The biting hot water ran down Kate's body. Her hair collected behind her back in one thick, dripping rope. Steam billowed out from the small cubicle of the stall. It still ached every time she swallowed from where his hands had clutched her neck. She ran her fingers over her throat. Already, it was considerably bruised. Deep purple and black streaks the very shape of Parker Dallas's fingers.

Memory was a funny thing. She hadn't consciously thought about that moment on the subway for a long time, but she was dwelling on it now, in the shower, under the hissing showerhead. She supposed she was *always* thinking about it just beneath the surface. Her face contorted into a grimace of pure rage.

She closed her eyes, steadied herself. *How could I have let this happen to me again? By this fucking asshole, no less?*

She was so goddamn stupid. She wouldn't fall for this shit anymore. She couldn't continue to be the victim and still retain a shred of self-respect. No, she was done.

Her fingers curled into fists and she punched the tiled wall as hard as she could, sending a threaded fracture up through the center of the green, ceramic square. The pain shot jolts of electric shock up through her forearm, into her elbow, exploding into fireworks in her shoulder and jaw.

Now her hand hurt like hell, but she preferred that sharp fire to the dull and depressing ache consuming her mind. She flexed her knuckles. They were bright red. She worried that maybe she'd broken a few bones in her hand, but she didn't think so. A small gash had opened above her ring finger where her engagement ring had cut back into the skin.

Her mind was ready to run away from her again, and she suspected another blackout was imminent. These were the moments that frightened her the most, when she sensed it coming, knowing terrible nightmares lay in wait. Bad thoughts swirled. She punched the wall again, but nothing would make it stop. So, she punched again. Again. Again.

"You okay in there?" a concerned voice called from somewhere beyond the hiss of the shower.

The distraction ripped her away from the maw of another blackout. Instantly, she was back in her body again. She halted, held her breath, but then decided that would make things worse.

"Yeah, I'm fine," she croaked.

She did not sound fine but hoped it would be enough to assuage the Good Samaritan. Kate waited until she felt she'd faint from holding her breath. There were no follow-ups.

It took ten minutes for the spray of the shower to wash away all the blood. Her breathing slowed. She calmed down and cut the water. With the shower off, it was quiet aside from the thrum of the water pipes and the murmur of faraway voices of other women. Fresh blood was pooling in all the cuts and scrapes around her knuckles where the skin had been beaten away. It soiled the towel wrapped around her wet body. Drops of the stuff fell to the floor as she made her way over to the lockers. Her hair was a tangled, wet mess.

It was not that she was unaware of the other women in the shower room, but she had found a way to focus so intently that she moved and acted as if she was the only person left in the world. Immediately she flashed on Richard Matheson's *I Am Legend*. Another one of her favorite horror books. In it, a lone human in a sea of vicious creatures – but who was the monster? She saw two ER doctors getting ready for their shifts. One changing into a clean pair of scrubs while the other brushed her teeth. Both women stopped as soon as they saw Kate and observed her, silently, as Kate moved from the shower stall to the lockers in her blood-stained towel.

Kate focused on the ache in her hand as she moved past them. She would be lucky to be able to move her fingers for the next few days. The pain was pushed below, tamped down, and right at this moment, it wasn't enough to slow her down. Her eyes were heavy-lidded. How long had it been since she'd last slept? She'd do anything to stay awake. After the incident with Molly on the train, she had nightmares for weeks. She couldn't imagine what demons awaited her now. In the dark, that's when monsters hunted.

Coming out of the water, she felt brand new, reborn. Where previously she was anxious about constant failure, now there was smoldering anger. The anger felt like fiery coals priming the steam boiler of her psyche to explode. She could rip concrete with her fingers, chew through the metal wire.

The tile floor was cool under foot. She dressed, and by the time she'd finished, the locker room had cleared. It was calmer when she was by herself, as if the others had known to let her alone by the smell in the air. *Stay clear. This is Kate White's territory now.* She grabbed the first aid kit from the supply closet and bandaged her hand. Now it thumped with a dull ache and she was so very thirsty. Kate stood before the

large mirror over the side-by-side sinks. Her comb worked
through the snarls of her tawny hair. She palmed a cupful of
water into her mouth, swished, and spat. She put the comb
down on the counter, wiped away the steam from the mirror,
and just stood there, observing her own reflection for a very
long time. The look on her face was not a look she recognized.
Then it hit her why the monster wasn't chasing her. It was
looking back at her.

★★★★★

The underside of her hair was still damp and stringy, but she
had every intention of going back to class. At home she'd stew.
Here, she could at least try to beat back this hungry beast inside
her that was slavering for revenge. It took every ounce of will
not let the image of Parker Dallas's terrifying, red eyes squash
her.

   Walking the corridors, she nursed her raw and bruised
knuckles and spotted a face from the corner of her eye that
stopped her. There was an obvious halt in her step as she
debated turning and running in the opposite direction but then
relented. It was Dr. Louis Fenton, a man who was usually but
a ghost in the halls of this hospital. Here he was, in the flesh,
with a duffel bag under his arm, headed into the men's showers.
Dark half-moons hung beneath his eyes. This was a man who
hadn't slept in days. He stuck out to her because it was in his
presence, Kate realized now, where she had started concocting
the plan that had gotten her on Lucas's good side. He had
become the face associated with her own fall from grace.

   She walked another five steps and watched as he
disappeared into the men's room. She was ambivalent but
ultimately pivoted on her heels, turned back down the corridor,
and slipped inside behind him. It was dark and humid in the
men's showers. She slipped into a hiding spot within the
janitor's closet and cowered there patiently. The smell of

chlorine bleach brought her back to summers at the community pool.

Other than Kate, who squatted like a spy in the closet, Fenton was alone. She cracked the closet door just enough to peek through and see him pass in and out of view in quick, hazy blurs. It turned to a game, Fenton sighting, like a grainy video of Bigfoot.

She carefully watched as Fenton packed his discarded clothes into his gym bag and crammed everything in the nearest locker. He removed his glasses and shoved them, along with his security key card, into the soles of his shoes. Wrapped in a white towel, he entered a shower stall and drew the curtain closed behind him. *Kishhh!* The water roared to life.

Kate huddled, silent and still. A nervousness crept in. She felt like she had to pee and couldn't hide n the dark of the closet for another minute. She made her move. Kate opened the door. As she crept over the tile flooring, the steam from Fenton's shower filled the room. She approached his locker and pressed her whole body against her hands to muffle the metallic sound of the lock mechanism sliding free. The rickety metal door swung open. She prayed that no one would enter the men's locker room and catch her out here in the open.

First, she snagged Fenton's shoes. Tucked inside the first was his glasses which she promptly returned. Tucked inside the other were Fenton's key card and cell phone. *Jackpot.* His security access card looked just like hers. The only difference was that his name was stamped within a red box. On her card, the name KATE WHITE was stamped within a yellow one. The color-coding must be related to access credentials or something. Below Fenton's name, his date of birth was listed along with his employee ID. This was also like the format and layout of her own card. Fenton had a June birthday just like her. Geminis. *Did he have a secret self, a double nature too? Was he a monster underneath like her?* She doubted it.

She pocketed his key card and then held his cell phone in the palm of her hand, careful not to lay her fingers on the glass surface. A few months back, when she began to worry that Sean was having an affair, she researched online how to access someone's locked phone. She didn't know Sean's four-digit code. He didn't know hers. It was one of the few secrets they had allowed each other. The website said that most people use the same code for everything, whether for the ATM card or the garage door keypad. She knew Sean's garage door code. When she typed it into Sean's phone, it let her in. At the time, she couldn't believe that it worked. But once she had the access to Sean's phone, she lost the urge to spy on him. Turns out that the act of breaking in was enough excitement.

The sound of Fenton humming cascaded over the pulse of the water. Kate grabbed the penlight from her lab coat pocket and clicked it on. A small cone of light shone onto the cell phone's glass. She drew the light in a slow, smooth orbit around the phone's surface until the angle was just so and she could see distinct fingerprint smears where the pads of Fenton's fingers most often landed. Digits from the keypad lined up perfectly with where the oily residue of his fingers left marks. There were four areas on the phone's surface with the most action. She mentally recorded the underlying numbers: *two, four, six, eight.*

★★★★★

Even with several recent visits through the cold corridors of St. Christopher's basement, this was the first time she'd noticed the security camera aimed at the entrance to the laboratory. If she had known, she likely would have folded on the entire plan before coming this far. If anyone on the other end was watching, she'd be toast.

The large, metal door was a final bastion. One last reminder to yield to common sense. A moment to reassess and give up the entire bestial plan. But Kate had already come this far. The door proved no obstacle and slid open with a quick wave of Fenton's key card.

The thing about lab researchers, Kate had learned from her time with Lien, was that they were so goddamn focused on the work in front of them that they often failed to notice their surroundings. Maybe it was an over-generalization, slagging off an entire group of people, but the stereotype was proving true at this very moment. Kate kept her head down and moved forward. Not only was no one trying to stop her, no one was even paying attention that she was here.

It was early afternoon. The lab was relatively empty. Kate rounded the corner. From her one class visit, it all came flooding back. She moved along the rows of workstations, past the genetic experiments, and past the small group of three researchers immersed in a computer display of microscope slides.

There it stood, cast in a single arc of golden light, calling for her: the specimen freezer. She approached it warily, a sleeping dragon, snoring lazily with its electric motor. Kate found the computer screen with its security-lock keypad, and she steadied herself. At this angle, she was shielded from view from the main room. She rubbed her thumb and index finger rapidly like a pick pocket warming up for the grab and dash. Then she pressed the numbers she had gleaned from Fenton's cell phone. *Two. Four. Six. Eight.* Enter. The red LED light flashed three times. Denied.

Too many failed attempts would certainly lock her out. Worst case, it would sound an alarm. Kate reasoned she had two more tries at most. And she still had to return the stolen ID card to Fenton's locker before he finished showering. The clock was ticking, ticking, ticking.

Kate held up Fenton's key card, looking him right in the cold, vacant eyes of his ID photo. She wanted to psychically pull the code out of him through some sort of mental telepathy. She wanted to communicate the way a rogue's gallery of monsters talked to her in her nightmares. Just through thought. That was when she saw it and suddenly, it all fell into place. Below the photo. Below his name. His birthdate: June 2. 1948. She typed again. *Six. Two. Four. Eight.* The LED light flipped green.

Immediately, the sound of a mechanism unlocking with a thud. Then the sound of some electronic beep. The computerized symphony accompanied the motorized freezer. The first of two large, hydraulic cylinders emerged, driven upward with a steady, mechanical hum. A ghostly, blue light emanated from within the deep freeze. Wrapped around the elongated, frozen core were dozens of small vials, each the size of a pencil nub worn all the way down. Wisps of nitrogen vapor filtered out like cigarette smoke.

She was keyed up with adrenaline. It was all happening now. This entire plan had come together not as some calculated affair. What was it they'd say in court? Pre-meditated? No, Kate was operating on pure id and following one chemical impulse after another. She was no different from the cockroach.

She stood before the erect cylinders, each holding a dozen or so biological samples. *Focus, Kate.* She closed her eyes. There was Parker's face with his terrifying, all-seeing red eyes. She felt the bruises on her throat. She was reminded of them every time she swallowed. She pictured Parker—sick, weakened—and then imagined Dr. Lucas lavishing praise upon her. She saw herself in a white coat with her name stitched on the lapel: *Katherine White, M.D.*

Her eyes opened. She realized she was nearly out of time—if she wasn't too late already. She needed to get Fenton's things back to his locker. She stretched out her hands, reached into the depths of the second cylinder, and craned her neck as if reading the spines of books on a library shelf. Everything here was labeled in code, so she didn't know one from the other. She snagged a vial at eye level. It was simply labeled *Compound 112A.*

That'll have to do.

★★★★★

She ran. Her lungs burned. Her stomach cramped. She didn't wait for the elevator, taking the stairs up from the basement to the first-floor shower rooms instead. She reached for the heavy door to the men's room, but before she could exert the strength to push it, it swung open by itself. She lost her balance and tumbled inside right into the open arms of Dr. Louis Fenton.

Kate let out a small yip of fright. With her frazzled appearance and high-pitched whine, she must have appeared to Fenton like a Pomeranian. He staggered backward but caught her before she fell to the floor.

Kate didn't realize it was him at first. When she righted herself, they were standing eye to eye, no more than six inches apart. She could smell cigarettes on his breath.

"So sorry!" she said. "Wrong room."

"Don't mention it," he called back. He politely chortled.

Kate backed up, turned around, and pushed her way into the women's shower room. She felt Fenton's eyes burning a hole in her, but when she gave in and turned back, he wasn't looking at her at all. He hadn't given Kate a second thought. He was headed for the elevators.

Fenton didn't seem like he was in a huff. He gave no indication that he even realized his key card was missing. But he wasn't going to get back into the lab without it. *He'd have no reason to suspect me, right?* She sat worrying on a toilet for fourteen minutes, chewing the skin off her thumb. After enough time had gone by, she snuck back into the men's showers and tossed Fenton's key card into the dark rear of his locker. Soon after that, Kate was running through the corridors on the second floor. She passed the same nurses' station where the same three nurses were fielding calls and delegating patient assignments.

Kate plowed through the crowded hall and finally arrived at room 217. Her hands were balled into little fists that held the stolen vial. In the pocket of her lab coat was a fresh needle, capped and ready for a jab. This time, however, there was a fundamental difference from before. The police officer stood guard at the door. Officer Jim. *Why couldn't he be flirting with the nurses today?* Upon Kate's arrival, he deliberately stepped between her and Parker's door. A bouncer at an elite club.

"Excuse me," Kate said, "but I need to get in there."

Officer Jim was chewing gum, open-mouthed, rather like a cow. "Can't let anyone in without explicit orders from the doc in charge," he said. "Especially after yesterday."

"I have permission. It's fine."

"Sorry. Can't do it." His arms crossed over his large, barrelled chest.

"He's been heavily sedated, though, right?"

"Doesn't matter. We're taking no more chances with this one."

She stood nose to nose with the cop. It required a little push on the balls of her feet to meet his height.

"I'm sure your superior would love to hear how well you stood guard yesterday," she said. "You know, when he had a knife to my throat, and you were too busy trying to bang Nurse Ratched in the linen closet?"

This pissed Officer Jim off royally. He stopped chewing that wad of gum. Those big muscular arms rippled. The threaded vein in his stolid face flexed. He swallowed hard then, so hard he swallowed his gum. There was a brief twitch in his eye, and he stepped aside.

Kate's hand grasped the handle. As she was about to enter, Officer Jim's hand landed atop of hers. Kate was taken aback. A hitch in her throat. Jim leaned in close and whispered in her ear, "I'm not the stupid cunt who untied him."

It was a punch in the gut. Her other hand, the one not on the doorknob of room 217, wrapped tightly around the syringe hidden in the pocket of her lab coat. It was a weapon she'd desperately wanted to deploy on all the men in the world in that moment. Shredding them to pieces.

She entered room 217.

★★★★★

Parker Dallas was unconscious in the hospital bed. With the soft light falling on his face, he appeared as harmless as a young child. It was the complete reversal of how she'd last seen him. Kate stepped slowly toward the man, looking for a sign, any sign at all, that he might be faking—waiting to lunge at her again. His breathing was slow and deep. His eyelids fluttered with dreams.

If Parker had awakened, she thought, Kate would have appeared standing over him with the iridescent glow of the hospital's machines behind her as some angelic vision. An angel of death. Or mercy. In her brain was the image of a painting—Bloch's *Christ at Gethsemane*. She didn't know much about art outside of the one art history class she'd taken during her undergraduate years.

She tested the leather straps holding down Parker's arms. They were tight. He remained unconscious. She reached into her lab coat and removed the syringe. It crinkled as she unwrapped it, carefully, tucking all the detritus back into her coat pockets.

She leaned in close to Parker's ear. "Parker?" she whispered. "You awake? Can you hear me?"

She waited with bated breath. There was nothing. She inspected the vial. Its translucent contents shimmered like hot oil in the light. The needle pierced the plastic lid of the vial. She pushed down on the plunger, dispelling all air, then pulled it back up, inhaling its contents. The spent glass vial joined the other evidence in her pocket.

She rested the needle on Parker's food tray, right beside the half-eaten green JELL-O and tied a rubber strip around his arm.

"Compound 112A" she said, having read it off the vial label. "I have no idea what this shit is…but I hope it hurts like hell."

She plunged the needle into his median cubital vein. It only took her one attempt. Her hand was surprisingly steady. Her thumb depressed the plunger. The compound solution disappeared from the syringe and into Parker's veins, flooding his bloodstream. The needle was removed, recapped, and returned to her coat pocket. She stepped back from him.

Parker's chest rose dramatically, as if he had emerged from swimming underwater, and inhaled a big gulp of air. Then all resumed as if nothing had occurred.

Her hand on the doorknob, she turned back to him and said, "That was fun. Let's do it again real soon?"

★★★★★

Kate White wound her way through admissions, back towards the main lobby. The pallid, fluorescent lights enveloped her as she passed through obstetrics and then the neurology wing. She was in a rather dreamlike state, being pulled by invisible cables. She weaved through a sea of people: doctors, nurses, orderlies, patients. This godforsaken hospital was always at capacity.

She wanted to burn away the evidence. But she couldn't. There were just too many people scurrying about. The shame of her dark secret was but a small bulge in her lab coat pocket. Her stomach turned. *It's the little things that always catch up with you. You know, little things like leaving DNA evidence in your coat.* At least, that was the lesson she took away from all those true crime shows her mother was always watching.

Just a few minutes ago she'd felt invincible. But the air had shifted. When walking through the halls, a heavy chain of guilt slung around Kate's neck. It was like the way a beautiful summer evening can suddenly turn disastrous when funnel clouds send tornados through town. Common sense was returning. Weirdly, it felt like pins and needles, the blood flow normalizing. Oh God. What if she had given him something really nasty? A novel coronavirus? Ebola? What if it didn't end with Parker? What if, unlike an allergic reaction, she had created patient zero. What if this was the start of some global pandemic?

Suddenly, she felt woozy. She wasn't thinking straight. There was a sharp pain in her chest and she was struggling to breathe. She thought about guilt and whether it could give a person such distinct physical symptoms. *If the deed was bad enough,* she wondered, *could it kill me?* She rounded the corner and bumped into Sean.

"Oh Kate, sorry." He looked her up and down. He could see she was frazzled. "You alright?" he asked.

"Don't worry. I'm fine. I just keep bumping into people."

She tried to walk by him, closing her eyes and hoping he would leave it be. Of course, that didn't happen. He was always good about assessing when something deep within her was wrong.

"I wanted to talk to you," he said.

"Yeah?" *Please go away. I'm toxic. I'll bring you down with me. You were right to go.*

"I heard about what happened with that asshole Parker earlier." He seemed attentive, warm, as if he hadn't broken up with her two days ago. "You should've called me immediately. I want to be there for you."

"That's sweet, but those are boyfriend privileges."

"The hospital never should have put you in that position."

She couldn't bring herself to admit that she'd gone in simply because Parker had asked for her. That she'd once again flaunted all the rules.

"I don't know" was all she managed to say. "Everything got crazy for a second. Tell you the truth, I don't remember much."

Sean drew closer. His feet scuffed on the linoleum, and he pulled her in for a hug.

"I'm glad you're okay."

She felt warm and secure all over again. In his arms, all the messy shit from the past week washed away, leaving only that feeling of dependence and powerlessness.

"We should talk," he said. "I don't like how we left things. There's got to be a way through this. We can make it work."

"You think so?"

"Can we talk later?"

"I don't know, Sean."

"Please. I have stuff I need to say to you. But I'm needed in surgery right now."

"It's all right. I've gotta get outta here too."

Kate watched him leave. His green OR scrubs were dotted with dried blood around the shoulders. Two days prior, he'd been her fiancé. Today, they were ships passing in the night. And she was late for class.

★★★★★

From the first floor, by the back, a glass corridor connected the main hospital to an entirely separate building known as Gaige Hall. Gaige was one of many other smaller buildings within St. Christopher's sprawling campus. It contained the academic classrooms for the medical students.

Kate loved stepping through the glass corridor. In the chill of late autumn—or even in the dead of winter when she hated the sharp, blustering cold—that glass corridor remained warm. It took the suns rays the way a New England apple pie fresh from the oven stays warm for hours. She felt like Alice tumbling through the looking glass, passing through time as she left the historic relic of the ancient hospital and moved into the futuristic, sci-fi world of Gaige Hall.

The largest amphitheater off the main lobby had been designed in a format resembling a theater in the round. It was nicknamed the Globe, an homage to Shakespeare. Tiered stadium seating encircled a stage in the room's center. At capacity, the Globe held nearly two hundred students. Today, with a smattering of first-through-third years gathered, a meager eighteen took their seats for another Patient/Doctor class with Dr. Childers. Kate grabbed the seat beside Daniel. He smiled at her. A face full of pity. Kate knew instantly that everyone must have heard about her and Sean breaking up by now. God, news traveled fast.

Childers stood in the center of the round in his pristine, white lab coat. The lab coat was the extent of his polish. Patchy, white stubble dotted his red neck down to his Adam's apple. He'd gotten on his soapbox again. Kate had seen him do it a hundred times. He'd turn his back to the class, grab a piece of chalk, and start scrawling in giant, scratched letters on an ancient blackboard that had been rolled onto the floor. The painful, scraping sound wormed its way into Kate's ears. She closed her eyes and looked away until she heard Childers finish the final stroke and drag a long, slow underline beneath two large words. The board read: *HIPPOCRATIC OATH.*

Childers addressed the class: "The Hippocratic Oath is one of the first statements on moral conduct for physicians."

As Childers droned on, Kate looked down at her engagement ring. The petite, French pavé crown diamond that she'd picked out for Sean to give to her. It was a small rock starting to feel like an insufferable boulder. Some bad luck totem. One of the students raised their hand. Kate tried to clock who it was, but the face was on the other side of the amphitheater and the spotlight was in her eyes.

"Yes?" Childers said.

The student spoke: "Wasn't the oath abandoned like two hundred years ago?"

"This specific oath isn't in practice any longer, but any institution accrediting students with the power of medicine should have a strong code of ethics. And all of it is rooted in the history of the Hippocratic Oath." Childers spun around, using the opportunity to meet the gaze of each student, emphasizing his point. He looked directly at Kate, and she could feel his stare piercing her soul.

"They may not make you take the oath at graduation anymore. But I demand my students do." He raised his right hand. "So come on," he said. "Stand up. Raise your hands." The class obeyed.

Daniel leaned into Kate. "Isn't this patronizing?" he asked. "What does he think we're gonna do out there?"

Kate shrugged. "Just go along with it." But beneath the placid sea of her surface, a tempest raged within.

"Repeat after me," Childers said. Then he inhaled and began to recite like a grade school student giving the morning's Pledge of Allegiance. "I swear to fulfill, to the best of my ability and judgment, this covenant..." He paused, allowing the class to catch up.

They responded all together: "I swear to fulfill, to the best of my ability and judgment, this covenant…"

His right hand was still held high. "Most especially must I tread with care in matters of life and death. If it is given to me to save a life, all thanks."

The students responded in kind. They continued the back-and-forth, call-and-response.

"But it may also be within my power to take a life; this awesome responsibility must be faced with great humbleness and awareness of my own frailty. Above all, I must not play at God. May I always act to preserve the finest traditions of my calling, and may I long experience the joy of healing those who seek my help."

When the students finished repeating Childers's words, the doctor let the echo in the round settle to complete silence. He motioned to the students to take their seats.

"Good. Don't we all feel better now?"

The students laughed, all except Kate.

"Okay, let's continue our discussion, shall we?"

★★★★★

In the early evening, the lone dish that sat under Kate's microwave Lean Cuisine sank beneath the suds in the sink. The street was quiet now that the late autumn chill had settled in. It got dark now before dinner. The world felt sleepy, and it wasn't even time for *Jeopardy!* The only sound was the hum from her refrigerator, louder than usual, creating a low, unsettling, industrial tone.

She rummaged through her drawers and ripped through the closets and under the bed, clearing away everything that belonged to Sean. She hadn't allowed herself the opportunity to cry. No sad songs, no combing through old love letters in a shoebox under the bed. It was the great purge.

The fervor was broken by a gentle knocking at the front door. Sean was ten minutes late. Kate opened the door. He stood there, awaiting permission to enter, even though he still had a key, even though it was his money that had paid for her to be here.

"Is now still good?" he asked.

"I suppose," she said, backing up, allowing him to enter. "I put everything of yours that I could find in boxes." Mismatched cardboard boxes littered the living room like a small perimeter fence.

He crossed by her to the other side of the living room, ensuring not to make physical contact.

"Look," he said. "I've been thinking, and…can we just, like, talk for a few minutes?"

She shut the door but didn't say anything. She was wondering if she really wanted him to apologize. Would it be easier to wallpaper over the past few days if he let her? Find a way to work it out? After what she had done to Parker, though, the bad thoughts kept coming. Blackened tendrils of mold were creeping through her veins. She'd have to come clean. She'd have to tell everyone what she did. It was the only way she could ever sleep again, even if it was within the cold confines of a jail cell. She wanted to confess everything to Sean right at this very moment, but her heart couldn't handle the way he'd look at her. It would be the rape of his idealization of her.

"I'm sorry about today." Sean took two steps closer to Kate, testing the waters. "I'm sorry about everything. I know, I've been saying that a lot lately."

"Forget it."

Sean stepped closer yet again. He grabbed her hand and gently pulled her back into the center of the living room by the coffee table they bought when she moved in. It was one piece her mother hadn't had to donate.

"Come on. Talk to me. I shouldn't have run out of the chapel on you like that."

"I shouldn't have sprung a surprise wedding on you."

"I thought about that for a long time afterward," he said. "It was a really sweet gesture. I'm just, I don't know, it's me. I fucked everything up."

"No, I knew we were over. I think I tried to force us to fix it. It's just…" Kate paused, struggling for the right words. "My father. God, this sounds so lame. But he died and then there was a long stretch of emptiness and then I found you. I used to feel like we were meant to be. But it's stupid."

"It's not stupid. And we don't have to give up on each other."

Kate looked up at the ceiling and exhaled. "Just tell me you weren't with someone else."

Sean tried to put his hand on hers. "That doesn't matter. Not if we agree to start over right here, right now."

She pulled away. "While I was going to class fourteen hours a day and planning our wedding and being eaten alive by stress, were you screwing around?"

He glanced away.

"You did, didn't you?"

"I'm not going to lie to you. I respect you too much."

She took the framed picture of the two of them sitting on the edge of the TV stand and thought about hurling it at him. But that would be so melodramatic. She slammed the framed photo down on the top of one of his now full boxes of stuff. The glass shattered into the pile of clothes within the box.

"We can't, Sean. It wasn't meant to be. I see that now. It's not just you. I'm all messed up."

She grabbed one of the boxes she'd pulled together and shoved it into his open arms. The force sent him stumbling backward until he was against the wall separating the living room from the kitchen.

She ran forward, closing in on him, the space between them now just a sliver of light. Leaning in, it was as if she planned on consuming his face. With her mouth against his ear, she whispered: "You need to go. You have no idea what I am capable of."

There was a clatter as Sean dropped the box he was holding to the floor and tried to wrap her in a hug. But Kate screamed. A visceral, rage-filled scream directed right into his ear. If only she could scream loud enough, then maybe he would disintegrate.

Sean fell back violently against the wall, his eyes those of prey caught in a trap.

In the distance, her phone began to ring. It pulled her out of the darkness and Kate saw her reflection in the hall mirror. The image looking back was not her own self. Her eyes had yellowed. She grabbed her phone and slid the green Accept button open. "Yeah?" she said.

The voice on the other end of the line was familiar and excited. It was Daniel. "Kate?" he asked. "It's me. You home?"

"Daniel, what's wrong?

"Sorry to bother you. I didn't think you'd want to miss this, though."

"Miss what?" Kate asked.

Sean was standing in the doorway, a box of his belongings weighing down both arms. He could see the magnetic pull of the conversation was big enough to trump their fight. He waited patiently, eyes aglow.

Daniel's voice was shaky on the other end of the line. "That crazy guy who attacked you, what's his name?"

"Parker Dallas?" Now she was confused as all hell and started pacing the hall. She clocked Sean's confused face.

"Yeah, that's it!"

Kate's heart began to thunder in her chest. Had they caught on? She wouldn't sleep for another hundred years with the fear and adrenaline pumping through her now. Could she hear the sirens of the cop cars flooding the lot outside her apartment? She tried not to betray anything in her voice. "What about him?"

"He's fucking dead!" Daniel yelled. "There's going to be an autopsy. It's in the exam room annexed off the morgue. You should be here. Sean too. I'll call him next?"

Kate's vision began to tunnel.

"Don't bother," she said. "He's here."

Kate clutched her phone tighter, a physical talisman to keep her in the present. In a white-hot panic, she lost her balance and started tumbling. Then, the blackout took over, and she disappeared into the ether.

Chapter Eleven
THE WITCHING HOUR

The entire return trip to St. Christopher's was a soundless haze of barely conscious activity. Kate felt like a bug, or some other lesser life form, operating from moment to moment on chemical impulse. *This must be what finally happens when you go crazy,* she thought. Emotional relationships dry up, and life becomes a linked chain of cause and effect: do, react, do, react. No bigger picture, everything completely devoid of deeper meaning.

She ran to the hospital from her apartment. It had taken her only twelve minutes to make the mile and a half; the best time she'd clocked since junior varsity track. Her side cramped, but she pushed away the pain, driven entirely by her deepest, darkest fear: that she'd finally killed a man.

With her heart thumping wildly in her chest, she rounded the corner to the hospital and nearly keeled over against the railing by the large, locked employees-only door.

"Shit!" she said, rummaging through her pockets.

She had forgotten her key card. Through the thick, glass panel of the door, she could see people inside scurrying about. She watched them with a kind of dazed avidity, adrenaline surging through her body, mixing with the blood coursing through her veins into a cocktail that literally made her shake.

"Hey there!"

She spun around. Dr. Fenton was behind her. She thought it was so strange that the universe was keeping them sutured together in this moment when throughout her entire history at St. Christopher's she could barely count the number of times they'd crossed paths.

"You're the one that fell into my arms the other day, right?" He laughed politely.

Without the pristine, white lab coat, he was just a schlub with mismatched socks and wrinkled khakis. His overstuffed briefcase pulled on one arm, throwing his posture off-kilter. A plastic bag swung from his other hand; a trench coat draped over the arm. The corner of a key card was poking from between his first two fingers.

"You mind?" he asked. "Arms are full."

It took her a moment to realize what he was talking about. She stood there, slack-jawed, as the first dew drops of perspiration released from her hairline. A slow trickle cascaded down her right temple, a spider slow walking the side of her face.

"Of course not."

She was trying hard not to look like her lungs were ravenously hungry for air. She grabbed the key card from between Fenton's fingers and opened the door for them both. When they were inside, Fenton dropped his briefcase on the unmanned security desk by the door.

"Thanks. I'll just take that back now."

She looked at the key card still in her hands. It was different from the one she'd stolen from him. This one had a brand-new photo. In it, Fenton wore an exasperated, "I don't have time for this shit" expression on his face.

"Third card this year." He laughed, largely to himself. "Just can't stop losing the damn things."

Kate cracked a mirthless, polystyrene smile, only for his benefit. One worry could be removed. He didn't seem to suspect his card had been stolen. But it amounted to plucking a grain of sand from the beach. At the moment, one floor below her feet, a man she'd recently injected with some godforsaken compound was lying dead. They stepped into the elevator.

"Going up?"

"Down," Kate said.

If things kept going the way they had been, the floor of the elevator was about to open over the very fires of hell.

He pressed the down arrow. "What've they got you students doing down in the big, spooky basement today?"

"Cadaver dissection."

"Ohhh," he said, intrigued, but then trailed off, unsure of how to continue. "I'd say that was my favorite, but I think that would make me sound like a serial killer or something, huh?"

"Guess so," Kate feigned polite laughter.

The drop of the elevator car made her stomach flutter. They rode in silence for what seemed an eternity.

"First time?" he asked.

"First time?"

"You know," he said. "Human dissection."

She nodded. "Yeah. We've watched the videos and read everything under the sun, but-"

"There's no substitute for the real thing."

There was a small ding as they hit the basement level and the elevator doors rocketed open. Well, good luck," he said. "Thanks again for your help."

At the T-junction. Kate peeled to the left. Fenton went to Davol lab on the right. The morgue was set back past the employee locker rooms, behind a simple set of brown, wooden doors with a small, plastic sign affixed to the wall. She found her locker. Inside hung the lab coat from before, still filled with evidence of her transgressions. She slung it on and headed for the morgue.

The wooden doors opened into a small foyer. To the left was yet another door. It led to the squat tiled room where nightmares found inspiration. Along one wall, the cabinet. Four columns, two rows. Eight squat doors. Room for eight dead bodies in refrigerated cocoons. Daniel said the autopsy was to take place here. Trays had already been set out, prepared with shiny, sharp instruments. A wall of windows looked back into the tiled, OR prep room filled with large basin sinks where Dr. Lucas and Daniel were scrubbing their fingers raw.

Kate entered. She had nothing with her, save the phone in her pocket, having erupted like a rocket from the apartment. The whole exchange was hazy now, though it'd only taken place a few minutes earlier. Sean said he'd be right behind, asked if Kate wanted a ride. But then the OR called him in and she put foot to pavement like the Olympic gold hinged on it. Sean was probably only parking now.

Daniel and Dr. Lucas helped each other tie off their scrubs. Kate kept her head down and shoved her slender fingers beneath the hot water. Her eyes fixated on the flow at the bottom of the sink as it spiraled down the drain. To Kate, there was an apt metaphor here: spiraling, vanishing, death.

The air in the morgue smelled like smoke and tallow. Her mind reeled with a chorus of ghosts screaming. Her head, about to split open from hammering within, sent radiating waves of pain outward. Shards of glass cut behind her eyes. Her father, wasted away to eighty pounds, leathery skin pulled over crumbling bones, was hissing at her through a mouthful of bloody fangs. She could see it all, somewhat translucent like a coating of fog, superimposed over the real world.

There was a muffled sound, far away. At first, she couldn't place it, but slowly it came into focus like the image on a new Polaroid picture.

"Kate? Hey Kate?"

Once she connected to the sound of Dr. Lucas speaking her name, she turned. The nightmare, like a fog, receded.

Everything felt in slow motion. Reality was set at the wrong frame rate.

She connected with Dr. Lucas's gaze who was wild-eyed with alarm. Kate looked back down to see that she had scrubbed layers of skin off the back of her hands. Rivulets of blood mixed with the stream of scalding hot water.

"Kate, that's enough!" Lucas was yelling.

Kate cut the water with her latex-covered hands.

"Jesus, are you okay?" Lucas asked with her gloved hand on Kate's shoulder.

"Sorry. Guess I just zoned out there for a minute."

"You're not kidding. Wrap your hands and head inside."

Kate nodded. Daniel patted her on the shoulder. "Can you believe this?" he asked. There was glee in his voice. Daniel was looking forward to cutting someone open.

Kate regained her bearings as Lucas was about to enter the exam room.

"Dr. Lucas?" she called.

"Yeah?" The doctor stood with her back propping open the door, arms aloft to not contaminate the PPE she had just painstakingly put on.

"What happened to him? To Parker, I mean?"

"That's what we're here to find out."

"Is it, like, appropriate that I'm here? Since, you know, there's a police report and an assault and everything?"

"Kate, I'm supervising, he's dead. Who cares?"

"Nervous?" Daniel asked, trailing Dr. Lucas as they entered the maw of the exam room.

And they were inside the main room of the morgue, leaving Kate to fumble into her operating scrubs, gloves, and mask.

From Kate's vantage point at the sink, she could see into the exam room where two morgue attendants rolled a gurney topped with a large, black body bag into the center of the room. One of them flipped a switch on the wall. A giant spotlight illuminated the body in sharp relief. The men unzipped the bag and gently rolled the corpse out of it. There was Parker, but from this distance, obfuscated through the glare on the window, his skin looked cold and gray.

Kate's stomach fluttered. She put on her plastic safety glasses and entered. The exam room smelled overwhelmingly of bleach. On the walls of the lab, whiteboards contained hand-drawn diagrams of the body accompanied by lists of scientific terms. This was a special occasion. Dr. Lucas had sent Daniel to wrangle up everyone he could from the cohort. Only he and Kate were here.

Kate and Daniel both approached the body slowly. Kate's eyes wouldn't leave Parker's shape. She searched for signs of what she must have done to him. Parker's pale body lay cold and naked under a plain white sheet pulled up across his chest and tucked beneath his lean, muscular arms by the two attendants. Up close, Parker's skin was capillaceous, bruised, and had already begun to flake in patches around his temples. Ashes to ashes, dust to dust. In what had only been a matter of hours, Parker was crumbling before their eyes.

Kate and Daniel took one side of the gurney beside a small table of various jagged operating tools. Lucas stood directly opposite. She adjusted the overhead lamp.

"I don't understand," said Daniel. "It's not common practice to perform autopsies, right? So why are we here?"

Because he's likely riddled with some crazy, infectious disease or something that I gave to him, Kate wanted to say. *Pierce him now and we'll all have Ebola.* But she couldn't get it out.

Dr. Lucas spoke instead. "All available indications suggest that the patient lapsed into cardiac arrest and was gone before anyone intervene." She was staring intently at them.

"With everything he'd gone through, there's just too much in his chart for us to not have a closer look."

Dr. Lucas pulled back the sheet, exposing Parker's chest. Harsh bruising covered his torso, where pockets of blood had settled. It made his body look like a sculpted heel of bleu cheese.

Daniel winced. Dr. Lucas noticed the nervousness in him.

"I'm sure everyone has been anxiously awaiting this day," the doctor said, attempted to inject some levity.

Kate said, "I wish Lien was here."

Daniel smiled warmly. "Knowing her, she'd be in up to her elbows already."

Dr. Lucas pointed to the table. "Okay, pay attention," she said. "Grab your scalpel and forceps."

Daniel grabbed for the tools and immediately, with trembling hands, passed them over to Kate.

The doctor guided her: "We'll work our way down into the body layer by layer. Start by making a light incision into the skin. Be careful not to go too deep. We'll want to start by looking at layers of the epidermis."

Kate positioned the blade of the scalpel over the body. With a slow and methodical pull, she easily sliced through the top layers of the corpse's skin. A hot wire through softened butter. Her hands trembled. It didn't feel real. She was playing a cosmic video game, standing outside of herself, watching the avatar work. The incision took on the jagged edge of a serrated knife blade.

"Steady," Lucas urged. Her words were not at all condescending. They were supportive.

Daniel leaned forward, watching closely as Kate's blade drew through mottled, grey flesh. "Nice job, Kate."

"Okay, good," Dr. Lucas added.

A pus began to ooze from the wound. Daniel's eyes fluttered, and he choked back a wretch. Lucas gave him a sharp look, which forced back the sickness with the power of her gaze alone.

"Daniel, move the sheet lower."

Kate was finding focus now. Besides, she needed to be the one interacting with Parker's body. Whatever he had died from, if there was a risk, it was hers to own, and she knew it.

Daniel slowly rolled the sheet covering Parker's body down to his lower abdomen. The blade of the scalpel reflected the overhead spotlight with disco ball pops of light across the exam room. With a long pair of tweezers, Kate lifted a pocket of Parker's skin, exposing viscous and congealing layers of fat and muscle. She started working her way down his chest.

Suddenly, out of the corner of her eye, Kate saw a small fluttering. There was movement coming from Parker's lower abdomen. The bunched wad of sheet began to rise and fall as if it was breathing.

"Are you guys seeing this?" Kate choked out.

It couldn't be real. She must be in another blackout or a fever dream or maybe she'd finally separated from sanity altogether. Kate glanced over and knew immediately that Daniel and Dr. Lucas were seeing it too. It was in the horror written all over their faces.

"What is it?" Kate called out.

Dr. Lucas reached over Daniel and pulled the sheet even lower to the line were Parker's wiry pubic hair poked out. In the space between his groin and his navel, the skin itself began to move, pulsating, as if something were inside of him trying to push its way out.

"Oh my God," the doctor muttered.

Clang! The surgical tools hit the floor. Everyone took a big leap backward. It was as if Parker's body were electrified.

"Is this supposed to happen?" Daniel asked.

"Uh, no," Lucas said. "Dead bodies are not supposed to move, you twit." But Dr. Lucas was no longer in stoic control. Panic was lapping at her shore.

The rise and fall of Parker's grey abdomen grew more intense. The soft breathing effect became more pronounced. Hyperventilation. Oil derrick. Engine pistons. Then the mechanical up and down changed, unfurled, and rotated in a serpentine arc. It looked as if a snake were trapped beneath his skin.

"Shit!" Daniel was freaking out. He began rambling, a nonsensical slathering of half-formed words.

"What would do something like this?" Kate squealed. But within, she knew there was no textbook explanation. Nothing but the truth: it came from Kate.

Dr. Lucas ripped the scalpel away from Kate. "Stand back," she said.

With the knife, the doctor made a deep incision across Parker's lower abdomen as if performing a C-section. Kate tried her best not to look at Parker's mutilated body. Instead, she kept her eyes on Lucas's determined face.

"Forceps."

Daniel was standing frozen in fear, the forceps in his hands by his side.

"Daniel!" Dr. Lucas screamed, snapping him back to the here and now. "Forceps!"

In the moment that Lucas turned her attention away from Parker's body, a long, serrated muscle erupted from the corpse's body cavity. It looked like a bloody snake flipped inside out. It wrapped itself around Dr. Lucas's wrist. The putrid thing was the color of fresh bruises. Something not human, something alien.

Daniel began to mutter. "What the..."

The fleshy mass coiled itself around Dr. Lucas's arm. It began to climb upward, slithering, inching toward her shoulder. She was screaming. Kate covered her ears. It was a blood-curdling scream of fear and pain. The beastly thing, whatever it was, lapped at the doctor's skin, ripping away pockets of flesh.

Kate was paralyzed, holding one side of Parker's chest cavity open, watching it all unfurl. Parker's body was convulsing from the sheer force of the thing protruding from within him. The body's fingers and toes twitched.

Kate snapped to, rushed around the side of the table, and grabbed Dr. Lucas around the waist. She pulled and pulled, trying to force Dr. Lucas free.

"Help me!" Kate called to Daniel. "Help me, please!"

Daniel was in the room physically, but not mentally. A vacant house. She yelled again. Again. Again. Then Daniel's eyes found focus. His head turned in Kate's direction. Everything was delayed, but eventually clicked. He joined Kate at Dr. Lucas's side.

The doctor was screaming. Guttural tones, a language of pain. The fleshy tentacle constricted around the doctor's upper arm, some monstrous blood pressure cuff, squeezing and squeezing until there was the sound of the doctor's bones snapping like brittle twigs.

From Parker's abdomen, something else drew forth. It looked like the skinless head of a rabid dog: snarling teeth snapping, eyes rolled over white. It was connected in some unnatural way to the protruding tentacle. A half-formed beast still in gestation.

Kate and Daniel had the older doctor by the waist and pulled with all their strength until, in a searing flash, Lucas's body ripped away from the table, but her arm did not. A geyser of blood shot out from the gaping hole where only a fragment of denuded bone and torn sinewy flesh remained. All three tumbled backward. But before Lucas's limp body could crash to the floor, a second tentacle blasted its way out of Parker's abdomen and caught her right in her dark, screaming mouth. It crammed down her throat, a train passing into a tunnel, and Lucas's screams muffled. Daniel and Kate scrambled across the green tile floor.

Dr. Lucas was all sucking, gurgling fear. Her eyes contained absolute terror, more frantic than anything Kate had known possible. With her air supply cut off, she began to asphyxiate.

Kate helped Daniel scramble to his feet and pushed him toward the doorway. Then she grabbed a new scalpel from the table beside her. In one swift motion, she hacked at the tentacle. The blade sliced deep and wide. The insides of the fleshy appendage splattered like ejaculate around the lab. The ropey arm went limp, recoiled from the doctor's mouth, and reeled itself back into Parker's abdomen.

At first, Kate couldn't tell if the doctor was unconscious or dead. She'd collapsed, bleeding like a live fire hydrant from the gaping hole in her shoulder. Kate grabbed a nearby towel and created a makeshift tourniquet for Dr. Lucas.

"What the hell was that thing!?" Daniel was shrieking.

"I don't know!" Kate said.

"If we run into Sigourney Weaver in the hallway, I'm gonna throw myself off the god damn roof."

"Shut up," Kate said. "We've got to get Lucas out of here. She's not gonna make it."

"We have to warn everyone," Daniel said.

Daniel ran to the wall and grabbed the flat red fire alarm lever and jerked it down. All around, alarms began to sound. Emergency lights started to flash in harsh, radiating blasts of hot light. He ran over to the intercom on the wall and fumbled across the keypad until he hit the right button. There was an explosion of static.

"Go for security" the garbled voice on the other end said.

"This is Daniel Parks" he screamed into the intercom. "We're in the morgue exam room. We have a CODE ORANGE. I repeat, CODE ORANGE. Infectious outbreak."

"Help me!" Kate screamed.

Daniel ran from the wall. The intercom was a blaze of chatter and static, but they ignored it. Kate and Daniel laid Dr. Lucas down on the gurney that had brought Parker in from the morgue. It had been pushed up against the back wall. Kate stepped off the locks on the wheels, and they rushed out of the morgue.

"Hurry up," Kate said.

Kate finally looked back. Parker's body was left on the table, a gaping hole in his middle, slack arms fallen nearly to the floor. Blood and viscera were smeared across the once sanitized, shiny metal surfaces.

But the room was quiet and still.

★★★★★

Sirens rang out through the hospital. Spinning orbs of red-and-white light flashed along the dark corridors of the basement. It made it hard for Kate to see straight. She and Daniel pushed the gurney with an unconscious Lucas through the halls, fighting the current of patients and staff who were evacuating the building.

As per St. Christopher's protocol, a pre-recorded message started playing over the hospital's PA informing everyone to leave *calmly and efficiently*. It called out: "*Code Orange:* All individuals must evacuate the premises immediately."

In the gurney, Lucas had gone as pale as a crisp hotel bed sheet. Her eyes were merely slits. Her face was slack as if all the muscles had let go at once. The blood loss was nearing irreparable by this point. Kate could see it in the doctor's color, in the bluish tint of her lips, in her vacant, empty stare. The gurney's rubber wheels sounded out a rapid *ch-chug, ch-chug, ch-chug* as they rolled over the linoleum flooring. Kate wanted to puke.

"Where are we taking her?" Daniel asked. He was covered in Lucas's blood. The look in his eyes was like nothing Kate had ever seen before.

"I've got to find Sean," she said. "You get Dr. Lucas to Trauma immediately."

"What the fuck was that thing?" Daniel screamed.

What the fuck was right. What was it? And where did it come from? But then she heard a low moaning sound, gurgling, coming from Lucas's throat. The doctor's head moved slightly to one side.

"We'll figure everything out, I promise," Kate said.

She was solemn. Her tremors had disappeared. She wasn't ready to see this woman—a monument of St. Christopher's residency program—slip away. There would be time to talk monsters later, she supposed.

★★★★★

The hospital could be a rat maze if someone wasn't familiar with its twists and turns. That was what happened when a building was expanded, section by section, wing by wing, over the course of so many years. Kate wasn't sure where Sean was but had a feeling that he must be here somewhere. She ran like never before, screaming his name loudly into each of the rooms as she passed.

Up ahead were several of the hospital's security guards in their white uniform shirts, eyes ablaze, directing anyone and everyone they could see to the nearest exit. They had been trained for significant events like this and so rarely got the ability to spring into action.

"Miss, you've gotta exit the premises!" one of the guards called out as she blew by him.

"I will," Kate called back without looking over her shoulder. "I need to find someone."

"He's probably outside! Miss, you're going the wrong…"

The security guard's voice was already fading into the distance as her charging feet pushed onward into the halls. Her thighs burned. The hospital was starting to empty now as she pushed deeper into the intestines of the building. She passed the harried patients and staff members packing emergency bags, racing for their lives from some unknown threat.

She was ready to collapse. Her vision swam. Finally, she stopped to collect herself for just a second. A quick moment to catch her breath. Her hands fell on her knees as she sucked in gulps of air. It was then that she realized she was at the emergency room.

Suddenly, the doors opened, and Sean Carraway emerged. He was wearing blood-stained scrubs. Behind him, two more surgeons were pushing a gurney of their own. It held a patient, unconscious, fresh from surgery. Sean's eyes went wide when they locked on Kate.

"Sean!" she called through rapid breaths.

"Kate, what're you doing here? You're covered in blood, are you alright?"

"I need you. We need you. We're in trouble."

"Kate, Code Orange is serious. That's a potential pathogen outbreak. We need to go. Right now."

"Something's gone very wrong," Kate said.

"What?" he yelled over the sirens. It was impossible to hear with the racket of the alarm system blaring. "We've gotta go. It's a Code Orange!"

"No, you don't understand!" she screamed. "*I'm* the Code Orange!"

★★★★★

Daniel had rolled Dr. Lucas into the emergency room. Scores of nurses, doctors, and staff flooded the area as they attempted to flee. Lucas's body jerked and swayed as the gurney shuffled awkwardly into place when Kate and Sean had finally caught up.

Sean grasped the railing of the gurney; it was the only thing keeping him up.

"What's happened?" Sean asked in alarm, finally seeing the extent of Dr. Lucas's injuries.

Daniel was crying now. "Someone…something…attacked us…" He trailed off in shock.

"We need to staunch the bleeding, now!" Sean screamed.

Kate backed away. "I'll be back."

"Where the hell are you going?" Sean asked, incredulous.

"I need to figure out what did this to her," Kate said. "Maybe we can stop it."

The look on Sean's face said that he didn't have the time or the energy for another Kate White argument. He looked down at Dr. Lucas's body. "Daniel, go with her. I've got this."

"Will she make it?" Kate asked, her eyes reflecting the shards of red and white emergency lighting.

"I don't know. It's bad. Real bad."

★★★★★

Kate led the way, running down stairs two at a time. Daniel lagged, seemingly unable to keep up, his ashen-white face was bled of all vitality. In lockdown emergencies, the elevators were taken offline. It was the standard operating procedure. They'd have to hoof it.

Together, they raced through the back stairwell, that concrete cocoon of seemingly endless repeating floors with the same view: gray cinderblock walls around them, gray cement stairs under them, black railings in their hands. Their stampeding footfalls resounded with charging crashes. It felt like an eternity with Daniel trailing behind. Finally, they landed in the hospital's basement.

"Where are we going?" Daniel called out.

She, too, was nearly out of breath. She managed one word at a time. It was as much as her lungs allowed. "Davol. Lab. Must. Find. Fenton."

"This is crazy."

Kate knew that if she didn't push with everything she had, Lucas might die too. That, she couldn't handle. Like a marathon runner rounding into the final bend, she dug deeper, chugged on. When she looked back, she saw Daniel skid, twist his ankle, and hit the wall with a solid thud.

She thought he might be dead until in one instant his eyes popped open. Daniel gasped for air in a raspy, hectoring whine. The wind had been knocked out of him, luckily nothing else. She dropped to her knees and propped him up a bit.

"You okay?"

He nodded, still straining to breathe, and held out a lone finger to indicate he needed a moment. Slowly, across what felt like minutes, he got back up to his feet. Then he closed his eyes and his lungs caught up with him.

"What makes you think…" He paused for breath. "That anyone in Davol will have the slightest idea as to whatever that *thing* was?"

"Fenton will. I'm sure of it."

Daniel tilted his head inquisitively. "How?" he asked.

She put her hand on his shoulder and met his solemn gaze. "Because behind that big, metal door is where that monster came from."

Hearing that was like a punch in the gut to Daniel and tantamount to a confession for Kate. "What? How do you know—"

"Not now. We need to find Fenton. Can you walk?"

"Yes."

Kate retook the lead and charged down the hall back to where they had started, just outside of the morgue. However, this time they broke in the other direction toward the lab. The lab's researchers were fleeing through the propped-open biohazard door.

There the man emerged. It was as if he'd been summoned on cue, with his overstuffed briefcase and his half-tucked shirt. At least, this time Dr. Fenton had the goddamn sense to put on a pair of shoes.

At first, Fenton didn't notice the two wild-eyed med students—drenched in blood—charging at him full steam. Then, Kate was on him. She violently grabbed him by his lapel and pushed him back into the laboratory like a kidnapper taking a hostage at gunpoint.

"Hey, it's you!" Fenton said, recognizing her for the second time in an hour. "What the hell are you doing?"

"The three of us need to have a chat."

"Code Orange! We need to follow protocol."

"We're not going anywhere."

And when it was clear the lab was empty of everyone else—the workstations having all been neatly covered over with tarpaulins—she shut the heavy, locking door back into place, where it sealed them inside with a final-sounding knock.

Chapter Twelve
KALEIDOSCOPE

Detective Oscar Ramirez had been idling in his car for the better part of an hour, waiting for the clock to strike six. He was here tonight to meet a man who had rung him up. No name provided. It was all very cloak and dagger. Someone just called, said that he'd had information. Information related to a case. The stranger's voice sounded like someone who was panicking and trying not to sound that way: artificial, aloof. He just kept repeating that he needed to tell someone. When Ramirez asked the man on the other line where they should meet, the man suggested Del's Place.

While Ramirez sat in the big car, he mulled everything over. He'd arrived thirty minutes early so he could watch the cars puttering in and out of the gashed asphalt lot. Putting the pieces together usually required reviewing the same loose threads, fixating on them. Repeat, over and over, until, suddenly, these once loose threads miraculously formed a finished tapestry. All night long, no matter how much he'd tried, Ramirez couldn't shake thoughts of Kate White. She was a lovely young woman. Very attractive. She had a haunted look, but one that invited pity. It wasn't just her appearance catching in Ramirez's mind. There was something else there too. A coincidence too large to ignore. Ramirez had meant to talk to Kate for a few days about the missing medical student. He'd had trouble connecting with her. Then, out of the blue, the woman he's looking for is the victim of an attack. Maybe it was nothing after all. Still, Ramirez couldn't move past her. Coincidences rarely occurred in real life.

He sipped from the flask that he kept in the inside pocket of his cheap wool overcoat. God, he was such a cliché. At least it was filled with iced tea, not whisky or scotch. Ramirez never drank on the job, rarely ever drank at all. After hours, when the gun came off, he was too tired for anything else. His father had been a louse, a man who drank himself to death. It was his father's flask that he kept by his heart. Ramirez's life was a shambles even without tempting fate. There was the wife that walked out on him, the kid not seen in three years. Work was all he had.

Again, that thread. There was something there. Something in Kate White that he recognized from personal experience. They'd barely spent any time together, a single interview at the hospital, but the young woman was exhibiting symptoms of something. Invisible sirens. She looked like a clear case of PTSD to him. He would know. Two tours, one in Iraq and one in Afghanistan. That'll show you the mouth of the beast. When the Humvee you were scheduled to—but missed because the sergeant held you back—is incinerated by an IED. When you hear that your squadron was torn apart. When God spares you from the theater of battle only so you can return home every night to an empty apartment. Ramirez saw a kinship in Kate White. She'd been through something too.

Ramirez was shaken from his thoughts by the alarms. They sounded distant, faint, from St. Christopher's across the street. Del's Place was the diner all the doctors and cops hung out at between shifts. Nothing had come through over the radio, at least not yet. But Ramirez had line of sight to the east entrance of the hospital. Suddenly, it seemed, everyone was stumbling out into the dark night, gathering in shivering groups to keep warm. *Kind of cold for a fire drill,* he thought.

Finally, the clock struck six. He hadn't seen anyone that looked like his man enter Del's. Of course, he had no idea what his man looked like. He expected to see a single person, one who maybe constantly glanced back over his shoulder, maybe a young man from the sound of that jittery voice. One more sip from the flask and off with the ignition. The frigid air stung his lungs. A light snow was starting to fall. The first flakes signalling winter.

Del's Place was a small, twenty-four-hour diner, the kind with a big, neon sign and crusty cheese clinging to the plastic menus. Half of the diners were dressed in their scrubs. They came in to grab bites after long shifts, to shoot the shit, maybe play a little stick. Inside Del's, it was always dark. The windows had large, aluminum blinds that were shut tight morning, noon, and night.

Ramirez hadn't been here in years. When he'd started on the force, after his discharge, he routinely patrolled this corner of Boston. Back then he had his fair share of greasy-spoon plates in all the hole-in-the-wall dives around town. Since his promotion to detective, that had become less common. Now a fast-food salad in the driver seat was as good as it got.

An old boom box sat on the top shelf behind the counter, alongside the health department certificate, and a litany of dead flies. The radio was tuned to WKLT, some far-away station that played Motown and soul amid pops of crunchy static. It was as if the radio had tuned to a frequency from the past. Right now, Smokey was seconding that emotion. Anyone who ever asked Del to change the station never ate there again. Ramirez had seen it himself.

He shook the dusting of flurries from his coat and hung it on the rack by the door. Then he saw him. The guy in the back. Not that he knew that for sure, but the body language gave it away. The man was young, with a torch flame of greasy hair swooping over his head.

Ramirez made his way through the restaurant toward the back booth. He took in his surroundings, noting all the individual people and their demeanors, access points, potential weapons. It was a habit developed from basic training, and it never left. Eight diners, two doors, six windows, a blind spot to the bathrooms and kitchen.

There was a man he recognized at the counter. He'd already talked to Kieran while investigating the missing person case. Smart doc. Kieran sat on a stool reading the *Wall Street Journal.* Two other docs he recognized played a game of pool in the back. But this new guy, the one in the booth, this had to be his man.

As he neared the booth, the man with the greasy hair locked eyes with him and nodded. Ramirez moved into the seat on the opposite side. The pockmarked vinyl let out a wheeze as he collapsed into it.

"Evenin'," Ramirez said.

He sized up the man across from him. Ramirez knew this part of the conversation—the first impression—was the most important. He had to present as trustworthy and approachable. He knew how to ascertain whether this guy was worth his time. The look in his eyes indicated he was.

"I'm Detective Oscar Ramirez with the Boston Police. You the guy who called me?"

The young man lifted his gaze, held still for a moment, then answered with a nod.

"And you are?" Ramirez asked.

"Justin. Justin Ames." His words came out clipped and jittery. Ramirez could see his jaw chattering with nerves.

"Nice to meet you, Justin." Ramirez saw that he was sitting with an empty place mat in front of him. "You want something to eat? My treat."

"No, thank you." Justin said.

"What made you reach out to me?"

"I'm friends with some of these guys," Justin said. He was nodding toward Kieran and the two docs at the pool table. "After you started talking to them, you know, asking questions about Lien, I got your card. I didn't, I mean, I don't know where else to turn."

"I'm heading up Lien's case, yeah. Do you know something?"

"I think so."

"Look," Ramirez said, "A young woman has gone missing. She doesn't fit the model of someone who'd up and vanish without a trace. I don't know what happened to her. But I see this shit a lot. My gut tells me it's not good. Statistically, by this point, we're pretty much out of time. Any information you have, I need it."

Justin kept his eyes fixated on the table's surface. When he spoke, it was in a low murmur. Ramirez could tell Justin didn't want anyone else hearing what he had to say. Ramirez wondered why on earth Justin suggested Del's. That's the worst possible place for a clandestine meeting. That would have been like Woodward summoning Deep Throat on the White House lawn.

"I work at St. Christopher's. I'm a researcher in the Davol lab."

"Same lab where Lien interned?"

"Yes. Under Dr. Fenton. I don't know how to say it, so I'm just going to put it out there: she's dead."

Beneath the table, Ramirez's hand instinctively found its way to the grip of his pistol, but he made no sudden movements. He needed more information.

Then, before Ramirez could respond, Justin added: "It was my fault."

"What do you mean?"

"I killed her."

"You what?"

"In a way," Justin said. "I promise, I never wanted her to die. I never wanted to hurt anybody. Ever." His eyes were red, wet slices of slimy tomatoes.

A waitress stopped by, but Ramirez flashed her a wild-eyed glare that sent her on to the next table without a word.

"We didn't know what we had" Justin said. "We never thought it'd incubate so quickly."

"I'm not following."

Kieran peered up and over his paper. Ramirez knew that Justin was conscious of the others in the room. Men who knew him, could identify him, had worked with him. Justin was shaking, but Ramirez knew the truth when he heard it. There was no doubt. Lien Chu was dead. He'd been chasing a ghost. But this kid was no killer.

"You want to tell me the full story or what?" Ramirez asked him. "It looks like you're carrying the world on your shoulders."

Justin pulled himself together. He grabbed a napkin from the dispenser and wiped his eyes. Then, the young man bounded out of the booth.

"Hey, where the hell are you going?" Ramirez asked.

"You want the story?"

"Yeah, of course I do."

"You wouldn't believe me if I told you." Justin put his jacket on, zipped it up to his neck. "So come with me."

"Where to?" Ramirez asked. He also got up and made no pretense that his left hand was on the butt of his revolver.

"Where it happened."

Justin reached into his back pocket. Ramirez unbuttoned the holster of his gun. Justin slowed his movements in response. When he brought his hand back up, there was a little, plastic rectangle in it. Ramirez looked closer. It bore the

St. Christopher's logo and Justin's smiling face. The face of a young man with boundless optimism. It was his ID card.

"We're going to the lab."

★★★★★

As the two men crossed the street, the flurries were coming down harder, making it difficult to see ahead. When they reached St. Christopher's, a large group huddled in the parking lot—patients, nurses, attendants—all of them covered in a fine coating of pure, white snow. The alarms blared. A recording kept reiterating a message: "*Code Orange:* All individuals must evacuate the premises immediately."

"What the hell is happening here?" Ramirez asked.

A look of horror splashed across Justin's face. "Oh shit." The look on Justin's face was grave. It was the look of someone staring into hell. "It can't be."

Security attempted to stop them at the door, but Ramirez flashed his badge and they were in, fighting the current. Ramirez had become accustomed to St. Christopher's. Over the past few days, he'd trekked most of these halls several times over speaking to anyone and everyone who had ever met Lien Chu.

Justin moved with the stealthy purpose of a hungry shark and led Ramirez to the back stairwell. When they spoke, they had to yell to each other just to be heard over the alarms.

"Where are you taking me?" Ramirez asked.

"Davol Laboratory. It's right down here. God, we need Fenton. He knows what this is. He's seen it before."

"If I find out that you're screwing with me, Justin, I swear to God, I'll shoot you."

The detective's heart was pumping so fiercely that he could feel the thrum in his temples. His hand went to his heart and felt for the solid metal outline of his flask. It was a totem that comforted him. The noise and the lights were fearsome, and the sound and fury combined with the fact that Justin was adamant Lien was dead was enough to make his adrenaline surge through the roof. It felt like being back in Afghanistan.

Once downstairs, Ramirez followed behind Justin as they hit the T-junction. Ramirez tapped Justin's shoulder; it wasn't worth blowing out his vocal cords and trying to scream. When Justin turned, Ramirez pointed to the ground. He saw Justin's eyes go wide. Together they followed the long smears of blood trailing from the elevator down off the hall in the other direction.

"You seeing this?"

Justin nodded.

Ramirez pointed to the corridor on the left. "What's down there?"

"The morgue."

Ramirez unholstered his gun and held it out before him. He pushed Justin behind him and together they slowly followed the trail of blood, step-by-step, inching toward the morgue. Something was clearly very, very wrong. They slipped into the pre-op room and stood at its doorway. Lights flashing. Alarms blaring.

"What did this? Was it the same thing that killed Lien?" Ramirez shouted.

Justin was flailing like a marionette. "I think so. We synthesized a compound. Called it 112A."

"What did it do?"

"Instantaneous recombination of key DNA string proteins."

"Talk to me in fucking English, man!" Ramirez yelled. He could taste bitterness on his tongue and knew his own breath was rank.

"It's like a synthetic kind of parasite. A big bug. One that grows immediately. And it kills."

"It killed Lien?" Ramirez asked. "Why should I believe you? This is madness."

"Fenton told me you'd say that. That night, he told me to go home. Told me to be quiet. He said he'd take care of everything. I trusted him."

Ramirez was stalling at the entryway of the examination room. "What happens when we go in there?"

"I don't know."

"How do you not know?"

Justin was gesturing in the dark, his limbs making phantom movements by Ramirez's face. "Because Fenton and I burned it to ashes. What we're seeing right now–"

"Yeah?"

"Well, it's just not possible."

"What do you mean?"

"We kept it contained. When it attacked Lien, it never got out. I made sure of it. That's why we work in the burn room. It's protocol."

"Who is *we*?" Ramirez needed to know.

"Me and Doctor Fenton."

"You're the scientist. Tell me, how could it be alive and out of your lab?"

A little light went on in Justin's eyes. They were aglow with the fierce burn of St. Christopher's emergency lighting. Ramirez could see the wheels turning

"The compound," Justin said. "It must have been used again."

This was all so crazy. One day ago, Ramirez had been following up on a routine missing person's case. Now he was center stage in *War of the Worlds*. Ramirez pushed forward into the dark room of the morgue. The alarms were head-splitting. Dizzying strobe lights turned the room into a demonic rave.

Ramirez knew he had to go in there. He was first on the scene and the situation needed to be assessed. He cracked open the door leading into the morgue. His eyes took a moment to adjust to the lowlight.

His gun jutted out before him, aiming into the abyss, a talisman. Ramirez padded along with the jitteriness of a cat. Justin's hand was on his shoulder as they walked together in train formation. His peripheral vision triggered with every flash of light.

As they neared the center of the morgue, Ramirez's feet slipped on the moist tile floor. His body almost toppled over but his right hand caught the edge of a desk. His gun wavered. Justin helped him back up. When the lights pulsed again, Ramirez saw rivulets of blood so thick and dark it looked like chocolate syrup.

They came across a gurney. On the bed, the body of a young man. The figure was face down. Limbs bent in odd vertiginous angles. Human bodies shouldn't move like that, Ramirez thought. He reached out and gently lifted the man's face off the bed and angled it for a closer look. With another pulse of light, Ramirez saw that the dead man's teeth had completely shattered. It was ghastly, creating the jagged effect of a mouth filled with bloody razor blades, something out of nightmares. Ramirez knew he'd see that image every night for the rest of his life.

Then suddenly, the dead man's body began to heave and flex. Several tentacles emerged from beneath it, creeping out across the gurney's mattress and down over the rails towards the floor. The fleshy arms slithered toward Ramirez and Justin like roots from a tree growing in time lapse.

The detective's heart nearly stopped. What this was, what he was seeing, was wholly impossible.

"Justin, run!"

In the dark, they scattered like roaches. The train was derailed. Ramirez retraced his steps back to the doorway from which they had come. His own breathing surprised him. He could hear it over the hospital alarm system, a wheezing whine. It was a sound he'd never heard his body create before. Not even during deployment.

Every few seconds, Ramirez caught a fleeting glimpse of freedom before being returned to darkness. The basement was so dark, and he didn't know this morgue, but his training was kicking in and a sixth sense guided him out the way he came.

Ramirez peered into the corner, waiting for each pop of lightning. He saw, in one of those moments, Justin slip in the dead man's blood and fall to the floor, screaming. He rolled onto his back. Ramirez was about to run back to the young man when he saw the monstrous beast falling upon Justin. Ramirez fired into the dark, his gun throwing sparks of firelight. But the bullets had no impact. He watched as Justin's heels pushed against the large sink in the center of the room. In a matter of seconds, Justin was thrashing wildly as the monstrous eruptions looped around him. Another tentacle intercepted his scream and penetrated his throat.

Ramirez turned away from the horror show. He hurtled his body through the absolute void of darkness until his footfalls were echoing in the hallway.

By the door, he saw a janitor's mop bucket left unattended. Ramirez grabbed for the pole of a mop and shoved the long, wooden bar through the handles of the double doors of the morgue. It was probably of no use. If the arms of that creature could lift a grown man like Justin off the ground, then there was little he could do to contain it. But it was something.

Then, Ramirez ran. He ran until he hit the stairwell. He ran until he burst forth onto the main level of St. Christopher's. He ran until he was outside in the open air of the parking lot, where fresh, white snow was falling gently upon him.

Then, finally, he screamed.

★★★★★

Ramirez reached his unmarked car and slammed inside, locking the doors behind him. He jammed his key into the ignition. The engine roared. He turned on the police band scanner. From the radio rang a shriek of static, and then it came: "All units, all units. Report to St. Christopher's Hospital for outbreak quarantine." The message was repeating. Like that damn alarm in the hospital. What the hell was happening?

Holy shit. They're asking for every officer in Boston.

He couldn't go back. Wouldn't go back. He had just seen the impossible. It was seared on his brain so that every time he slammed his eyelids closed, Ramirez saw that fleshy beast violating Justin. It moved fast. And it was merciless.

When Ramirez realized the loop on the band scanner was unchanging, he shut it off and sat in silence. He reached into his pocket and pulled out the flask. It was heavy in his hands, and his tongue ached for it. He thought of his son. He would see this through for him. He would tell his boy he'd bravely faced down a monster, tell him he remade the world for him as a safer place. Ramirez reloaded his revolver, took another swallow from the flask, and got back out of his car.

As Ramirez approached the front entrance of St. Christopher's, he once again flashed his badge and once again crossed the line inside. The hospital was mostly empty now. It was the parking lot that was a circus. Inside, the sirens and emergency lights were still full tilt.

Up ahead, just outside of the doors, he saw the uniformed officer. Instantly, he recognized Sergeant Andy Macmurry. They had come up together on the force.

"Mac! Hey, Mac!"

The tall, uniformed officer turned to Ramirez. He was still tucking in the back of his uniform shirt, adjusting his belt, assessing the situation. When he saw Ramirez coming towards him, his eyes lit up.

"Ramirez! What a sight! I certainly didn't expect you to respond to the call."

"I was already here."

"Have you heard?"

Ramirez was shaken, bone tired, more frightened than he'd ever imagined a human could be. "I don't need to hear. It's god damn hell in there. What'd they tell you?" Ramirez asked.

"You were inside?!" Mac was incredulous, he took two steps backward. "They're saying it's some kind of biological contagion. But no one's sure what that means. Is it bullshit?"

"It's not bullshit. They're underselling it. This isn't the flu." Ramirez felt himself getting hysterical and his voice clipped like his body was infused with an overload of caffeine. "The life you know, it's over, man. Game over."

Ramirez didn't want to see Mac go down. "Make sure you keep your weapon loaded. And whatever you do, stay outside." Ramirez pointed down the empty blackness of the interior of the hospital. "Under no circumstances should you go in there."

Mac laughed. He had a twitchy mustache, and his eyes were set back like he had been punched in the face a few days prior. "Don't worry. I'm planted right here. Orders are easy. We ain't doing shit except getting people out. CDC and military will be running the show."

"Military?" Ramirez asked. Maybe folks in this hospital knew more than they were letting on? "No shit."

Mac shrugged. "Beats me. Viruses and dirty bombs? Cyberattack and pandemics? I don't understand this place anymore. Whatever happened to good guys and bad guys?"

Mac pulled Ramirez over by him to let a few stragglers out of the doors. The group was pushing and shoving one another, further knotting everyone up.

"Hey!" Mac shouted. He yanked at someone in the pileup to get them moving again. "Orderly fashion, folks. Slow is smooth and smooth is fast."

As Ramirez watched the crowd disperse, he thought of Justin. The young man had been wracked with guilt, called him out of the blue to say he needed to talk. What was it Justin had said back in the lab? There was someone here who knew what they were dealing with.

Ramirez shut his eyes.

The tip of his nose stung in the cold. He let the sound of panic in the parking lot fall away. The alarms became but the white noise of ocean surf. He tried the circular breathing exercise he had learned in a beginner's cardio class. Inhale, one, two, three. Hold, one, two, three. Exhale, one, two, three. Inhale, one, two, three...

His mind flashed back to the darkened basement. With eyes closed he mentally retraced his steps. The flashing lights. Justin's hand on his shoulder. Following the long trail of black blood back into the morgue. Instantly, a name popped into his head. He envisioned it as a neon sign, sparking in the darkest night. First, a black void, and then—drumroll—cue electricity.

Lights.

Camera.

Fenton.

★★★★★

It only took Ramirez about forty seconds to round the entrance of St. Christopher's, dash across the street, and return to Del's Place. When he entered, it was like a time capsule. A tableau of a 1950s family moments before the big one exploded. Inside, the diner was warm. Music was blaring from the tinny radio.

Ramirez stood in the doorway, catching his breath. The aroma of hash and eggs permeated every pore of his skin. In this place, it was still peacetime, a demilitarized zone. He envied them their ignorance and wanted nothing more than to just sit down, pull from his flask, and forget about Lien Chu and Justin Ames and the tendrils of ropey flesh that came out of that corpse on the gurney.

But everything he'd been taught to believe about the supernatural was wrong. Monsters were real. He learned that today. There would be no sleeping after this. But, Ramirez guessed, monsters had always been there. The world was cruel. It would not stop grinding everyone down: poverty, disease, racism, sexism, until nothing was left but a mass of wet pulp. A globalized mold, blighting civilization and returning it back to nature. Ouroboros. Humanity eating itself.

The young men he recognized from the hospital were surrounding the pool table. Ramirez approached Kieran. He'd folded up his newspaper and was loosely watching the game. The rings under his eyes indicated a level of exhaustion one would expect with med students ramping up their clinicals.

"Detective," Kieran said, shaking his hand. "Back already? Didn't I see you in here talking to Justin just a bit ago?"

Ramirez nodded, the full weight of the world on his shoulders.

"Let me cut right to it," the detective said. "We've got a problem. A big one. I need to know who Fenton is?"

"What?" Kieran asked with eyes glazed over. He was trying to make sense of it all. "Is this about Lien? Have you found her?"

There wasn't any time for small talk. Ramirez grabbed Kieran by the shoulders. "Lien's dead! So is Justin. And I think a lot more people are going to be dead soon too."

The pool game ceased. Zach and Greg were looking at Ramirez and Kieran as if aliens had just landed. Kieran's knees buckled. He fell back against the pool table, knocking the placement of several balls.

"What are you talking about?" Kieran asked. "I don't understand."

Ramirez ran over to the counter, grabbed a step stool, and unplugged Del's radio. He flipped on the old, black-and-white television mounted in the corner, which was riddled with cobwebs. The static gave way to a breaking news segment. At once, all of them saw it. St. Christopher's was on the local news station, and the banner on the screen said something about an attack and subsequent quarantine at the hospital. This Third World war zone coverage was happening in real time right outside of Del's diner.

The double doors from the kitchen crashed open. Del erupted with a grimace on his round, potato face, the look of manslaughter in his eyes. He was ready to cuss the whole goddamn place to high hell until he saw what his customers were watching. Del grabbed the grease laden TV remote and cranked the volume up as high as it would go, until the tiny speakers buzzed from clipping.

On screen, one of the station's anchors stood angled on the side entrance to the hospital. A dozen or more police cars blocked the perimeter. The reporter addressed the camera, talking about some sort of biological contagion. Evacuation. Behind her, people were flooding out into the cold, snowy air in droves.

In the diner, the roar of the television was suddenly blighted by an even louder commotion. It was like hearing a plane pass by overhead. Ramirez looked around. Everyone in Del's stood motionless, their breath held, listening. Del pressed the mute button on the remote. The television fell silent. The roar outside the diner got louder.

At once, they could hear the chaos, the terrified voices, muffled slightly by the walls and glass of the dilapidated diner.

A police officer was pleading for order on his squad car loudspeaker. Above that, a dull roar that ramped louder. Finally, Ramriez clocked the source of the feverish symphony when a fleet of incoming military vehicles tore by. The trucks rolled within inches of the restaurant. Everyone ran to the vibrating windows.

"What the fuck is going on?" Greg asked.

"You ever see anything like this before?" Del asked.

"No, I've never seen this before," Ramirez said. "It's bad."

"Maybe it's a drill?" Greg asked.

Del flung open the front door for a better look. A blast of cold air tore through and sent a shiver down Ramirez's spine.

The military descended on South Boston. Soldiers came in trucks. They came in Humvees. They came in armored attack vehicles. They came with guns. They came with semitrailers filled to the brim with equipment. They came as a convoy, a traveling circus. First nothing, then an entire city erected in a moment.

Ramirez turned back to Kieran. "This is no drill," Ramirez said. "I saw it. I was in the basement, and I saw it. I need to find Dr. Fenton."

Ramirez watched with steely eyes as the soldiers quickly erected a large tent in the parking lot. The troops moved very quickly. They were wearing gas masks and hazmat suits.

"Del," Ramirez said. "You better go turn off the gas."

Ramirez watched as the grease-stained fat man ran back into the kitchen. Then, Del snagged a paper menu and a cup of crayons from a drawer under the counter and scrawled something on the menu in green crayon. Del came back to the main entrance and hung the makeshift sign in the window with an arm's length of duct tape. Even Ramirez knew it was the first time a *CLOSED* sign had ever been hung at Del's Place.

★★★★★

The searchlights were marble pillars that touched the heavens. The lights hit the hospital from giant, metal cans set in a perimeter around the sprawling campus. A barrage of military vehicles, SWAT trucks, and police cruisers, all with flashing lights, encircled St. Christopher's, creating a moat of screaming metal. The CDC arrived in their own emergency vehicles. They were erecting decontamination stations. Big, white, oblong tents with plastic walls and chemical spray stations.

Ramirez was amazed at how fast the infrastructure went up. These were teams of people who practiced for this type of event. God, the circus really had come to town. Where were the elephants? This was no longer a Boston story. This was like September 11th or the Kennedy assassination. This was going to be one of those moments people asked you where you were the night when the monsters came from St. Christopher's hospital.

Ramirez could not wait a moment longer. He rallied Kieran, Zach, and Greg and together they ran toward the hospital. Along the way, Ramirez brought them up to speed. He started with the story of Justin's confession and then transitioned to what he had seen in the basement. The look in the eyes of the men was one of disbelief. He needed them to help him scan the faces of the people gathered outside of St. Christopher's. Somewhere, if they were lucky, they would find Fenton.

Ambulances ferried patient evacuees to other area hospitals and makeshift clinics. Propane heaters emanated small pockets of orange warmth for those still stranded. In this staging area, nurses tended to their patients and attempted to reassure them that everything would be alright. One overweight patient was tethered to a breathing apparatus in a wheelchair. He was yelling to anyone who would listen. Ramirez watched him cussing out nurses.

"What the hell is going on here?" his fat mouth screamed. "My TV cut out. Next thing you know, I'm freezing my ass off in the parking lot. This is crazy!"

But he was one ignored voice amid the chaos created by the throngs of people flowing through the area in all directions. *If only he knew,* thought Ramirez. *Then maybe he'd shut the fuck up.*

Kieran tapped Ramirez on the shoulder. Ramirez followed Kieran's finger which pointed up to the sky. First, he could only hear the *ticka-ticka-ticka* of a helicopter's rotor blades, but soon saw it shred the dark clouds and descend, casting giant beams of light down on the sea of people.

Runners of early-evening fog had layered into the parking lot around them. The mist danced in the wild vortex of wind from the helicopter. The reflective lamps of the helmets of the National Guardsmen looked like soft halo rings. A hulking soldier in camouflage strode through this mist. He had stars on his breast pocket and walked with a stiff, confident gait that could only be attributed to men in absolute power. In his hands was a bullhorn, but his voice cut through the night air just fine without it. Ramirez stopped Kieran, Zach, and Greg so they could listen.

"Do not panic." The military man spoke with a voice as clear as a clarion call. "There has been a small incident pertaining to one isolated area within the hospital. We're asking everyone to remain calm. Those of you who need immediate medical attention are being relocated to nearby hospitals."

"God, how he can say it's a small incident!" Ramirez whispered to the others.

"Maybe they don't really know." Zach then said, "Did you radio in what you saw?"

"What?" Ramirez asked, incredulous. "You want me to tell everyone I saw some hideous creature disembowelling a man in the basement? Have them lock me up? No thank you."

As if on cue, the quick chirp of a rescue truck's siren rang out briefly with two *bleep-boops* as it pulled away into the night. The fat man on the gurney yelled out again, "What time do you expect this to be all wrapped up?"

A passing nurse waved the fat man away with a quick flip of her hand. "It's over when it's over."

The military man with the bullhorn disappeared as mysteriously as he arrived, into an unmarked evergreen army tent. The flaps opened; the mouth of the tent swallowed him whole. Standing outside were armed guards with large rifles.

Onlookers were gathering across the street shooting video on cell phones. The military's makeshift barricades kept everyone back. Even with everything he'd already seen, Ramirez was still having trouble believing it. He looked back one more time to the hospital. Another throng of patients, staff, doctors, and nurses charged out of the front door through a battery of National Guardsmen. The soldiers monitored each person that came through by holding small, electronic scanners up to their bodies. Once cleared, they were directed into a single-file line to pass through the decontamination tents like cars in a car wash.

They know, Ramirez realized.

When that burst of people cleared the hospital's entrance, soldiers barricaded the doorways and set up men with rifles to stand guard at each post. Anyone left inside was staying there whether they wanted to or not.

Ramirez left Kieran, Zach, and Sean at the tent to help look over patients. They had described Dr. Louis Fenton and what to look for after confirming he was not in the parking lot. Kieran had seen him earlier in the afternoon, figured he must still be in there.

Ramirez searched for an unguarded entrance, a way to sneak in, but the gaps had all been plugged up by this point.

The large campus had evolved over time, grown larger, and the transitions between eras were not exactly well coordinated. The ancient stone walls of the original building gave way to the smooth, glass edges of Gaige Hall. Ramirez found an unguarded door at the back and stepped inside. The space was neat, quiet. His footsteps echoed loudly. Up ahead, a young police officer stationed at the door to the bridge that led back into the older hospital. He looked like a high schooler dressed as a police officer for Halloween. His nose was riddled with pock marks from a recent acne attack.

Ramirez didn't know the officer, so he flashed his badge and attempted to walk on through. The young officer stepped in his way.

"Sorry, can't let you in."

"It's okay, I'm with Boston PD."

"Sorry, sir. Explicit instructions from my CO. No one goes in. That means you too."

"You have any idea what's going on here?"

"No, sir. Nobody does. But I've got my orders."

"Well, I do. And I need to get in there."

"No can do."

Ramirez knew this was an existential crisis. This rookie was in the wrong place at the wrong time. He was just a kid. Power was going to his head. Ramirez could see the beads of sweat on the young man's temples. The twitch in his eye. They were the ones who went off the deep end when things went sideways. There were plenty of men like this back in Afghanistan. They were the ones who'd mow down a family just because someone put their hands in their pockets.

Ramirez pushed him out of the way. "Sorry, buddy, but I'm going in."

"You can't do that! Get back here!" the officer screamed.

The officer fumbled for his service weapon. Ramirez didn't care. Cops don't shoot cops. There was too much chaos around. This place was nuts. He pushed through the doorway, turning his back on the young officer.

At first, Ramirez didn't feel a thing when the bullet slammed right into his heart, tearing a massive hole in his aorta. He went down immediately, the light fading quickly. The only pain he could discern was that he'd fallen on his father's flask. *That'll bruise,* he thought.

Now on his back, bleeding out, he saw the young officer's hands. They were shaking. A wisp of smoke peeled away from the gun's muzzle.

"I said no!" the officer screamed. "You're under arrest! Now get up, asshole!"

But, for Ramirez, there was only darkness. He flashed on his son, smiling. And then, nothingness.

Chapter Thirteen
POLYMORPHIA & UTRENJA

There was only a small desk lamp to light their way. Kate, Sean, Daniel, and Dr. Fenton were scratching in the dark. In the last few hours, everyone's lives had flipped entirely upside down. Here they were now, trying to stitch Dr. Lucas back together. All of the, were desperate to retrieve her from the brink of death.

Sean directed Kate. In the moment, she didn't mind. Their breakup, their history, her issues of confidence, all of it was irrelevant now. In fact, Kate preferred ceding control over to Sean. He somehow had managed to maintain a sense of calm. Her deepest, primordial fears had externalized into monstrous shapes in the real world. It felt as if a threshold had been crossed where demons were no longer relegated to the darkest confines of her head.

Sean tied Lucas's upper arm by the shoulder where only the bloody pudding of a nub remained under wads of compression bandages. Kate saw just how pale Lucas had become. A sickly alabaster, rimmed with blue around her lips and eyes.

When the bleeding subsided, Kate wiped the sweat from Sean's brow. She could see he was trembling. It made her feel better. In some small way she could be there for him.

"Kate, remove the tourniquet," Sean said.

She did, with a delicacy as if she were cradling a nest of robin's eggs. Lucas was barely conscious. Kate winced as the towel slid to the floor with a wet plop of pulp. Fragments of bone and blackened skin remained beneath the tourniquet.

Daniel and Fenton stood back, watching, as Sean and Kate worked with urgency.

"What the hell could do something like this?" Daniel asked.

Sean jumped in: "I have no idea. But look at this."

"What?" Kate asked.

"These wounds," Sean indicated the torn flesh and puncture marks on Lucas's upper body.

Lucas slipped from consciousness, head lolling to the side. She had the deflated limpness of a rag doll. Kate followed Sean's gesturing hands. He was pointing to the toothed edges of her flesh where the skin puckered beneath the tourniquet.

"These wounds," Sean said, "are almost parasitic."

"No way," Kate said. It wasn't making any sense. She knew what she'd seen. This wasn't some invisible bug. "I mean, I saw it happen just fifteen minutes ago. It was an attack. Something, I don't know what it was, something massive erupted out of Parker's body."

Kate turned to Fenton while she said this. The old doctor shrank back against the wall, his hands in balled up fists by his sides.

Outside, searchlights swept across the windows of the operating room. It had grown quiet once again. Kate looked back down at Dr. Lucas. Her chest rose softly with shallow breaths. Her blood pressure was dropping, and her lungs were filling with fluid. Her heart wasn't getting enough oxygen. Kate had no trouble diagnosing that death was imminent.

"Think we can save her?" Kate asked.

"I don't know." Sean lifted his eyes from Lucas's wounds and met Kate's gaze. "I know I messed everything up," he said. "I just want to say that I'm sorry."

"Forget it." She spoke. "Now is definitely not the time for marriage counseling."

"This just feels like one of those times in the movies where people clear the air. You know? Before it gets bad all over again?"

"You're being stupid," but she smiled as she said it. This pretentious man that would push her away from base cultural offerings was suddenly pretending he was living in *Love Actually*.

"Besides," she said. "I'm the one who messed everything up."

"You can't beat yourself up," Sean said, and Kate realized that he still had no idea what she had been up to.

"We've done all we can, right?" Kate asked.

"I guess so. Go. You should get out safely while you still can. I got it from here."

"No, I need to talk to Dr. Fenton."

Kate pivoted to the back of the room with the self-determination of a cyborg on a programmed mission. In the darkness, with the panicked expression on his face, suddenly the old man looked feeble. What Kate saw before her now was the man who'd synthesized this thing. She marched forward, driving him backwards, until his back was up against the filing cabinet on the rear wall. Fenton's heels nearly lifted off the ground. He stammered with surprise and submission.

Catching the commotion, Sean blurted from back across the room. "Kate, what's going on?"

She held up a hand, index finger pointed to the sky, telling him to hold a minute. Her eyes did not break from Fenton's. Kate felt anger taking over, overwhelming her body. Her fingers curled into small, hard fists.

Kate reached into her lab coat pocket and slammed the empty vial of Compound 112A down on a lab bench. Fenton crouched until he was at eye level with the little, glass vessel.

The flashing orange emergency light shimmered off the table and caught his eyes just so, causing them to take on a crazed and manic fire. It hit him just what he was looking at, and he scooped up the vial, turning it over in his shaking fingers.

"Where did you get this?" Fenton whispered.

"From your lab. Where else?" When Kate spoke, it was low and seething. Her words frothed through clenched teeth.

Sean called out from Lucas's side, "I need to know what's going on back there!"

Kate and Fenton ignored Sean while the dance continued.

"Unbelievable! And this," Fenton inspected the vial closely as all the puzzle pieces fell into place. "This is what got out? This is what happened to-" With one limp hand, he pointed to Lucas's body, life fading from it, on the other side of the room. "-to Vivian?"

Kate sneered, "You really shouldn't use your birthday as a password. That's like security 101."

Fenton was overcome with emotion. Kate watched him trying to tamp it all down. A bucket of sand poured on a campfire, embers smoldering behind his eyes. Fenton chucked the vial away. Somewhere in the dark, it clattered to the floor.

"Do you have any idea what you've done?" he asked incredulously.

Daniel stepped forward, no longer content to just observe the show around him. "Kate, what was that stuff?"

"It's a compound we synthesized in the lab," Fenton said, answering for her.

"I'm not following. How did whatever was in that glass vial make this happen?" Daniel asked.

"Because, Kate, here, stole it," Fenton said. "And it looks to me like she did a lot worse with it too."

Kate pushed in closer to the old man, until their faces were mere inches apart. "How do we stop it?"

"First, you have to tell me what happened," Fenton said.

Daniel still seemed stuck on the revelation about Kate and her dirty secret. Kate could feel the wheels in his brain trying to churn this new information. In his confusion he sat on the floor, back against the wall.

"Kate? What, I mean, how? Why? I don't, I don't understand." Daniel was stammering, unable to right the train on the tracks.

Kate paid no mind to Daniel's chattering and turned her back on him to address Fenton. "It's still in the basement right now. It killed a patient, and right now it looks like it may have killed Dr. Lucas too."

Fenton laughed. It wasn't that he found the moment funny. It was just his body's reaction to it all. Some form of insanity.

"Doctor," Kate said. She modulated her tone to be less aggressive. "Tell me. What is it?"

Daniel was still unsure of what they could ever possibly do. He kept asking the same questions over and over again. "Can someone tell me what is happening?"

Fenton erupted, and he grabbed Daniel from up off the floor. There was no power left in Daniel's legs. Should Fenton have let go, Daniel would have collapsed back on the floor like an invertebrate.

"You want to know what's happening so bad? You're raving about a monster here in the hospital? You're right, my friend. You're standing next to her." He pointed at Kate. "She killed Vivian."

"That's not true! We're trying to save her," Kate said.

Fenton released Daniel. He approached Kate with that very same fire in his eyes. "You don't understand, do you. Look at what you've done." he growled. "You better hope she doesn't make it."

"Why would you say that?" Kate asked.

"If that thing touched Vivian then she's likely already infected. By keeping her alive, you're making more of them."

The sirens of St. Christopher's emergency management system hushed. Suddenly, the room went from a whirling disco show to the hush of a library. Low crackling static whispered through the hospital's PA system. The repeating message had stopped but the emergency strobe lights continued to flash, throwing glass-like shards of light around the room.

Fenton padded over to Dr. Lucas. Sean had just tied off the last of the bandages. The old doctor reached for the Vivian's hand and held it in his own. She was barely alive. Kate knew they were nearing the end. The only option now required an infusion. Intubation. There was no way she would be able to breathe on her own much longer.

"My God," Fenton muttered. His voice came out in a soft hush.

Resigned to the fact that there was nothing more to do, he turned away and crossed the room where he collapsed on a bench. When he did, he exhaled a slow, long breath.

Kate sat down beside him. "I never meant for any of this to happen."

His eyes were bloodshot. "I still don't understand," he said. "How did we get here? What would possess you to fool around with some compound from my lab?"

Possession was the optimum word here. She hadn't felt herself at all these past few months. Kate White had been asleep at the wheel and some demonic entity had taken over.

She told Fenton everything, from initiating the allergic reaction in Parker to the attack in room 217. She told him that she had trouble remembering much of it. She told him about the blackouts. She told him that she believed she'd gone crazy.

Finally, she said: "You know, I'd give anything now to trade places with her."

"Kate?" Sean had overheard the whole thing. He was looking at Kate with the expression of a wounded child.

"You're a despicable human being," Fenton said. "What a trite thing to say. None of this would have happened if you had behaved with even a modicum of rationality."

She had nothing to say. She didn't want to make excuses. It was not about some mental condition. They were not choices that could be explained away. She had to own it, all of it. And now her head fell, defeated, into her open hands.

"I know," she said. A long beat of silence. "What is 112A?"

"It started as a vehicle," Fenton said. "To marry with anything. Ideas were endless. Of course, didn't take long for someone to request that we marry it with a parasite."

"And Lien?" Kate asked. "She saw it?"

"It seemed so powerful. Completely beyond the realm of anyone's expectations. But when we saw what it did to her, that poor girl, we knew we had to shut it down. I hid the remaining vials from Father's men. I was going to destroy them. It was never supposed to get out."

"Wait," Kate said. Her mind was reeling with the impact of a punch to the face. "Lien's dead?"

"Oh my God" Sean bellowed. "What the fuck is happening?"

Daniel couldn't face sitting on the sidelines anymore. "Guys, I agree that there's a lot to talk about here. But, how do we get out? Lucas needs proper care and from what I've been able to gather, there's still a pretty big bug somewhere in the hospital."

Daniel turned to Fenton. "Surely, there must be a way to stop it. Please, help us."

Fenton started to laugh. At first, it was but a churlish giggle, but soon evolved into the cackle of a raving lunatic.

"I don't see what's so goddamned funny!" Kate exclaimed.

"What's so funny?" Fenton asked. "We already stopped it once, but you only have a small window. I didn't sleep for days wondering if we missed something. We dodged a bullet when it was just Lien. It was, frankly, a miracle that only she died."

"You stopped it before. Let's do it again."

"With Lien it was different. Don't you understand? The experiment was controlled. Within minutes every scrap of biological tissue was incinerated."

Kate stood. Ideas were forming. There could be a drop of optimism somewhere in this ocean of pain.

"Then we'll have to lure it back to Davol lab and kill it again."

Kate saw Fenton genuinely considering her idea. "The team from Father will be here any second. They'll shut it all down."

"What's Father?" Daniel asked.

"It's the name of the government team that funded our program. They're the group who forced me to build this."

It hit Kate. "The men in suits scurrying around your lab a few days ago."

"They charged in here, went over everything with a fine-tooth comb, dismantled everything."

Kate was pleading now. "I'm not trying to get away with anything anymore. I'll admit everything and happily sit in a jail cell for the rest of my life. None of it matters. I just need to fix this."

"You won't fix this, Kate. Hell, you won't even survive this," Fenton's voice slithered.

This sent the group of survivors spiraling back into a silence of despair. The gravity of the situation was too much to bear. Daniel coughed.

Fenton continued. "It's a perfect organism. A work of art. And if it's the size you now claim it to be, then what we have is an efficient killing machine. It's over."

Kate was feeling woozy. It was all too much. The people around her were dead and dying. She grabbed the spent syringe from her pocket. The one that infected Parker and yanked the cap off with her teeth.

"Then I deserve this," she said as she thrust the needle into the side of her soft neck, pushed down on the plunger, and felt the few remaining drops of compound 112A marry her blood stream.

"Oh my god!" Daniel cried out.

In an instant, Fenton and Daniel were on her and trying to wrestle the needle away from her. Finally, Daniel swatted it. The needle tore from her throat, blood shooting outward.

Daniel was apoplectic: "Kate, you're insane! You want to end up just like Parker, with that thing inside of you?"

Kate collapsed onto the floor and started to sob. She didn't know what had come over her. An overwhelming dread that the world was worse off because she was in it. Now she didn't want to get up. *Leave me alone,* she thought. *I deserve it.*

Daniel picked up the spent syringe. He urgently gestured for Fenton and Sean to join him. In the corner of the room, they whispered back and forth while Kate lay in her depressed fugue on the floor. To Kate, they sounded far away, in another room, their voices floating over clouds.

Sean asked: "How does it work?"

"You take a parasite or virus, something that's already extremely volatile." Fenton took the syringe from Daniel and held it up to the light. "In the case of Compound 112A, it was the ascariasis parasite."

"What's the ascar—"

Kate sat up, dazed and wobbly, wiping away blood and snot. Her hair had slowly become a tangled mess.

"Ascariasis. Nasty stuff. Roundworms. They live in the lungs, lay eggs in the intestines of its host. Flesh eaters. Even at microscopic sizes, they'll eat you to death, from the inside out."

In her mind's eye, Kate had fixed on an image of the parasite on one of her disease-themed flash cards she had reviewed regularly with Lien. God, she missed Lien. Now knowing this damned parasite had taken Lien like it was about to take Dr. Lucas made her sick. She pictured that ghastly thing that had erupted from Parker's stomach. For something that powerful to have grown that large was unfathomable.

Fenton was impressed with Kate's quick diagnosis. He joined in. "And when you add this particular gene sequence, it attaches itself to host cells and replicates. Quickly. The parasite and host merge. Until all that's left are—"

Daniel was white as a sheet. "This isn't happening..."

"Just tell me one thing," Fenton said.

"What?" Daniel and Kate asked in unison.

"Tell me you locked the door to the morgue after you ran out of there."

Their silence was his answer.

"I'll be back," Fenton called out, running at a breakneck pace out of the surgery.

Kate and Daniel followed, and the three of them crashed through the double doors out into the corridor. However, the gruff old man pulled away into the dark.

They could hear a burgeoning commotion through the walls and windows of the hospital. Kate pulled a chair over and placed it beneath a small window that was set six feet off the floor. She climbed onto the seat and looked out. Down several stories, an alien landscape below, soldiers running the circus city in the hospital's parking lot. She could see the decontamination stations. Trucks and tanks and squad cars with their lights all whirling. Overhead, Kate could see teams of helicopters cruising the skies. She saw men in hazmat suits carrying sci-fi contraptions around. She figured it was that stupid group with the stupid name. Father. If they knew everything, then they knew what Kate, Sean, and Daniel were up against. And they'd deployed an army.

"What the hell is happening out there?" Daniel asked.

Kate didn't respond at first. She was too busy watching armed men take their positions from the roofs of satellite campus buildings. The weapons were trained on the exits.

"Uh-oh."

"Uh-oh what?" Daniel asked.

"Fenton was right," she said. "We're not getting out of here alive."

Chapter Fourteen
BEWARE THEM NIGHT TERRORS

Fenton had run the labyrinth of the hospital's halls and descended the back stairwell. The basement was still shrouded in darkness. Pops of lightning striking from the emergency alarms pointed the way. Within minutes, he was back in the very familiar territory with the locked door to Davol Laboratory before him. But he didn't enter. Instead, he turned away from his lab and sprinted in the other direction until he reached the morgue, out of breath.

This was not the clean and orderly morgue he'd been accustomed to working beside. What he saw was Grand Guignol theater. The double doors had been locked with a makeshift broom handle barricade; the wooden stem shoved through the door handles. Fenton slid the broomstick aside. The doors opened. He entered.

With each slow step, another strobe of white light, fleeting, and then darkness. Inside, in the center of the morgue's tile floor, he found the body of Parker Dallas. Horrendous, gaping wounds littered the corpse. Blood was everywhere. It was so unlike anything he'd seen in his time at St. Christopher'. It didn't feel real, more like maintenance had spilled cans of red paint.

They really weren't kidding, Fenton thought. Not that he had any reason to believe they had been. *Whatever did this was big and mean.*

Fenton wished he was armed, not that he'd ever shot a gun in his life, but he needed something physical. A weapon to put his faith in, to feel alright about what he had to do now. The static PA cracked and popped.

He thought of Sunday mornings from his childhood, when his father brought him to church, and he sang in the choir. Those old hymns came flooding back. He wasn't sure why. Human beings were funny creatures. HIs firing synapses called up "All Creatures of Our God and King." Fenton found himself whispering it just beneath his breath while stepping through the darkness.

"All creatures of our God and King. Lift up your voice and with us sing. O praise Him, alleluia. Thou burning sun with golden beam. Thou silver moon with softer gleam."

His father had come to this country from Armenia with nothing but a claim against the American dream. Everything saved was poured into Fenton's education. First, the chemical engineering program at McGill. Then, grad school at MIT. Much of it was a case of right place, right time. Like Bill Gates or Steve Jobs in computing. When he was a student, biochemical engineering was new. St. Christopher's came calling with the keys to Davol Laboratory. When he started, he had never envisioned a life that could have led to this moment. Who could?

For a second, Fenton wasn't thinking about creatures or death. He was thinking about the decades of time and the barrage of faces that had traveled through St. Christopher's. Important work had been done in this institution. Work that forwarded the mission of science. Work that sought to define the unknowable. He wanted to leave the world in a more hopeful place than he found it.

He felt as if he were in a lifeboat bobbing in the detritus of a massive shipwreck. Looking up the corpse of this dead young man. It was just like Kate had described. The hairs on the nape of his neck stood on end. His arms broke out in gooseflesh. He was simultaneously cold and sweating.

The gurneys and shelves and trays within the morgue had all been turned over. Tools and electronic equipment were strewn across the floor. This place resembled pictures published in the newspaper the day after a tornado touched down in some midwestern farm town. Devastation.

With each step, his brain summoned more memories. *Flash.* Two failed marriages. *Flash.* Two kids, now fully grown. *Flash.* 1973, flirting with the cute, new intern, Vivian Lucas. They had kept their relationship a secret, not just then, but forever. Every few years, between children and marriages that would spiral out, they' find their way back to each other like magnets. God, Vivian was beautiful. And now she was one story up, bleeding to death, infected with a creature he had incubated in his lab.

"A mighty fortress is our God. A bulwark never failing. Our helper He, amid the flood. Of mortal ills prevailing."

Fenton crept slowly through the room in a broad, sweeping circle. Beneath each footstep was the crunch of glass and metal. Something in the distance, a lump in the dark. This was not a tool or a piece of equipment. The shape was too jagged, too organic. He was having trouble, but he plodded forward into the darkness, each step shaky, each crunch beneath his feet deafening.

He crouched down and reached out for the unmoving shape, and when his hands were upon it, he immediately knew what it was. It was Vivian's severed arm. The flesh was grey and cold to the touch. Sinews hung from the torn end like strands of red spaghetti. He was going to be sick.

A black cloud had moved into his head. His stomach was a white-hot ball of fire. Every B-horror movie with a mad scientist usually had a scene where the creature turns on its master and there is some epiphany—too late, of course—of the damage done trying to play God and all that hubris bullshit. *Was this him? Was this his story now?*

He didn't make monsters.

In the near distance, a booming crack pulled Fenton back. He exhaled slowly, trying desperately to not make a sound. He rose and scanned the room. There was nothing but the hectoring sounds of his own shaky breaths. Then something else. Some horrible swishing sound that started swirling around him. Wet and repeating: *Plop. Plop. Plop.* Water leaking from a broken faucet? It was dripping from the ceiling, splattering to the floor all around him.

He tried to keep calm. Flash. His uncle telling him "Don't ever show that dog that you're afraid." He tried to swallow his fear. Clenched his jaw. Outside he projected stillness. Inside, he felt pinwheeling fireworks. *It's just the neighbor's big dog. Walk slowly out of the room. Don't ever show it you're afraid.*

He stepped backward. His eyes wildfire. He felt his way back, trying not to trip over the mess all over the floor. *Plop. Plop. Plop.* The sound was following him from above. He didn't dare look up. Now halfway to the morgue doors, and he was wet. The rain was above him. One drop hit him square on the top of the head and rolled down his forehead, over the bridge of his nose, and sloped down his cheek.

A gurgle above. He stopped, looked up, couldn't help it. At first, there was nothing. He was squinting into the darkness. There was a brief sound like wet sheets on a clothesline slapping in the wind, and then everything happened so quickly.

The creature's slimy, serrated tentacles unfurled from the ceiling like a flag. Its movements were lightning fast. Fenton was paralyzed by the fear and left to just watch it all happen to him. Now, it came into view.

Flash. Long and powerful arms of flesh, jutting out of the giant, insect-like body.

Flash. Gory humanoid parts, a head with two empty eye sockets. It must have once been Parker.

Flash. The tentacles wrapped around him and then he was hoisted effortlessly up the ceiling.

He issued a blood-curdling scream. Pieces of him plopped to the floor like rain drops. Slosh. Crunch.

Flash. Gnashing teeth.

Flash.

Oh, he thought at last, *today I've seen things I did not know how to dream.*

Flash.

Chapter Fifteen
A SAVIOR COMPLEX

The emergency room doors crashed open. Sean was pushing the gurney. In it, Dr. Lucas was an unmoving sack of flour. The wheels kept careering to the right and the drywall came away pock-marked and scuffed.

Kate and Danieel jumped up to the front of the gurney to guide it as Sean pushed from behind with all his might. The cords of his neck were bulging. He'd said Lucas was sutured up. They'd hooked her up to an O-negative transfusion line to try and stave off hypovolemic shock. Now they were in the realm of prayer.

The group headed toward the front entrance. Dr. Lucas needed to be loaded into an ambulance immediately. "Maybe," Sean said, "we can speak to someone about a medevac flight, just to be safe."

"There are plenty of helicopters buzzing around," Daniel noted.

"Hey, Sean, look," Kate said.

Sean looked at Kate and followed her gaze down to see the fingers on Lucas's remaining hand starting to flex and curl.

"Vivian, if you can hear me, hang in there. You're doing good. Real good," Sean said.

"Think she can hear you?" Kate asked.

He shook his head. "No. But she's the one person I'd never underestimate at a time like this."

At that moment, as if on cue, Lucas's eyes fluttered open. Her pupils were enormous, unfocused. She gagged from the intubation line in her throat.

Sean looked down at Lucas's face while continuing to push the gurney through the empty corridors. With Sean, Kate, and Daniel all guiding, they quickly hit cruising altitude.

"Vivian, you've been in a serious accident." Kate was trying to comfort her as they careened through St. Christopher's. "We had to intubate you. We've just come out from surgery. We're gonna get you out of here."

Lucas's eyes darted around. She acknowledged Kate by nodding slightly. Then her eyes closed, and her head lolled. She was out again.

Sean brought the gurney to a stop in front of the elevators. He hit the button, but there was no reaction. It took him a moment to realize the service was off. "Shit!" he cried. Elevator's out."

"So that's it?" Daniel asked.

"No. We've got to get her out of here. She needs proper care."

Kate said: "You haven't seen it outside. Soldiers. Men with big guns on all the roofs. They don't want anything—or anyone—leaving this hospital."

"We have to try," Sean said. "We owe her that much."

"All right," Daniel said, "We'll need to carry her down the stairs."

They moved the gurney from the bay of elevators over to the double doors leading to the stairwell. Sean brought up the rear. Daniel and Kate each grabbed one of the opposite corners by Lucas's feet.

Kate caught Sean eyeing the needle wound on her neck.

He asked her: "You okay?"

"Yeah, fine." She focused them on the task. "Ready: one, two, three, lift!"

They hoisted the gurney up. The wheels of the heavy, metal frame lifted from the ground. Kate's arms quaked, the metal bed was so heavy, and they hadn't even hit the first step yet. They were looking at a slow crawl down one long flight to get back to ground level.

"I have a bad feeling about this," Kate said through gritted teeth.

"Why?" Sean asked.

They stepped over the threshold, each of them with a rickety hold on a corner of Lucas's gurney and proceeded down the first few stairs. They stepped slowly, trying to ease the rattling impact on Lucas.

By now, she was probably dreaming of a boat ride on a choppy sea. They hit the half pace and started descending the last half-flight of stairs. Kate's hands were moist. She was losing hold of her corner. Then, in an instant, the bar was out of her hands. The corner of the bed crashed down, the force causing Daniel and Sean to lose hold too. The bed crashed down the remaining seven stairs and slammed into the concrete wall below.

"Oh god!" Kate screamed.

Sean and Daniel leaped down the remaining stairs to make sure Lucas was okay. Rattled, but fine. They steadied the metal frame. Kate counted to three again, and together, the group got the wheels moving. They were on their floor and Dr. Lucas seemed to be regaining consciousness.

Up ahead, the main entrance was visible. Kate could see the shafts of blinding, white search lights obscured only by the black cutouts of soldiers flittering between them like moths to a flame.

They made it to the central lobby, by the admissions desk, through a waiting area with three-year-old magazines stacked on tables. *10 Minutes a Day to a Brand New You!*

From within the gurney, Lucas's arm raised slightly. She was half-conscious, grabbing at the air in a daze. The group came to a stop in the middle of the floor.

"What do you think?" Sean asked. "Leave her intubated?"

"Yeah," Kate said. "Let's try to wheel her out the front door."

Lucas's movements were becoming more pronounced. Now she was pointing at the tube that ran down her mouth and into her chest. Her head was fixed to the gurney with a strap to keep her from hurting herself and she strained against it until the cords in her neck stood out like thick ropes beneath her skin.

"I think she has something she really wants to say," Kate said.

Sean looked from Kate to Daniel, who was nodding in agreement. He concurred. "Okay then. Remove it."

Sean leaned over Lucas. Her eyelids were fluttering, but she was awake. "Okay, Vivian, I'm going to remove the tube in your throat now. On the count of three, I need you to exhale as hard as you can, got it?"

She grunted the affirmative around the plastic tube. A gentle warmth was starting to return to her skin. The area around her mouth looked less blue.

"Kate. Daniel. Hold her shoulders down," Sean said.

They did. Kate exerted physical force on the same woman who had as recently as a day before terrified her. Once this frail old woman had seemed magnanimous, mythical. Now, she was an endangered species.

"One, two, three," Sean counted.

Then he yanked the long, plastic tubing up and out of her lungs. The old woman started to gag, cough, and wretch. Instantly, it was out. Lucas's head settled back on the pillow. No longer was she straining against the head strap. Slowly, she regained her composure. Kate and Daniel relaxed their hold on her shoulders.

"Shhh. Don't try to talk," Sean said. "If you need to say something, whisper."

Dr. Lucas curled the fingers of her hand inward a few times. *Come closer.*

Sean loosened the strap around her forehead. Lucas's eyes were open and rolling around. Finally, they found their focus and landed piercingly on Kate.

Kate leaned in very close. "Dr. Lucas," she called, "can you understand me?"

Lucas nodded, and then she opened her mouth, but only guttural sounds emerged.

"That's okay," Kate said. "Take your time. Sean patched you up pretty good. You'd be very proud of him."

Kate's eyes were flooding over realizing once again that all of this was all her fault. "No one else is in the hospital. They've been evacuated. It's just us. But we're going to get you out."

Lucas's cracked lips curled, trying to form words. She spoke, but it came out very softly. Too softly to hear. Kate leaned in even closer. The doctor's breath was putrid. Kate was embarrassed for even thinking such thoughts at a time like this.

"What are you trying to say?" Kate asked.

Lucas formed the words again. Slowly. Deliberately. Pushing them forth with all the available air in her shriveled lungs. Finally, it connected with Kate. The word tumbled out of Dr. Lucas's mouth slowly. Three distinct and clipped syllables:

"In. Fec. Ted."

Kate felt her stomach drop. She grabbed Dr. Lucas's hand in her own. Squeezed it tightly. Fenton had been right. It was folly, Kate thinking she could mess with things she didn't understand. She had laughed in the face of her oath. The dread squirmed in her guts. This was what it felt like when you were doomed.

"What'd she say?" Daniel asked.

"Please, Dr. Lucas," Kate said. "I'm so, so sorry for everything."

Kate stepped back from the gurney and doubled over with her head between her knees. Now was not the time. She had to keep it together.

From behind her came Sean's voice: "Kate, what'd she say?"

"Daniel, stay with Dr. Lucas," Kate said.

He nodded. "Of course."

Kate got up and laid her hand on Dr. Lucas's for a quick moment. Then she crossed to the other side of the main lobby where Sean was waiting for her.

Sean brought her in close. "She said she was infected, didn't she?"

Kate nodded.

"Do you think-," he asked, then, starting again. "Is there any chance there are another one of those things growing inside of her?"

Kate struggled. Her mind was a flat, brick wall of nothingness. She recalled her conversation with Dr. Fenton. He'd talked about how this thing had started. The bug he had used to engineer it. *Ascariasis.* What did she know about that?

She began to pace fervently. Head down, she moved quickly, her mind not all present in the here-and-now but traveling through her mental Rolodex of medical knowledge, mining all the thousands of associations between words and their meanings she'd crammed in.

Ascariasis...

"Come on, Kate. We need you now. More than ever."

Kate's mind left her body. With her eyes slammed shut she was sailing in a black void, conjuring everything she could possibly remember about parasites. In its conventional form, it could mature to become infective. But typically hosts had to ingest eggs. That only happened in parts of the world without good sanitation. Where people lived and farmed in their own shit. Kate envisioned the enormous creature with its spindly, tentacled arms and how one of them had gone right down Lucas's god damn throat.

"She's infected," Kate said solemnly.

"Are you sure?" Sean cried out.

"No, *of course* I'm not fucking sure! But I think so. We've got to get her out of here. There's gotta be something they can do."

Sean was evaluating things, looked at the soldiers and searchlights up ahead at the front entrance. "They'll never let us take her out," Sean said. "Not with something inside of her."

Kate glanced back at Daniel, who was stroking Lucas's hair. She'd slipped out of consciousness again.

"Guys!" Daniel called out. "Whatever we're doing, we need to do it now."

Kate held up one finger to let Daniel know they would just be another minute. She lowered her voice to address Sean in a near-whisper.

"So, you're suggesting we leave her here and let that thing come bursting out of her?"

Sean cast his eyes to the ground. Kate knew Sean well. His expression said that he had no idea what the right next move would be. It was the same look he had given her when she had asked him if he had been with another woman.

"No. No way in hell am I leaving her here." Kate was ferocious. She would wheel Lucas out of there by herself if she had to. She returned to the gurney with newfound purpose. "C'mon, Daniel. Let's go."

"Are we leaving now?" Daniel asked. His voice cracked. He sounded so young and so afraid.

Kate nodded.

They each took a corner of the gurney and began to push. Sean exhaled and then jogged over to catch up, resigning himself to help. They approached the front door and Kate could hear the chopper blades and the sound of a muffled voice on a megaphone. It grew louder as they neared. Help was all within reach.

Then suddenly, a rustling came from behind. Something back, behind them, in the dark.

"Whoa, shhhh," Sean said. The gurney stuttered to a quick stop. They held their breath, listening.

"Hear that?" Sean asked.

Kate peeked behind. There was nothing but the darkened lobby, beyond it were unknowable lengths of corridors, jutting back into oblivion. She watched the room for signs of movement. The sounds were growing louder, intensifying. Squishy, fluttering, membranous sounds. Her heart was a galloping wild horse. Whatever it was, it was getting closer.

Suddenly, it was on them. At first, all Kate could see were its scaly legs bristling with the coarse, black hair of a tarantula. But this tarantula was the size of a Buick, each leg, several feet long.

The creature loped wildly, propelling forward. It lashed toward them, not on the floor but across the ceiling. Its misshapen body slid left a trail of blackened slime across the ceiling tiles which were churned up like paper through a shredder.

The flashing red-and-blue lights from the cruisers just outside were winding their way across the room in jerky loops.

They cast upon the creature, sending large, elongated shadows spiraling out at strange and horrible angles. It looked huge. It looked heavy. It looked hungry.

Kate thought she was in the middle of one of her nightmares again—just like so many others—but the spell was broken when she realized that in all her fantasies she was alone, and if Sean and Daniel were standing here with her, then this was very real. They leaped backwards. It closed in on them. Thirty feet...twenty...ten.

"Oh shit!" Daniel screamed.

"Run!" Kate urged.

They grabbed the gurney and pushed with all their might. Overcoming the weight was tough going at first, but they quickly got it up to speed, and then inertia helped shoulder the burden. They raced toward the main doors. Just a few more feet out.

Kate glanced behind her. It was gaining. It was fast. "Oh my God!" she cried.

"Keep moving. Don't look back!" Sean ordered.

They charged toward the front door. It was close enough behind them that they could hear its mouth and a horrible sucking sound. A fleshy, red hole ringed with razor-blade teeth. Kate kept imaging one of those long, undulating tentacles descending from right above her and pulling her up to the ceiling. She wondered if it would be slow and painful or if it would be over quickly.

They could see soldiers gathered on the other side of the front door's glass panels. With each step, more came into focus. The soldiers were wearing Hazmat suits and wielding M16 rifles. Two of them crouched at the door, then there was a flash of blinding light.

"Hey! Hey! Let us out!" Daniel started screaming.

"Help! Help! Open the door!" Kate chimed in.

They bellowed with what little breath they could muster. Still, they ran, closing in on the last little gap of lobby between them and an entire army that could blast this thing into ribbons. As the group neared, it finally became apparent that the soldiers weren't opening the doors. They were welding them shut.

Lucas's gurney crashed into the main door with a force that caused it to buckle, but the doors didn't open. Sparks flew inward from the welding in bright, fiery arcs. For half a second, Kate and the others stood there, separated from the outside world by a thick pane of glass and two metal doors. They peered at the soldiers on the other side. Their eyes hidden behind the blacked-out glass of their masks.

The creature was slithering in and out of the whirling lights as it scuttled across the ceiling. One of the soldiers rolled over one of the massive searchlights and aimed it directly inside the door. It was so fiercely bright it blinded all of them. They staggered in a cloud of white darkness. The creature screamed and receded from the shine of the light.

Kate felt something soft on her arm. She looked down. It was Dr. Lucas. She was pulling at the back of Kate's lab coat to grab her attention. Lucas's body seized in a spasmodic cramp, sending her pelvis up into the air, some pained version of a yoga pose. Her body shuddered violently.

"Help me," Lucas mouthed, unable to put any more force behind the words.

Sean and Daniel kicked at the door. Each blow barely rocked the metal frame. The soldier crouching on the other side of the glass completed the weld and put down his torch. Then he picked up his rifle. The rest of the soldiers raised their guns. It was a death squad. Muzzles aimed right at Kate, Sean, and Daniel.

Lucas lifted her torn shirt, exposing her bare midriff. Soft folds of doughy skin spilled out over the waistline of her pants. There, much like Parker before her, were the little protuberances of fleshy tendrils slithering within her.

With guns pointed straight at them, Daniel and Sean froze and lifted their hands in a manner of surrender. \

Daniel cast his eyes upon the creature within Dr. Lucas. "Oh God," he said.

The bandage Sean had looped around the stump of Lucas's other shoulder began to unravel. A small and squirming tentacle wormed out of the gaping, bleeding wound, popping stitches with violent tearing cracks. Then gray, fleshy spindles fell out of her open wound like a bucket of eels. Dr. Lucas's body was seizing uncontrollably. Her eyes rolled back into her head and foam ran from the sides of her mouth.

Kate, Daniel, and Sean began pounding their fists on the door. Behind them, the beast on the ceiling was coming back in from above.

"Let us out of here!" Kate screamed.

"You're gonna kill us!" Sean added.

Then it leaped and the big beast fell onto Lucas's gurney. Kate spilled to the right, Daniel, and Sean to the left.

"Noooooo!" Kate cried.

The large creature wasted no time wrapping all its sinuous tentacles around Lucas's body. It began to devour her. The doctor finally found her voice. She began to scream painful, wretched cries that quickly turned into gurgles as one of the creature's tentacles looped around Lucas's neck and punched violently through her ribcage.

Kate watched as the soldiers saw it happen. They fell backward. For the first time, their terrified body language betrayed their emotionless, masked faces. The muzzles of their guns lost their aim. Only when Lucas's body had finally been torn to shreds did the soldiers sail into action. Lifting their machine guns, they fired on St. Christopher's doors, right into the bulletproof glass. The doors marred and buckled, spiderwebbing fractures rippled through the glass.

Kate yelled over the explosive sounds of war. "We have to get out of here!"

"Where?" Sean asked.

"Go to Davol Lab. We'll lock ourselves in."

Sean chimed in: "How will we get in?"

Kate addressed Sean directly. "Split up. You two make your way down there now. I'll find Fenton's key card. No time, just go."

There was no time to argue or strategize further. Gunshots were exploding around them. Glass from the door had fallen away in jerky lifts and pops. The smoke was overwhelming, enshrouding the lobby in blinding fog.

Sean and Daniel ran off in one direction, Kate the other. The armed guards continued to rain machine gun fire at the beast, which had all but appropriated Lucas's body into itself.

★★★★★

Kate was in the east wing now and running for her life. She didn't think she had been followed, but who knew how this thing moved. Maybe it was in the air ducts right above her and ready to pounce? She charged down the hall, every three or four steps, instinctively glancing behind. All seemed clear.

Finding Dr. Fenton would be difficult, but if the soldiers weren't letting anyone them out, then Fenton must still be here too. She slowed to a stop and bent over to catch her breath. Something about this part of the hospital made her feel queasy. Then she realized what was making her feel this way. She was standing before the door to the chapel.

A small pulse vibrated on her leg. Her heart leaped as she thought that the creature had finally caught her. But it was just her cell phone buzzing. The screen said two simple words:

MOM CALLING. She ducked into the chapel and swiped to answer.

"Kate?" the voice rang out in a tinny whine on the other end.

"I'm here, Mom." Kate spoke in a hushed whisper, not sure if it was stalking the halls nearby.

Someone's overcoat was left behind on one of the chairs. A pair of reading glasses were folded over the page of a hymnal. Flickering candles danced. Kate instinctively got nervous about the unattended fire, but when she saw the candles were battery-operated.

"Oh, thank goodness, you're okay!" Kate's mother said. "There's all this stuff on the news. What's going on?"

"I'm fine, Mom, but I can't talk right now."

"Are you home?"

"No, I'm here. At the hospital."

Kate ducked under a nearby table. On it was a ceramic star, some interfaith symbol. Crouching under the table like a child, Kate cupped her hand around the phone and made herself as quiet as possible.

"Are you sure you're alright? I'm so scared," her mother said. "I've been calling for an hour but couldn't get through. TV says the hospital is on lockdown"

"There was an accident."

"What kind of accident?"

Kate closed her eyes, nearly dropped the phone. She tried to keep her voice from wavering. "I did a bad thing, Mom."

"Oh honey. Just tell me that you're in a safe place. I'm sure everything will be fine."

Kate had to bite down on her lip to keep from openly weeping. Her mother jumped in when there was too much silence on the other end. "You're making me nervous," she said. "Why can't you talk?"

Kate slammed her eyes shut. Saw herself as a young girl beneath the dining table in her childhood home. Her hands covering her ears. *No peeking!* Her parents scurrying around the kitchen, emptying the cupboards of all the snack foods they could find to make Surprise Plates. An Oreo cookie, a few gummy worms, a handful of Cap'n Crunch cereal. Every time, it was different. Her mother tapping her on the shoulder. Kate giggling, opening her eyes, and uncovering her ears. Her father slipping her the plate, and she gobbling it all up.

"Just listen," Kate said. "I don't have time, but I need to tell you I'm sorry for being such a shit. You and Dad were everything to me. You're going to hear some terrible things about me when this is over."

Kate rubbed her neck. Something didn't feel right. There was a bitter taste in the back of her mouth, like in the seconds before vomiting. It felt a lot like the start of a flu. Nausea. Aches. Chills.

"Kate? You're scaring me."

Sean and Daniel were waiting for her. Without her, they didn't stand a chance.

"I have to go," Kate said and hung up choking back a sob.

She slung the phone back into her pocket. Her fingers reached into her shirt and grabbed for a simple locket she always wore around her neck. She didn't bother reaching for the clasp and instead just ripped the thing off. Links of the chain, as thin as a cat's whisker, went sailing off into the chapel. She drew her finger along the rim of the pendant and then opened it. Inside, a tiny photo of her and her father from childhood. Her finger traced its shape. She smiled. It was hard to see through the tears, but it meant the world to her. She peeled back the photo. Beneath it was an engraving. *TBYIAWTICTTMYSEITMSA.* The long, strange sequence looked like a snippet of genetic code, but, it was an abbreviation for one of her favorite sentiments, from Ralph Waldo Emerson:

> *To be yourself in a world that is continually trying to make you something else is the most significant accomplishment.*

She grasped the locket in a clenched fist and slipped it into her pocket, where it mingled with her cell phone. She left the chapel with purpose. There was work to do.

★★★★★

Kate ran back to the basement but stopped momentarily when a hacking cough overtook her. Twice now, she'd coughed and when she pulled her hand away, there was a small dot of ruby-red blood. That scared her, yes, but what scared her more was that the monster would hear her, and because of something as stupid as a tickle in her throat, she'd be eaten alive.

She could hear it. It wasn't far. Loud, rumbling sounds. It was looking for something. Looking for her. It overturned heavy objects, moving from room to room. She braced herself against the wall, waiting idly. She had never been hunted before. This was what it felt like to no longer be at the top of the food chain.

Right before the stairwell that would take her back to the basement, she stopped. Something caught her eye that sent her off into another direction. Across the hall was a pitch-black room with glass walls. From her vantage point, there was nothing inside except for a few blinking electronic lights. On the door were two simple words: *SECURITY OFFICE.*

Askew in the middle of the hall was a large, rolling bin stamped *LAUNDRY*. Inside were piles of soiled bed linens and lab coats, all of which had been in the process of being ferried away to the bowels of the basement when the alarms had started to ring. She snagged a long sheet and wrapped it around her elbow until her arm was a massively engorged, padded limb.

There was a muffled crunch as she drove her elbow into the glass pane of the door's window. She cleared away some of the sharper shards before reaching in to pull on the handle from the inside and entered the security office. This was yet another room of St. Christopher's that she'd never inhabited.

The office was small, little more than a cubicle fit for two bodies. A long desk, full of equipment: band scanner, CB, PA system, television. Kate had never been confident with electronics. She flipped the switch on the CCTV security monitors, but they were dark. She tried the CB. The small unit crackled to life with a roar of static. She pictured Wendy Torrance from that movie, trapped, hollering for help into a little, boxed radio. How her life had come to resemble a horror movie.

Kate flicked through the various channels. On each one, she paused to call out: "Anybody? Anybody?!" Flick; another channel. "Somebody! Anybody? I'm one of the survivors trapped within St. Christopher's Hospital."

The static crackled for another lengthy period. Kate's hand hovered above the power switch, silently praying to a newfound god, willing the universe to send someone's voice back to her. She had just about given up, but as she went to flip the unit off, there was a break in the static.

"This is Charlie One reading you. Go ahead."

The voice greeted her like sweet music. It was dispassionate, yes, but someone was there on the other end. Another human being. She slammed the talk button down with enthusiasm.

"Yes!" she cried. "Oh, thank God. We're locked in the hospital. Something's in here with us. We need help."

She released the talk button. Her heart was thundering. She wished Sean and Daniel were here with her. Now she would have to find them and tell them the good news. Only the voice on the other end wasn't responding.

"Hello?" Kate called into the CB unit. Another ten seconds of silence. "Hello?" she called again.

"We read you. Over."

She shrugged the nonresponse away, hit the talk button, and put the microphone to her mouth. "Are you gonna get us out of here?"

Another long moment of static. She asked again: "Are you going to get us out of here? Over."

Finally, the radio crackled back to life. "Sit tight, ma'am. We're doing what we can. Over."

"We can meet you at the door. We just need you to not shoot at us this time."

"Uh, negative, ma'am. We're going to need you to please keep off the line. Over and out." The radio went dark once again.

"Goddammit!" she screamed aloud.

She wasn't ready to throw in the towel. She may not be making it out of here, but she was sure going to get Sean and Daniel out.

She pressed the talk button once more. This time, she found herself clutching the handset with a white-knuckled grip of desperation.

"Wait, wait! We need help. Please! Somebody? Anybody? Please don't do this."

But nothing came. Kate tried again. "Hello? Please? How much longer do we have? Over."

There was nothing but the gurgle of low static.

With stiff fingers, she growled and then savagely tore the CB unit off the desk by yanking hard with all her might. The wires snapped back, sending a spray of sparks all over the desk. She chucked the unit against the wall, where it splintered into a blitzkrieg of black metal and copper wires and landed on the floor, transformed into a heaping pile of junk.

That was dumb. Kate knew it instantly. Not only because she had cut off communication with the outside world but because she would be lucky if that thing hadn't heard her.

But she couldn't leave yet. She hadn't tried everything. Her eyes fell across the emergency band scanner, and she flipped it on. Again, there was static, but she hit the Scan Frequency button, and the unit began to cycle through all channels until it found one that was transmitting.

It landed on a station where there was a voice at the other end. It took her time to realize the sound was pre-recorded. It was playing a message repeatedly. A message so horrifying in its finality that it stopped her heart cold.

The computer's voice said: "Evacuation complete. Detonation in T-minus eighteen minutes and thirty seconds."

Her eyes were as wide as a yearling's. "Oh shit," she muttered. She had to warn Sean and Daniel. Even if she never found them again.

Her trembling hands fumbled over all the equipment before her. Everything on that desk that had an on switch. Finally, she found the phone, lifted the handset from its cradle, and placed it to her ear. There was a dial tone. She dialed the number zero and then pressed the Star button.

After a brief electronic beep, she could hear something overhead from the speaker in the ceiling. It sounded like a vent opening. There was a low hiss. She blew into the receiver and listened to the sound she made coming out of the speaker in the ceiling above her. She was live, transmitting throughout all of St. Christopher's.

Kate placed the receiver down on top of the band scanner's speaker. The recorded message played again, but this time it echoed through every empty room and hallway of the hospital. She left the office the same way she had come in—creeping quietly—and on her way, the voice returned.

"Evacuation complete," it said. "Detonation in T-minus eighteen minutes."

★★★★★

Kate crept through the dissection lab of the morgue. It was difficult to make her way in the dark. The flashlight on her cell phone, with minimal battery life left in the device, cast a diminutive glow allowing her to see but a few feet in front of her.

She padded cautiously. At any possible moment, she expected danger to rear its head. The room was dark, so very dark, and the smell of death was rampant. Parker's gurney, where it had all occurred, was drenched in blood, and tipped on its side in the center of the room. Everything had been demolished. Torn to shreds. Finally, her phone sputtered and died. The light extinguished, leaving her in total darkness.

She grabbed for a long, slender piece of debris, a rod-length splintered piece of a wooden table leg. Beyond the debris, further into the room, was a rolled-up wad of white fabric. As Kate neared, she recognized it as the torn shard of Lucas's lab coat. She turned it over in her hands. The back side of the fabric was sticky with splotches of blood. Kate bunched it all around one end of the splintered wood post. Behind her, tucked into the wall, was a built-in shelving system for supplies. She rifled through it in the dark until she found the familiar giant jug of rubbing alcohol. The smell was pungent. She doused the fabric and lit it afire with a flint spark tool.

Above her, the mechanical voice continued to echo out: "Evacuation complete. Detonation in T-minus seventeen minutes."

The torch she built was hot and bright. The flame cast dancing shadows over the detritus strewn all around the room.

"Dr. Fenton?" she called. "Are you here?"

In the distance, there were sounds in the air ducts. Kate looked above her where the ceiling had been shattered, and only a vast, gaping chasm remained.

She tiptoed. Beneath her feet was the cereal crunch of broken glass. Her flame passed over every little piece of debris: surgical tools, medical supplies, a man's tennis shoe. It was the kind Fenton wore. Kate remembered his sneakers from rifling through his locker. Here she was again, looking for Fenton's key card and having to dig into his shoes to find it. Finally, in the light of the fire, her eyes fell upon a small, plastic card half buried in debris. She picked it up. On it, Fenton's face looked exasperated. *Bingo*. She pocketed it.

That was when the monster struck. As Kate backed out of the room, it unfurled from the ceiling. Its tentacles cast out far around the room. It was bigger than before. It was still growing. The beast towered over Kate. She was thrown to the floor and quickly scuttled backward on her palms and feet like a crab. Her limbs gritted over the mess, and she could feel the tears in her flesh from the scratching, broken glass. The torch crashed to the back of the room, casting warm, romantic light upon a supply closet and table. As she scrambled absently to her feet, Kate saw a trail of her own blood smeared in her wake.

The creature neared. A lone spidery arm reached out for her. Its bristling, wiry hair was razor sharp. The low, thin mewling spewing from its mouth dripped an oozing liquid onto the floor. She backed against the wall by the supply closet. There was nowhere else to go. She was cornered.

Kate's hand reached out to feel blindly along the tabletop. She wasn't even conscious of what she was grasping for—anything hard or sharp, preferably both—would do. Her hand fell the round, smooth plastic of the bottle of rubbing alcohol, and the idea hit home like a bolt of lightning striking her between the eyes.

She closed her hand around the bottle and squirted it in a broad arc onto the beast. The jug emptied in a pool at the creature's feet. The thing screeched, fell onto its back end, and violently brought one of its long arms down. She managed to tuck and roll, ignoring the razor slice of burning pain radiating up her side from the chips of glass and metal dicing her like an onion.

One of its tentacles landed where she had been only half a second before with a dull and splashy *thwick*. It brought down such brutal force that the floor tiles beneath it rippled with great cracks.

Kate reached for her homemade torch, her fingers just glancing off its thin, stem base. The creature reared up again, preparing for another strike, but Kate was faster. In one fell swoop, she had the torch in her hands and launched it toward the pool of alcohol.

It went up in a fireball. Flames licked at the ceiling tiles and turned them an inky black. The creature squealed and thrashed, bellowing in pain. Its insectoid eyes shimmered in the fire. Could she say she saw something like uncertainty behind them?

And then it was gone. With a whooshing roll, it disappeared back into the cavity of the ceiling from which it had descended. Kate could hear its thrumming, fluid movements as it fled through the air ducts. To her, it sounded as if a bowling ball were rolling down a huge lane, trailing off. Then the firelight died, and the room once again dimmed to black.

Kate's clothing was sticking to her now, soaked with her own blood. She wasn't sure how bad it was. That flu-like feeling was back, front and center. Once she had a chance to consider it, she realized her head was throbbing. It was about to split in two right down the middle—a buzz saw behind her eyes. But she lay on her back, looking up at the hole in the ceiling, and laughed. Kate White, of all people in this world, had stared down the monster of her nightmares, and she had bested it.

Chapter Sixteen
PARALLEL LINES

They heard it immediately, and when they did, it stopped them in their tracks. The dispassionate message from the ceiling. A countdown to imminent obliteration. Daniel and Sean collapsed on each other, not quite a hug, more an expression of pure physical exhaustion. At least hearing this meant that Kate was still alive, but the content of the message was terrible. It meant they had much more significant problems than just finding shelter and waiting out a military rescue. Sean was seeing with new eyes. He, Daniel, Kate. They might not make it after all.

There was nothing creepier than an empty hospital. Sean had traversed the halls of St. Christopher's nearly every day of his adult life and, until now, had never experienced such complete and total isolation. Each charging footfall echoed down the long, taupe corridors. Room after room, department after department, was utterly devoid of everyone. No doctors or nurses. No patients or family members. Not even a goddamn custodian. Everything was dark. The emergency lighting kept a low beacon lining the ceiling, a runway to follow, like streetlamps guiding the way along a quiet, dark road.

He and Daniel were moving through the west wing of the hospital and looking for the stairwell. Daniel felt like the little brother he had never had, always tagging along, ever present. Sean was bone tired. He looked at Daniel, who had started to lag a bit behind. Daniel was worse for wear: haggard, hair a mess, blood splattered across every inch of exposed skin and clothing. Even adrenaline wasn't enough to propel them much further at this point. The crippling fear was settling back in. Soon, he and Daniel would be hobbled. The creature could be anywhere. Hell, it could have gotten Kate after she set up the PA. How would they ever know?

"Sean, I'm scared," Daniel said. "I know I shouldn't say it. But I don't care. I don't wanna die, man. Can't we just find an exit and sneak out and let the guys with guns handle it?"

"Look, I'm scared too. But I think we continue with the plan," Sean said.

Sean stopped in his tracks. He was straddling a pocket of emergency light. The orange luminescence carved him in two.

"What's the plan?" Daniel asked. The fear in his eyes ballooned them into the iridescent orbs of an anime character.

"Daniel, didn't you see what happened back there? They'll kill us if we try to leave."

"Maybe that's the better way to go? I don't want to die with one of those things bursting out of me. God, Kate should never have gone off like that."

"I know, but that thing was right between us. It was our only chance."

"You know her, Sean. Probably better than anyone. How could she have done this?"

He'd have to confront it eventually. But not today, god, not today. When he closed his eyes, she was standing there in the chapel, looking up at him. Doe eyed. Innocent. All of that was gone now. Today there were obsidian clouds in place of her eyes. He probably could have stopped it if he had been there for her. If he hadn't screwed around. If he had agreed give her the life she deserved. Was it his fault? Had he broken her? In the past week, he had lost both of the only women he'd ever truly loved.

"I don't know, Daniel" Sean said. His voice was weary, sanded down. "But I know the real Kate and she was filled with nothing but love and determination and wonder. What happened here, that's not the Kate I knew."

"But she did it."

"Yeah, but maybe there's more to it. Something we don't understand."

"Like what?"

"Did you know that in this country, murders have risen more than 30% in the past two years? And it's everything. Gun crime, police brutality, deaths of despair. It's all up." Sean wasn't just shoveling shit, he believed in what he was saying. "Criminologists, historians, they're looking at this. There's a theory. It's called Anomie. It says there's this fundamental tension in society. This obsession with wealth and status and how it's so unrealistic for so many to obtain."

"So, Kate failed to be the next *American Idol* or something?"

"No, of course not. It's just that good people are being broken by the expectations of an unobtainable ideal. Think about Kate, think about where she comes from. This world is cruel. And it's getting worse. Pandemics. Genocide. Oxy-fucking-Contin. When I stop to really think about it, I don't understand how more of us don't lose our minds."

"I don't think some pencil-necked academic, sitting in his campus office, can so easily explain away what your girlfriend did."

"No, I don't suppose."

In the far distance, there was a large clatter. The two men stood motionless, breath held, waiting out another sound. Then it came. A thunderous roar from in the unseeable distance.

The aural nightmare was growing louder. It was as if someone or something were tearing through the halls, going room by room, upending the hospital, flipping carts, lifting beds, breaking windows.

Sean said, "That's not human. We gotta move."

They inched their way forward until they hit the big, metal door marked *STAIRS*. Together, they laid on the push bar with slow, creeping strength. The squeal of the metal striker releasing rung out sharply. They listened; the sounds of the creature had subsided. Was it listening for them?

Sean stood shoulder to shoulder with Daniel. They were half in and half out of the doorway, propping it open, waiting. Then the sound of the thrashing resumed, farther off down the hall. They ran like hell for the stairs and descended into the basement.

★★★★★

The door to Davol Laboratory stood locked before them. The morgue was at their backs. No sign of Kate. Without a key card to enter, they would be served up on a platter. Every minute, the pre-recorded message on the loudspeakers was counting down to their inevitable fiery deaths.

"Great," Daniel said. "Now we get to worry about whether this thing eats us before we're blown to hell."

Sean punched him in the arm, playfully but with enough oomph that Daniel got the message. He rubbed his triceps where he had been struck.

"So, I heard you before," Daniel said. "Really, I did. Kate's great. Yadda, yadda, yadda. But, we need to talk. About her and about what we're going to do."

"Uh-huh." Sean wasn't sure what else to say. Where was Daniel going with this?

"Do you think she's legitimately crazy now? Like, what if she doesn't want us getting out? What if we're next?"

"No way, man," Sean said. "I still think Kate's a good person in her core. Have you seen her today? She's killing herself."

"Maybe she deserves to go." Daniel wore a look as if to say he didn't want to get pushed around anymore. At some point, Sean figured, all little brothers start standing up for themselves.

"Look around, Sean," Daniel said. "First, she's *infected* a patient. I shouldn't even have to go on to number two. That's like *off-the-charts* crazy. But beyond that, she stole an unknown virus from a locked laboratory to do it. Maybe I just don't get women. But that's not normal."

"She's not the one who killed Lien," Sean stammered. "She's not the one making designer bugs for the government after hours in a basement laboratory. All she ever wanted was to help people, and do well, and life kicked her in the teeth." He hadn't expected this defense of Kate to erupt like that.

Daniel didn't relent. "You know we're probably going to die now, right?"

Sean exhaled. It was long and slow and deep and carried with it the weight of the world. In his mind, he was back in bed with Kate. Together, at her apartment, nuzzling in the early-morning hours. A warm blanket over them.

"I know."

Above them, the message played again over the PA system: "Evacuation complete. Detonation in T-minus fourteen minutes."

But maybe there was a way out of here?

Sean wasn't ready to cash in his chips. Not yet. They still had time. Besides, he didn't want to face this down alone with Daniel. If he was going to die, it was going to be arm in arm with Kate. Sean swiped at the air as if to shoo away the message coming from the PA.

"She'll be here with the key card. I'm sure of it."

Daniel heard it first. Sean could see it in his face, the way his head cocked upward. Then Sean heard it too. It was the sound of something moving through the air shafts. The sound of sheet metal buckling.

"You do hear that, right?" Daniel whispered softly.

"Sounds far away," Sean said.

"For now," Daniel added.

Chapter Seventeen
SHE CAME, SHE CAME – AND THE QUIVERING FLAME

When Kate finally arrived at Davol Laboratory, Sean and Daniel were a sight for sore eyes. Her body felt completely empty, a deflated balloon, but she knew deep down that she had only hurt the monster, not killed it. It was going to come back, and it would be pissed off. She ran for her life. Her clumsy, galloping gait had taken on a bit of a limp. Her entire left side was now soaked in blood.

Sean and Daniel bolted upright at her arrival. Sean urged her on. She had maybe fifty yards to close until she would reach the locked door of the lab. But she wasn't alone. Behind her, she knew that feeling. It was with her again—with them— somewhere nearby. She could hear it trawling behind her. The look was in Sean's face. Kate refused to turn back. She kept her gaze locked on Sean's eyes, which were frightened and wide.

"RUUUUUNNNNN!" Sean screamed.

The muscles in her legs burned fiercely. She pushed harder, lungs gasping for air. Sean was coming out to meet her. She was closing in, fishing into her pocket for Fenton's key card. She snagged it, held it up high to let them know she had it. Her hands were slick from a mixture of blood and sweat and she almost lost her grip on it. Her knuckles were a blistering, bone white.

It was getting colder in the hospital. The HVAC had been off for a few hours now. Despite the cold halls, Kate was overheating. Her vision wavered. Sweat poured from the damp strings of hair, carved down her forehead, burned her eyes.

"C'mon, Kate, hurry!" Daniel cried.

Kate knew that if she didn't make it, it was going to be like leading lambs to the slaughter for Sean and Daniel. There was a realization that this might be their ending, after a string near misses, after everything they'd gone through.

There wasn't anywhere else for them to escape. They'd be cornered back in the morgue where it had gotten Dr. Lucas and where it had gotten Dr. Fenton. What had felt like miles to go suddenly turned to feet that turned to inches as she closed in. Her palm slammed Fenton's key card down on top of the badge reader by the door. The red light flipped to green. The large, locking door slid open and they tumbled inside.

Sean punched the Emergency Lockdown button along the inner wall. It sent the lab door crashing closed behind them. Kate turned, and through the momentary glimpse of light from the whooshing door, she saw the blur of the creature barreling toward them. It was crawling along the ceiling with the grace and speed of a scuttling spider. But now its left side was charred black. Each of its tentacles pulsed like strong, squeezing pistons.

The door was halfway closed when it leaped at them. One outstretched tentacle flittered inside the lab and landed on Daniel's shoulder. It alighted, tearing away a chunk of flesh with a spray of his hot, red blood. But the heavy door slammed shut and sliced through the tentacle, lopping off the fleshy, membranous muscle like a lost finger. It fell to the floor with sudden, jerking spasms.

Daniel was screaming. Sean and Kate fell on him, propping him up and stanching the bleeding with one of Daniel's own shirtsleeves that Sean tore from his ZARA button down. Daniel's shoulder was as raw, shiny, and red as a fresh-dipped candy apple.

"Go," Sean yelled to Kate. "I've got him."

Kate moved for the nearest research station. Outside the walls of Davol Lab, Kate could hear the creature's thundering, unrelenting booms. It was just beyond the inner walls, throwing itself against the door, again and again. With every impact, Kate jumped. But the door was holding. For now, anyway.

After one minute, two, three, the sounds died away. Kate grabbed a nearby propane torch, turned on the gas, and clicked the button for ignition. There was the familiar whoosh of the hot blue flame. It gave them a makeshift lantern. Light in the dark. The flame cast the laboratory in a flickering glow. It felt to Kate as if they were teenagers telling ghost stories in the woods.

"Okay, guys," Kate said. "Any ideas?"

"What's your gameplan?" Daniel asked through clenched teeth as Sean tied off the shirt sleeve tourniquet.

"My gameplan?"

"Yeah, I mean, you got us this far, right? Now what? Shall we play parchesi? Or just sing Kumbaya until we roast?"

She wanted so badly to hit him. To grab him and shake him and let him know just how wrong he was. With his smug exasperated smile. But it was at this moment that the repeating message came through over the PA system. Time was sand through a sieve. Kate breathed in for four, held for four, exhaled for four.

Daniel pulled the knot of the makeshift tourniquet on his shoulder tight with his teeth. Then he rose and slowly backed up until he was against the wall.

"How could you do it, Kate?" Daniel asked. His voice, usually so inauthentic, like processed cheese slices, gave way to an organic mixture of pain, rage, and terror. It came out in hoarse, raw venom.

"Daniel, stop it!" Sean called. "In ten minutes, it won't matter. The more time we bicker, the less we focus on getting free."

But Daniel wasn't done. "You know, I could have been a great fucking doctor. A good dad. You took all of it away from me. You realize that?"

Kate began sobbing. Through the tears, she managed to choke out: "I'm sorry. Please."

"I need to know why you did it!" he screamed. "Before we all die, I just need to know that one thing. Just tell me that one thing. One little thing. Why?"

The room filled with their heavy breathing. Kate turned to Sean. He looked away, sickened. The compassion he'd so often directed towards her seemed entirely sapped from him.

"Because I'm a shit person," Kate said. No more excuses. No more equivocation. It wasn't stress, and it wasn't bad dreams, and it wasn't a dead daddy. The real answer was simpler: she was rotten, from the inside out.

Sean approached Kate and caressed her shoulder tenderly with his warm, heavy hand. It felt good, but wrong at a time like this. Kate writhed free of him.

"You don't mean that," Sean said. "And it's not true."

"Now you want to psychoanalyze me. Shall we talk about my relationship with my mother?"

"I'm afraid we're out of time," Daniel joked, sarcastically. "We need to find a way out of here."

Kate went to the Davol Lab door and put her ear up to it. She couldn't hear anything on the other side, but it was impossible to see, and for all they knew, it was sitting tight and waiting to pounce as soon as they tried to leave the lab.

"If it's out there, we won't get by it."

"There's always a way," Sean said. "I mean, that's what we learn here every day, right?"

"Sean, I am definitely not in the mood for your goody-goody pick me up."

Sean ignored Daniel's protestations. "Just think. Kate, what is it at its core? No one is better at this analysis than you."

Kate closed her eyes like she did in all those hospital rooms for all those questions from Dr. Lucas. With her mentor, out on the floor, her confidence failed her. Now finding it mattered even more.

"Start with the basics," Sean said. "What do we know?"

"It's some bastardized version of the ascariasis parasite," Kate said. "But that's the easy part."

"Who knows more about little bugs than you?" Daniel added.

She was tired. It wasn't clicking. "Maybe I can read some goddamn flash cards, but that doesn't mean that I can stop some flesh-eating, comic book monster."

Sean passionately grabbed her by the shoulders and shook her. "How do we kill it, Kate?"

"I don't know!"

Daniel stepped forward. Now he, too, was toe-to-toe with Kate. They peered into each other's eyes in some sort of game for dominance before Daniel wound back and slapped Kate across the face. Hard. The sharp, gunshot-sounding crack exploded in the soft air. Kate fell back as Sean interjected.

"Whoa! No hitting."

Kate reached up and touched her stinging skin that now bloomed bright red. "I really don't know!" she screamed. "I'm sorry I got us into this mess. I don't know how many times I can say it. But I don't know what to do."

Daniel pushed by Sean and slapped Kate again, even harder this time. Sean threw Daniel to the floor.

"That is not helping, Daniel!" Sean bellowed, grabbing Daniel by the wrist with force just shy of grounding bone to dust.

Above them, the voice rang out: "Evacuation complete. Detonation in T-minus eleven minutes."

Kate glowered. Her sweaty skin was lightly blackened from soot and ash caused by the fire.

Sean suddenly bolted upright. "Come here," he said, gesturing for Kate to follow.

An idea. He led her to the other side of the lab and gestured for her to sit on one side of a long workbench. Sean dragged a stool to table's other side so they found themselves seated directly across from each other. He moved equipment out of their way, clearing an open workspace. With the propane torch between them, it was almost like they were sitting across from each other at Arturo's. God, what she would do to be back in time with Sean's arm slung over her shoulder and the worries of the world receding.

Sean held up a bare, flat hand miming the shape of a flash card. "Which parasite is this?"

Kate waved him away. "This is stupid."

Out of the corner of her eye, she saw Daniel watching her with bated breath from a pool of darkness at the edge of the room.

"It's not stupid," Sean said. "This stuff is like muscle memory. It never leaves. Close your eyes."

Kate did so. Her entire world went black. She focused, her senses heightening. She could hear the thrum of her own heartbeat, the static hiss of the band scanner over the PA system, the low, muffled sounds of the military forces mobilizing outside. Beneath her hands was the gritty, dust-covered workbench. Her fingers burned and bled from a thousand small cuts radiating like hot fire.

Kate felt her recall moving slower than before. The way an old car engine that's been sitting idle for too long takes a little extra to turn it over. Her eyes scanned the darkness beneath her eyelids as if caught in the throes of a vivid dream.

Then it came flooding back all at once—a bucket of water crashing over her head.

"Okay, so we know it's the ascariasis parasite." When she spoke, she did so carefully, like when trying to remember a dream immediately after waking.

"Hosts?" Sean asked.

Kate's fists clenched and unclenched. She was willing the thoughts to mind. An antenna picking up some alien radio station. "Rodents, small mammals, house pets, humans."

"Good. Location?"

"Western Hemisphere. North and South America."

"How is it transferred?"

"Transfer? Um, uh, larval eggs by feces, and, uh, through entering the mucous membrane or wound."

"Good. Good. And that's how Dr. Lucas got it. Keep going down the list. Symptoms?"

"With ascariasis, symptoms include fever, abdominal pain, shortness of breath, and vomiting."

She was connecting the dots to how crummy she was feeling at this very moment. Her neck still burned from where the needle had torn at it.

Kate opened her eyes. Sean was looking at her with respect and adoration. He needed her in a way he never had before.

"Treatment?" he asked.

Kate was silent. There was nothing there.

Sean pressed her. "Treatment?" he asked with greater emphasis.

"No universally accepted treatment." She felt her words bleeding the world dry. Hope was fleeing as the air seemed to be sucked out of the room, hopes dashed.

Sean turned and violently punched the wall. "Dammit!" he screamed.

"Evacuation complete. Detonation in T–minus nine minutes."

Kate leaped up from the table, a fire under her. "But!" she cried. "Recent experimental techniques have included submitting the host to chemotherapy to kill the parasite."

Kate felt the magnetic pull of her words on Sean and Daniel. She watched as they lifted their heads and looked back with a profound sense of amazement.

Sean turned back to Daniel. "Told you she was the best."

"Wow. So, chemotherapy?" Daniel asked sarcastically. "How do you expect we get that thing out there to volunteer to sit for an eight–hour chemo session?"

They all fell silent. Kate began to pace the length of the room. Ideas filtered through, one after the next, her giant Rolodex of research stored and maintained in the mainframe of her brain. She chewed on the inside of her cheek, narrowing her mind's focus. When she caught herself doing it, she thought of her mother, who was always biting the inside of her cheek. Then she thought of her father, the many chemo treatments he had endured. All for naught.

All at once, razor sharp, it came. Her eyes clocked the fire extinguisher on the far wall and she saw everything clearly. There was a plan.

"I've got it!" Kate yelled. "I need alkylating agents and antimetabolites."

"The hospital pharmacy has all of that stuff!" Daniel said. "Upstairs. First floor."

"And I need an air compressor," Kate added.

"Maintenance," Sean said. "One level lower. Sub-basement two."

"You mean there's actually something below us?" Daniel said.

Kate walked over to the fire extinguisher and lifted it off the bracket on the wall. The big, red meta canister was heavier than she'd imagined. It was cool against her skin. She tested its weight. *Yes, this will do nicely.*

"I think I can kill this thing," she said. "But I'll need your help."

★★★★★

Facing an unforgivable countdown to certain annihilation, they all agreed it would be best to take their chances and open the lab door. If the monster was there waiting for them, they would make a run for it, knowing they wouldn't all get through. If the doorway was clear, maybe they could just make it.

Kate released the emergency lock. Inhale two, three, four. The mechanical lock released the bolt. Hold two, three, four. The Davol lab door slid open. Exhale two, three, four. Quiet.

Luck was on their side. The biohazard door opened upon an empty corridor. They listened carefully but couldn't hear anything besides the soft murmur of activity from the soldiers outside. Kate looked upward. Behind the drop-ceiling tiles was the hospital's labyrinthine mechanical system. It could be anywhere now. They listened to the recorded message play once again over the PA: the dispassionate countdown, unrelenting.

"We've got to hurry," Kate said. "C'mon."

Kate led them from the front. She carried the heavy fire extinguisher while the two young men flanked behind her. She tiptoed cautiously through the corridor as emergency lights strobed.

They turned the corner. Sean crept closer to Kate. "Look, I know this isn't the right time," he said, "but we may not get another chance. I need to say that I'm sorry about Lien. It never should have happened."

"I think I've got you beat on the terrible, no good, monster of a human being index."

When Sean laughed at her snide remark, she smiled too. It was the lightest she'd felt in days. Daniel approached. He'd been keeping a few feet back. His features were alert. He was tracking something.

She asked, "What do you hear?"

Daniel was tuned to a frequency that neither Kate nor Sean could receive on their mental radios. Kate saw Daniel's eyes go wide, and then his mouth parted to scream: *"MOVE IT! NOW!"*

She watched Daniel sprint ahead of her. Sean wouldn't let her fall behind. He was pushing her from behind. They were three separate, simultaneous bolts of lightning launched from the sky. Kate was so tired, her neck and shoulders burned. They cleared the corner, and, suddenly, it was upon them. Through the wall, crashing right in front of them, tumbling like a car flipping over an embankment.

For a moment, Daniel stood paralyzed right before the creature. He was frozen in his fear, unable to move. It raised up on its back end, and now Kate could swear that it was over ten feet tall. The son of a bitch was still growing. Half of it seemed to be a mouth with fangs, something Professor Van Helsing would dispatch in a Victorian horror novel. It was preparing to strike. Long strands of its milky saliva fell on Daniel's face, carving trails of slime into his mouth.

Then Sean was behind Daniel, pulling at him, trying to get him to move. Kate helped, pulling at Daniel's hand, scratching his arms. Suddenly, Daniel was back in his body, in control of his limbs. Fight or flight kicked in. They reversed course and ran back down the hall from where they'd come.

The group charged around the corner, pounding their way through door after door, driving for the stairwell at the end of the corridor. They reached it and tumbled inside.

The creature was gaining on them. All three clambered through the hulking metal doorframe, slammed the double doors closed behind them, and bolted up the stairs. Moments later, there was the horrible crash of the splintering metal doorframe giving way, the crumbling sheetrock raining a cloud of drywall dust over them like the plume of some volcanic eruption.

The creature slammed its body against the door again and again until the door folded under its unyielding strength, crumbling like wads of wet newspaper.

This time, they didn't wait for it to catch up. They were almost back to the first floor, to the world of the living. Behind them, the creature's horrible sounds echoed through the dark and empty halls. Screeching, corroding metal. The beast's wet flesh on the cement stairs. It all layered together like an atonal symphony from hell's orchestra.

Kate was living the terrible nightmares she'd been suffering for weeks. They had materialized into reality. She had willed them into existence.

They reached the first-floor landing.

"In here!" Daniel cried.

He led Kate and Sean through the door. All three poured out, closing it behind them. Then everything was quiet.

Kate caught her breath and glanced around. In the darkness, she reached out with her hands and felt strong, industrial steel shelves before her that ran from floor to ceiling. On the shelves were thousands of plastic bottles. She picked one up. It shook like a baby's rattle. Daniel had led them to the hospital's pharmacy.

"Shhh," Sean said. "Don't lead it here."

"We're goddamn lucky," Kate said through gasps, "that no one locked the pharmacy gate when the evacuation order was given. If they had, our plan would be over before it had started."

Kate's shoulders were burning from carrying the fire extinguisher. She placed it down delicately on the register counter, and the three of them pulled down the security gate for some semblance of protection.

"I'm gonna grab the stuff!" Daniel said. Then he vanished into the back room, leaving Kate and Sean to listen to the sounds of him rustling through all the pill bottles, boxes, and liquid vials.

Kate and Sean collapsed in a heap on the floor behind the counter. For a long moment, they listened to the din of the military, interrupted only by the PA system's continual countdown.

Sean whispered, "I never told you about the recurring dream I been having lately."

"Can't we talk about it later?"

"No," Sean said, grabbing for her wrist. She didn't fight him. She liked the feeling of his hand on her agin.

"You always hated it when I told you about my dreams," she whined.

"Listen to me."

"Okay, okay. Go ahead."

"I'm standing on the deck of a big ship."

"In your dream?"

"Yes, when the hell else would I be on a big ship?"

"I don't know. I'm just asking."

"Anyway, I'm on this ship and I see you running by. I try to call out to you, but I can't speak. There's no sound. And you look so happy and you're running towards something, but I don't know what it is. And you loop around again and again, like a record skipping. I see how happy you are, but I know it's not from me and I want to reach you and grab you but-

"But what?" Kate asked. In all their time together, he'd never shared the details of his dreams before. It was touching. Her hand felt for his in the dark.

"Every time I wake up," Sean said, "I'm shivering. I reach out in bed hoping to feel the shape of you beside me. But there's nothing there but cold sheets."

It made Kate's heart sing to hear this. She pulled Sean in close for a tender hug. They were finally alone, and Kate figured this was the moment—that classic movie moment— where in the middle of a crisis, the two on-again, off-again lovers managed to resolve their problems, realize they faced more significant obstacles in this life, and make up with a big romantic kiss for the ages.

But the creature launched itself at the pharmacy gate with a deafening crash. The gate buckled under its sheer strength. Kate and Sean screamed in fright. The gate wasn't going to hold much longer. Again and again, its great, thick, ropey arms pulsated against the metal gate.

Kate reached for the fire extinguisher and approached the gate where those thin rods of metal were all that stood between her and it. Her hands reached blindly for the pull cord. She didn't dare remove her eyes from its gnashing teeth. One of its smaller tendrils wormed its way through a drop-box hole. It was coming nearer, sliding along the floor, about to rise over her leg.

Below its mouth hung the blood-red, tubular vestiges of its body. Kate squinted. *It couldn't be, could it?* The thing's body appeared to have small protuberances that pushed out from its sides. It almost looked like the screaming face of Fenton. Its very biology was a coagulated mixture of everything it consumed.

Sean caught Kate's attention. She watched as he grabbed the heavy, metal cash register from off the counter, lifting it high over his head—God, the thing must have weighed sixty pounds, at least; his arms shook. He brought it down with all his might and obliterated the slimy tendril into an oozing mess of viscera on the floor.

The monster bellowed. It attacked the pharmacy gate harder. The metal buckled, the bolts sang and the wall surrounding cracked.

Kate raised the fire extinguisher, the two–foot–long rubber hose aimed right at its mandibles. Her fingers pulled the pin, and she clamped down on the trigger. The surge was immediate. The giant, metal tank kicked like a shotgun, and a freezing, white foam gushed forth. The foam lathered the creature, which released its hold on the gate. It fell away. The room was now a cloud of opaque white mist. Kate didn't let off the handle, blasting the extinguisher until it had exhausted all its contents, sputtering to nothing.

"Kate, you alright?" Sean called out from somewhere nearby in the fog.

"Yup, right here," she said. Suddenly the tank was much lighter.

They found each other. He held her until the white cloud dissipated. When it was gone, they glanced out into the corridor. The coast was clear again. Kate set the tank down on the floor. It settled with a hollow, metal thud. The gauge read *Empty*. Then she unscrewed the sizeable, levered handle on the extinguisher and peeked inside of the empty, blackened canister.

Daniel returned with his arms full of stock bottles. "Now what?"

"Start crushing pills. Grab all the powder and chuck it in here."

They opened every bottle they could and started smashing chemo meds into pieces with any object they could find on the desk – ceramic coffee mug, calculator, needle nose pliers - until they had a pile that looked like a bowl of sifted baking flour—enough for a wedding cake.

They dumped it all into the empty cannister of the fire extinguisher. To this, Kate added two bottles of saline and mixed it up with a wooden ruler she found on the desk until she had batter.

Daniel felt the need to ask: "Kate, do you mind, uh, sharing your plan with us?"

"I set it on fire once. It hurt it, sure, but it didn't kill it. What if blowing this building halfway to hell isn't going to kill it either? It's on us. We must do the job."

Kate started screwing the top back on the extinguisher when Sean placed his hand on top of hers and looked her in the eyes. "What if this doesn't work?"

The PA system chimed in overhead, re-emphasizing the sand was draining from the hourglass.

Kate broke into a smirk. "Well, then, we won't have to worry about it for long, will we?"

Chapter Eighteen
OUT

The maze of St. Christopher's was becoming second nature to them as Kate, Sean, and Daniel rushed down the maintenance stairwell into the deepest bowels of the hospital. Not one of them had ever stepped foot in sublevel two. It was almost mythical—a place where the mole people dwelled. There were only two departments that inhabited the lowest level of the hospital: laundry and maintenance.

Being so far underground, they were guided only by the emergency lights that marked every twenty or thirty feet along the ceiling. The walls were flat, grey concrete, a tomb. Around them, a topiary zoo of industrial-sized equipment: boilers, oil tanks, large, antiquated machinery. A long row of massive water heaters fanned out along the left wall.

Knowing not to strafe too far from one another, they ventured out across this unmapped terrain, searching.

"Remind me: what are we looking for?" Daniel asked.

"An air compressor. A big engine with a hose and nozzle connected to it." Kate said.

They craned high and low, searching amongst the shelves of supplies. Even on emergency power, with so much of the hospital on an as-needed basis, these ancient machines pulsed and pounded and kept up their duty as the circulatory system of St. Christopher's.

They passed fossils of a bygone era and came upon a gigantic, black, iron basin in the center of the room. It emitted no sound. A sleeping dragon.

"What is this?" Daniel asked.

"Must be the old, coal-fired furnace. It's probably been out of commission for forty years, at least." Sean said.

Stacked steam pipes that would have thrust up into the floors above had been severed with jagged cuts and now led nowhere. A large chute, its door rusted shut, flanked the right wall. Beneath the door, a fenced-in basin large enough to park a car was held over from the days when massive piles of coal were required to feed it. Anything left over from those early days was dyed black with coal dust.

The warning from the PA blared again.

"Let's pick up the pace, people," Kate called out.

There was a sound of scraping metal as Daniel moved crates of tools around in a back corner in the dark.

"Kate, here! I think I found it!" he called.

They congregated beside a tall, metal cylinder covered with hazardous warning labels. Fixed atop were a regulator and nozzle, and from the nozzle descended a long, rubber hose which looped on the floor like a snake.

Kate fished it off the ground and then cranked the pressure dial on the tank. Immediately, they could all hear the *sissssssss* of air flowing through the hose. Kate's hand closed around the nozzle. She squeezed it tight, and a strong gust of wind blasted out.

"Yup. This is exactly right. Hurry. Get the extinguisher ready."

"Finally," Daniel said. "Something goes our way."

Sean laid out the fire extinguisher that had been filled with a variety of strong medication. Kate jammed the nozzle of the air compressor into the female end of the extinguisher, and her hand laid on the lever. Slowly, the gauge on the extinguisher's readout began to climb. Higher and higher, a race car in the red. They were waiting for the needle to hit the charged indicator line at 690 kPa.

Sean and Daniel found their positions at the heavy, rectangular door that ran off the smaller end of the large furnace. Smokestacks of metal piping vented from the machine directly through the cement walls to the outside. The door had a large, red warning sign. Beneath it in big, black, block letters read: *INCINERATOR*. They could feel the heat dispersing from the furnace ten feet away from the door. It was like standing on the sun.

"Evacuation complete. Detonation in T-minus seven minutes."

Always curious about the firepower at the heart of the hospital, Sean found an oil-slicked, industrial work glove sitting atop a nearby crate of supplies and opened the incinerator door just a crack. Within raged molten, orange fire. He put his hand up to shield his face from the heat. Bright ambiance rushed out into the room.

Sean started to shut the door, but Daniel called out, "Not yet. One second."

"Hurry up. It's crazy hot."

Daniel returned with a three-foot section of a two-by-four from a pile of debris. It still had nails sticking out of it in places. He removed the rest of his torn-up ZARA button down shirt, leaving his undershirt on, and wrapped it around the end of the wooden post. His undershirt was covered in blood where his shoulder had been attacked, but he was no longer bleeding out.

To their right, a drum of spent oil lumbered a few feet over. Daniel dipped the end of the shirt into it. Then he walked back to the furnace and edged closer to the fire. As soon as the board crossed the gate's threshold, it ignited. He pulled it back.

Sean slammed the furnace door closed, chucked away the glove, wiping sweat from his forehead.

In the glow of the flame, Sean's eyes were dark and piercing embers. "Where'd you learn to do that?"

"Ever watch that show *Lost*?" Daniel asked. "All they ever did was wander around, make torches, and run away from weird-looking sci-fi monsters."

"If we ever get out of here, remind me *not* to add it to my Netflix queue."

"Deal," Daniel said.

Kate watched the extinguisher come to pressure. The line hit the appropriate mark; it had recharged. The familiar heft of the filled tank returned.

"Perfect," Kate said. "Now get me that length of hose."

Daniel shut off the air valve for the air compressor tank before unscrewing the hose connected to it. He handed it off to Kate, who then replaced the scrawny, two-foot length of tubing on her fire extinguisher with the one from the air compressor.

"How long is it?" Kate asked.

"Not sure. Twenty feet, maybe?"

"It'll have to do."

"Evacuation complete. Detonation in T-minus four minutes."

"Think we'll find it in time?" Sean asked.

Daniel led the small group with the torch while Kate and Sean each shouldered half of the load of the extinguisher. The torch threw rich, radiant light onto the walls, and as the fire danced, it compressed and elongated their shadows around them. The stick crackled as the oil burned off.

They headed from the rear of the basement to the stairwell. Along the way, they had to squeeze between the cold stone wall and the old coal furnace. As they moved through the small space, a quick puff of air licked the fire of their torch and almost extinguished it.

"Guys, hold on a sec," Sean said.

"What is it? What's going on?" Kate asked.

"Give me that." Sean was asking Daniel for the torch. Daniel gave it to him.

Sean brought it right up against the wall. In the light of the flame, it was clearer. The old stone blocks had a large, black crack running between them. Kate held her hand to the break and she could feel air rushing between her fingers. The torch flickered again.

Kate said. "How is that possible?"

"So what?" Daniel asked.

Sean glanced around, drawing the torch over the contents of the basement. Not too far away was an old, dented, aluminum garbage can. The can was filled with an assortment of shovels and rakes and brooms collected over time. Sean handed the torch to Kate, ran over, and grabbed a shovel and a pickaxe and returned to them. He handed the shovel to Daniel, who now looked at him suspiciously.

Crack! Sean brought the pickaxe down with powerful blasts directly into the wall. With the first strike, chunks of hardened mortar crumbled, elongating the black sliver of nothingness between the stones. More air rushed out.

"What do you think you're going to accomplish with this?" Daniel asked.

"I'm not ready to give in."

Daniel wheezed from the debris that had fallen from Sean's strikes. "We're two stories below ground. And this place is going to blow any minute!"

Beneath their feet, the ground began to vibrate. On the wall above them, a towering shadow emerged. Black, inky arms moving in serpentine arcs.

"Shit," Sean said. "I think it found us."

It was on them before they could turn around. Twelve feet tall now, cramped by the ceiling above. Eight tentacles protruded from its scabbed, insectoid body. They struck out with the ferocity of venomous snakes, aiming for Daniel and Sean. Kate ducked behind the old coal furnace out of view. She stopped for a moment, on the verge of throwing up. Her head was about to split open from within. Her heart galloped. Now was not the time to chicken out.

She swallowed hard and inched her way, step by step, rounding the back of the furnace. She could see the muscular back of the disgusting creature on the other side of the old machinery. Gingerly, she placed the extinguisher down so as not to make a sound. The creature was maybe seven or eight feet away. But to get to it, she had to round the old coal-fired boiler. She had maybe twenty feet of hose in her hands. The math was tight. *Close enough.*

"Hey, you ugly bitch!" Kate screamed.

Kate launched from behind the iron behemoth. The creature spun around, its body distorted, oozing. She saw a talon growing from its back, mid-mutation. In one swift movement, one of the tentacles wrapped itself around Kate's body like a python and pull Kate toward its gnashing, mewling mouth. Her body left the ground.

Sean screamed, "Kate! No!"

The creature lifted her high, prepared to bring her in. Its jaws open wide. Tendrils of black and yellow venom dripped from its mouth.

A second tentacle was around her now, running up her shirt, between her breasts. The soft, cotton blend lifting as it passed. It was shredding her skin apart as it wormed its way across her. The tentacle wrapped itself around her neck and began to squeeze. Kate felt blood pooling in her face. Her vision tunneled. She gasped for air, but nothing was coming in.

At that moment, Kate felt as if she were drowning. But in the beast's clutches, she was no longer afraid of dying. She was only terrified of missing her one chance and of letting Sean down. *Just give me one goddamn shot.*

Gasping for breath, she opened her mouth. A third tentacle fixed to enter her just like it did to Dr. Lucas.

Beneath the din of the battle, Kate's gurgle, the monster's cries, the screams of Daniel and Sean, there was one solitary, dispassionate voice ringing out over the speaker system: "Evacuation complete. Detonation in T-minus five minutes."

The creature was toying with her as it pulled her closer. She started to gag. Unable to breathe, she thrashed. Her vision was replaced with gray kaleidoscopic shapes.

With all of her might she looked down at Sean below. Sean had tears in his eyes. Daniel's mouth was agape. Sean then ran toward the beast, punching and kicking it relentlessly. Kate watched them ten feet below, and she wanted to cry out to get them to run. But she couldn't make the sounds come out of her bruised larynx.

Daniel picked up the nearby pickaxe and began slicing at the beast with long, swooping heaves. He struck hard, again and again. His blows splashed up pools of black and yellow slime as he penetrated its studded, membranous skin. Sean found the discarded shovel and began hacking away as well. The two men were on a chain gang, heads down, breaking rocks. The creature riled and roared.

For a moment, Kate felt the pressure ease up on her throat. There was enough of a let up so that she could inhale again. Dank, stale air bled into her lungs. Her vision swam back into focus. She watched as the creature swung in angry loping arcs at Sean and Daniel. Finally, it connected, and one particularly muscular swipe sent both men sailing across the room. Daniel knocked his head on the coal furnace. When his body hit the ground, he was already unconscious. Kate thought for a second, he might be dead.

The creature turned its speckled, dripping face back toward her. She was but inches from its mouth. She could smell its putrid breath fueled of dead flesh and bile. With her last ounce of strength, she took the nozzle end of the black hose that she'd somehow managed to hang on to and jammed it deep into the creature's vaginal throat.

"Suck on this!" Kate gasped.

It screeched. The nozzle sliced a gash within the soft flesh of its neck. Kate rammed hard on the length of tubing, ferreting it in farther and farther, like threading conduit behind drywall. The thing's wound secreted a disgusting ooze, but Kate continued to force more and more length of hose deeper inside until she felt it clear the thick, ruddy walls of its flesh and the resistance backed off.

"Sean, now!"

He was just getting to his feet and dizzily made his way back to the coal furnace. She prayed that he'd know what to do. The creature turned and went for him. It brought a long tentacle down hard, but Sean dove out of its way, landing right by the fire extinguisher. His hand clamped the lever, and he threw all his weight onto the release valve. Then came the sound of thunder.

All at once, the force of the extinguisher's pressure erupted. The chemical cocktail exploded like a supernova from the length of hose into the creature's writhing body. The long, serpentine arms that held Kate high into the air immediately released. She dropped back to the stone floor like a rag doll.

It felt to her that time had slowed. And then Sean was there at the bottom to help break her fall. It wasn't a clean catch, though, and she clattered, hard, grabbing at her neck, gasping for air, panting.

Slowly, Kate came to her feet. A few feet away, Daniel was waking, groaning. Sean ran over to the extinguisher and kicked it. It rattled onto its side, a large, metallic ping indicating that its tank was depleted. Every ounce of the chemo mixture flooded the beast. The three of them found each other and watched.

The death blow had been dealt. The dying creature struck about wildly and then collapsed with great force into the giant, coal-fired furnace. The impact toppled the iron dinosaur in one extravagant blow. A blinding plume of gray smoke clouded the room. Everything fell quiet. The effect of the silence was deafening. The monster was down, tangled among fiery, twisted metal. Yellow foam oozed forth from porous holes.

Then the silence was cut with the static from the ceiling. "Evacuation complete. Detonation in T-minus three minutes."

When the coal dust settled, Kate was struck with the most beautiful sight she had ever seen. That thing, that disgusting, monstrous beast, had fallen in such a way that it had knocked the iron furnace through the stone wall where Sean had been hacking away.

Now, there was a large chasm of open blackness where ancient rock once stood. It was clear they were standing at the mouth of some kind of tunnel. Cool air was circulating. It lapped at Kate's face with the promise of freedom.

"Kate! My god. Are you alright?" Sean screamed.

She turned to him, still half in a daze. Then she smiled and nodded. There wasn't time for anything else. They clamored toward the hole in the rock. The tunnel was something from another era, braced with wooden beams every few feet like an old mining shaft.

Daniel tentatively approached and stepped on the tail of the creature. Its springy flesh squished between the soles of his shoes. Then he was on the other side.

"I guess we have to try," Daniel said.

"Are we sure it's dead?" Kate asked.

Sean grabbed for the nearby shovel, lifted it high over his head, and brought it down onto the creature's body in one last, spiteful blow. The metal blade folded into its flesh and was swallowed up to the neck of the wooden handle. The beast didn't move.

Daniel wiped the sweat from his brow and stared off into the darkened cavern. "What the hell is this place?"

A revelatory smile crept across Kate's face. "Well, I'll be damned," she said.

"What is it, Kate?" Sean asked.

She couldn't believe it. It was just like that stupid show on the television in Parker's room. God, that felt like a lifetime ago.

"I think it's one the tunnels that fed Boston's first sewer system."

The three of them stepped through the hole in the wall and into the black, cavernous void. They shared a quick group hug. The embrace felt good even though they stunk of rancid death. But that was not enough. The computerized voice rang out another warning. Time was unrelenting.

"Come on!" Sean yelled.

He jogged ten feet forward into the darkness. His footsteps splashed through a pool of stagnant water. "Let's go home."

Kate knew they had all been through hell, but it wasn't over yet. Battered and bruised, she collected the torch off the ground. Miraculously, it was still burning.

*****

Sean led them through the darkness. Kate could still feel this thing inside of her, growing, incubating. Each breath burned. It hurt in every conceivable way, this pregnancy from rape, compressed into a gestation window of only a few hours.

She was happy to lean on Sean to lead them out. It was impossible to see so far below the Earth aside from the dim light cast from their dying torch.

"Come on, guys," Sean said.

He was trying to rally them. Kate guessed they were just about to clear the perimeter walls of St. Christopher's above. There seemed to be no end inside this tunnel.

"Where will this take us?" Daniel asked.

"Anywhere but here," Kate said.

"She's right," Sean added. "Just keep moving."

They picked up the pace. No matter how hard she strained, Kate could no longer hear the computerized countdown. Strangely, it had the opposite effect, unsettling her more. Since it was impossible to keep track of time, minutes felt like hours, and she expected the place to blow any moment.

The torch died out. Daniel cast it off behind them, where it bounced off the concrete walls and clattered onto the wet ground beneath. The tunnel was pitch black now. They moved like a train, Kate leaning on Sean, Daniel pushing from behind. Here, underground, the only sounds were the ones they made as they moved.

Together, they rounded a corner, passed through a slow bend. Sean's arm was outstretched, feeling the nothingness that meant another step forward. Without any light, they'd slowed to a crawl, feeling the bend of the tunnel by hand. Kate stumbled over an upturned rock, rolled her ankle, and fell to her knees.

"Gah!" she wailed.

Sean groped in the dark. His hand fell upon her stringy hair. What she wouldn't give for a bath. He got a hand under the crook of her arm and guided her to her feet. She relied on his strength as her legs struggled to find balance. Shooting pain roiled her bad ankle when she attempted to put weight on it.

"What happened?" Daniel asked.

"I fell. I can't walk."

"We must keep moving. Here—"

Sean put Kate's arm around his shoulder to act as a crutch. They loped forward. Their footfalls splashed in the wet, cavernous sewers until ahead of them they spotted small holes of light above. Stars in an obsidian sky. They'd stumbled upon a ladder built of iron rungs in the stone wall. The light above was from a manhole cover. Sean wasted no time and grabbed the rungs, one at a time, until he was at the top.

Kate collapsed to a crouch. She watched as Sean pushed, his corded neck and shoulders lifted the cover. She closed her eyes and thought of him stitching her up a few years back. That flutter of excitement. The world had a way bringing such joy.

She watched Sean climb out, glance around as his eyes adjusted. He inhaled deeply. Satisfied, he turned around and reached his arms back into the black hole. Daniel pulled Kate up from the muddy sewer floor and guided her to the ladder. With each step up, she ached but pulled herself higher and higher. Heavenly ascension. Sean reached down and pulled Kate up with blackened, oily hands.

When Kate cleared the surface, she collapsed on fresh grass and started to heave. Then Sean helped Daniel out. When Daniel emerged, he was crying, and joined Kate on the field. They rolled in the long, cold blades of wet grass. She inhaled the earthy aroma, and the release was altogether cosmic. Their breath came out of them in silver plumes. When they caught the exhausted expressions on one another's faces, they burst out laughing.

"I can't believe it," Sean said through large gulps of air. "I just can't believe we made it out."

Kate knew what she had to do. Her arms were around Sean's neck. He could barely stand up himself, but he wouldn't admit weakness in front of her. He kissed her long and hard on the mouth. Sean's kiss in the fresh air made her feel magnanimous, new, even though her insides were being torn apart. Her breathing shuddered. Her muscles trembled.

The underground tunnel had led them out and away from St. Christopher's. In the distance, the gun metal sky connected with the long shafts of white searchlights. The lights were a signal for the bombers to find their target.

From this knoll, St. Christopher's hospital was but a doll's house. Here, the sounds of nature rose above the cacophony of war.

Kate watched the hospital. Her home for everything good and bad these formative years. The lot was empty now. Everyone had been pushed back. Long poles erected from the tops of large white trucks aimed satellite dishes into the heavens. All the major news networks had parked just past the barricade along Chalkstone Ave.

They watched the helicopters take flight and the soldiers clear the area. Around them, chirruping crickets, and the soft hush of the gentle wind.

Kate, Sean, and Daniel had exited hell through an iron sewer cap. Now, Kate backed away from Sean and toward the manhole. The slow-burning light of the new day was sparking on the horizon. Kate was so happy to get to see one more sunrise. She looked at Daniel in the grass. Dirt and dried blood had caked on his cheeks and chin. His sweaty hair was swept back.

"Don't do it, Kate," he said. "We can figure something out. We made it this far already."

Sean was reaching for her, the muscles of his arms glistening. But she pushed his hands away. Now she was grimacing in pain. She couldn't hide it from them any longer.

"Are you crazy?" Daniel yelled.

She had tears in her eyes. It was hard to speak. "I can't go," she mumbled.

"What?" he said.

"I can't go with you."

"Why not?" There was only confusion. He still hadn't done the simple arithmetic to deduce what she was trying to say.

"I'm infected," she said.

It came out with a finality that was like the iron lid settling into place over the manhole they had just crawled from. Closing it up with her inside was precisely what needed to occur right now.

Sean wasn't giving up. "We'll fix you," he said. "We've seen what kills it. We'll find a way. Everything'll be okay. Remember our toast? We are the most badass doctors around!" He said this through tears.

She was in agony. She knew what needed to be done, and she had to remain steadfast in the face of their genuine compassion. If she had to go, it was good to go knowing you were loved.

"It has to be this way," she said.

She started descending back into the depths. Step by step, she receded down the ladder into the tunnel below.

Golden rays of sun disappeared as she descended, and she joined darkness once again. When her feet touched the bottom, she winced on her bad ankle. Then, she looked back up at the early-morning sky. Speckled stars studded the canvas of deep purple.

Sean leaned in from above. "Then I'm coming with you."

He placed one foot over the rim of the manhole cover, but she raced up the ladder to block his descent and started wailing on his legs as they dangled over the edge. He cried out and pulled himself back up and turned to peer back down.

She was hanging from the ladder just a few inches below the surface. Her eyes had gone glassy. She was about to lose consciousness.

"Are you sure?" he asked.

Kate nodded. "Seal it. Now."

He choked back the emotion and started to claw at the iron manhole. But he was too tired and too afraid to move it more than a few centimeters. "Daniel," he called out, "help me."

Kate watched from below as Daniel joined Sean. Together, with their hands clasped around the giant, iron disc, they pushed with all their might. The lid scraped in a low, jagged squeal over the rim of the manhole. It was like the dawning of an eclipse.

"Hurry up!" Kate screamed. "Do it now!"

"I love you, Kate White," Sean said.

Kate smiled. She still would've married him in a heartbeat. And she wanted to think—maybe it was wishful thinking, but who cared—he would have wanted to marry her this time too. With a final push, Sean and Daniel fit the heavy lid back in place, sealing Kate in a tomb of darkness.

★★★★★

She was straddling the ladder several feet off the ground when a sudden thrust of blindingly sharp pain seized her. She folded in half, and her hands opened. Her body crashed back to the slick, wet floor beneath. She whacked her head, hard, and bit down on her tongue. This began her seizure.

Overhead, faintly, she heard one of the last things she would ever understand: the rush of jet planes sweeping by.

They roared past with such energy the ground vibrated under her. Through the holes in the grating above, they appeared to her as shooting stars crossing the sky.

There was a big boom. So much of this day had turned out like the movies, but this, the big-bang finish, it was nothing like that. An explosion filled the sky. A giant fireball lapped at the heavens, and then, as quick as it had come, the light died over the horizon line, and the sounds of nature supplanted the world.

When the hospital was destroyed, it barely registered. The blinding pain began as she writhed in a shallow pool of stagnant water, sucking diseased air into her lungs. She lifted her shirt up a few inches and placed a hand on her abdomen. She could *feel* it in there. The tentacles inside of her were pushing at her skin. The sound of the explosion happened first. It rocked her where she lay so hard that she left the ground for a moment. Then there was a soft hiss, like a babbling brook, but it grew louder and louder, more aggressive, as it neared. It was the incoming fire.

Kate White smiled and closed her eyes as the flames engulfed her in the heat of a thousand suns.

★★★★★

BOSTON HERALD

Mysterious Sickness Spreading—City Count Grows By 12 Overnight

Jan. 4, 2022

Over the past 24 hours, 12 more cases of what the media has been calling "the Boston plague" have been confirmed in the metro area, raising the outbreak total to 734, including 512 deaths. Officials are still tracking suspected cases of the viral illness.

According to the most recent reports from the Centers for Disease Control and Prevention's multifaceted, epidemiological response committee, cases in the past few days have continued to spread outside of the Boston metro area as well despite austere lockdowns. In the past week, single-case counts have been confirmed, followed quickly by deaths of the infected, in Seattle, Dallas, and Miami.

The uptick in Boston cases was confirmed during a weekend of unrest throughout the outbreak region, where protestors of the city's lockdown mandates clashed with local police and CDC officials who were attempting to perform building decontamination in affected sites.

In the latest update from the World Health Organization's Western regional office, WHO says the new "hot spot" status of Boston is highly concerning and that if lockdowns do not immediately halt the spread of the contagion, intensification of the surge of infection in the greater US population is imminent.

Transmission rates have fluctuated in the past three weeks, with an increasing trend seen in the last half of December, WHO said. Officials note they are cautiously optimistic regarding the development of highly experimental treatment options, which they hope to be submitted for phase-one trials shortly.

Gary Gamache, staff writer

Epilogue

The weather was warming. Sean Carraway could feel it when he left work that afternoon and had to pull off his button-down to strip to an undershirt. Phoenix heat was overwhelming, even now in mid-March. Only six months back he was running for his life in a frigid Boston hospital. Now he was inadvertently working on his tan.

He piled into his Acura TLX. Everyone in Phoenix drove everywhere. It was typically too hot, and everything was spaced too far. Two days after landing, he'd gone searching for used cars. Just something to get by. When he found his Acura, dirt cheap in a want ad, he'd fallen in love. The car was a rental, had over 140,000 miles on it. Like him, the car had a previous life too.

Sean blasted the radio and sped off down the highway. The car purred when he took it up to about eighty-five. He couldn't drive like this back in Boston. Every fifty feet in the city was a red light. Seeing the world speed behind him filled him with calm. Standing still, now that was hard.

He hated his new boss. Hell, he hated his new job. But it sure as shit was better than nothing. After the day they'd climbed out of the sewer, Sean vowed that he would never set foot inside a hospital again. He left the old life behind. He'd heard that Daniel went to Chicago, working as an ER doc at Cook County. Sean sent him a Christmas card, hadn't even bothered to sign it. Just the default message: *Happy holidays.* That stuff had always been Kate's domain.

The holidays were painful without her and without Lien and without the hospital. It was easier just to cut ties. He hadn't spoken to anyone from his former life in a while now. Things were easier that way.

It was a shitty gig, selling life insurance over the phone, when he'd been a surgeon just a few months before. But slinging indemnity plans was the furthest thing from the old life. Between calls, his supervisor, Max, let him flip through magazines. Max was twenty-two, a face riddled in pimples, and his freshly minted online college degree printed and framed on his cubicle desk.

The job was escapist. A total bore. Essential workers, his ass. And he needed that right now. Maybe not forever, but definitely right now. Sean had gotten a subscription to the Harvard Business Review. He'd lend them out Max for brownie points. In turn, Max handed him the best shifts. Sean figured maybe he'd go and get his MBA. Maybe start a business somewhere. He liked the idea of being his own boss. Then again, other days, he felt like that just wasn't in the cards for him and that he'd work here the rest of his life. Or until the sickness caught up with him.

The Acura turned left on the interstate. A wide expanse of flat, sand-filled horizon unfurled into the distance. He was approaching the turnoff to his street, the neighborhood in view. When home, Sean inhabited a condominium complex that seemed to be full of clones of himself: late-twentysomething single men. They had all moved to Phoenix for the work. Labor was cheap, but so was the cost of living, so it all worked out in the end. Probably wouldn't be that way forever, he reasoned. More and more people were migrating from the East Coast every day. It was a new gold rush. But Sean kept driving.

He was hungry and didn't want to go home just yet, so he pulled into the parking lot of the Denny's down the road. There wasn't too much commercial development in his neighborhood. Looking around, all he saw was empty, barren dessert. He had lost fourteen pounds over the past six months. Most of it seemed to sweat right off. He hardly recognized himself when he looked in the mirror.

A Grand Slam and a Coke sounded like it'd really hit the spot, so that was what he ordered from the perky waitress with the stained jersey shirt. She looked a little like that actress Florence Pugh, and that made him smile. The television over the breakfast counter was tuned to one of those twenty-four-hour conservative news networks. Seemed like everyone out here in the dessert polluted themselves with that shit. Maybe it was the sun. Six months in, and they were still talking about St. Christopher's. About the Boston Flu. There were more and more infections every day. Entire towns in quarantine. The East Coast had been ravaged. The ticker on the screen said the total dead was somewhere north of 440,000 and climbing. Hell, people coming to Phoenix for work? Shit, they were coming to Phoenix to outrace death.

The news never mentioned the monsters though. Those in charge found a way to keep that out of the mainstream.

"Can we change the channel, please?" Sean asked the waitress.

The restaurant had just started to fill for the dinnertime rush. A fat man two seats down glanced over at him but didn't say a word. His face smothered in cheeseburger grease. The perky waitress looked up at the screen and then back to him.

"Honey, every channel is talkin' about it."

"Then can you turn it off?"

She did. None of the other patrons questioned Sean. They just went back to their breakfast-for-dinner specials. His food came, he inhaled it. The waitress brought his check. She even signed it with one of those hand-drawn smiley faces. He went digging for his wallet.

"Sean Carraway? That you?"

Sean turned as a young man took the seat right beside him. An instinctive double take as he realized he knew the man. It was Daniel.

Daniel was as lithe and fit as ever. He put his keys on the counter, swept the hair back from his eyes. It had grown out over the past few months but was still perfectly coifed. Sean was struck by how different Daniel seemed. It was in his look and in his posture. Or was it just the march of time? The effects of separation? Something about Daniel was more relaxed, less uptight. He carried a dog-eared magazine under his arm and when he laid it on the counter, Sean could see it was a copy of Writer's Digest.

"Daniel? My god. What's up?" Sean asked awkwardly.

Sean didn't know what else to say. He could only look back with a slightly goofy grin. For so long, he'd thought he wanted to never see anyone from his St. Christopher's days again. But it felt good, surprisingly, to be seated beside the one person who'd gone through it with him. The only one still alive, anyway.

"How've you been?" Daniel asked.

"Alright. You?" How does someone make small talk after going through what they went through? "Listen to us. It's like a high school reunion. Not sure what to say."

Daniel laughed politely. "Eh, you know. Every day is just filled with more and more cases of the sickness."

That's what some of them called it. The sickness. The Boston Flu. Whatever. Sean couldn't believe it. In the twenty-first century, man now capable of space travel, iPods, complex derivatives but we still had settled on calling it The Sickness.

"Any luck?" Sean asked. "Or are we just prolonging the inevitable?"

"Some," he said. "There's exciting stuff happening with mRNA vaccines. I'm sure that's the last thing you wanna talk about." Daniel's tone lightened. "What're you up to these days?"

"Nothing fancy," Sean said. "I get up, drive to work. Come home. Go to bed. Lather, rinse, repeat."

Daniel chuckled. "What is it you do now?"

He waved Daniel away. "Oh, you definitely didn't come all the way out here to hear about that."

"It couldn't be that bad."

"I sell insurance," Sean said.

"Insurance? What kind?"

"Car. Boat. Life. All kinds. Why, you need some? I don't think the actuarial tables have caught up to the fact that we're all going to be dead in a few weeks."

Daniel laughed and opened his magazine. Tucked inside one of the pages was a folded scrap of paper. He slapped it down on the counter and slid it over to Sean. Sean's own fingers were ragged at the nails. He'd been biting them. He pulled the paper back quickly in the hopes that Daniel wouldn't notice.

Sean held an envelope, the long top edge jagged where it had been torn open. It clicked after he turned it over. It was the envelope he'd used to mail Daniel's Christmas card. The Frosty the Snowman stamp was affixed to the corner. In the other was his handwritten return address.

"I saved it," Daniel said. "So, I could find you."

"You flew halfway across the country just to grab a plate of eggs at a Phoenix chain restaurant?"

"Nah, I stopped at your place, but you weren't there. So, I figured I'd grab a bite before heading trying again."

"Where are you staying?"

"The Radisson. The one by the airport. Nothing fancy."

"I'd offer you a place to stay, but I don't really have…"

He was interrupted when Daniel held up his hand. "Don't worry. I'm not fishin' for a place."

Sean looked down at the magazine. "What's that?" he asked.

Daniel met Sean's gaze. His once bright-green eyes now seemed gray, aged, the light having been turned down. His face held a stoic sadness in all the cracks and lines. That was new. Sean remembered Daniel always seeming so boyish.

Daniel thumbed through the pages of the magazine. The soft paper fluttered. He was dancing around something, Sean could tell.

"Know any place we can talk?"

★★★★★

The terrain was so flat in this part of the country. Sean could see through the rear-view mirror for a dozen miles back. He supposed it didn't make any sense to Daniel why he'd tucked himself away into this little corner of the world. But Sean knew why. It was where he came from. There was something really satisfying living in a place where nothing could sneak up on you.

Living out west had changed him. He felt it. He wasn't the same on-the-go man he used to be in Boston. He drove fast, but never anywhere important.

Daniel was struggling to keep up with him, though it was just half a mile back to Sean's place. Sean pulled into his spot. It was marked on the black asphalt with his condo number. As Daniel pulled in a minute later, Sean directed him to the row marked VISITORS. They'd given Daniel a big black BMW at the rental counter. He may be older and sadder, but deep down he was still Daniel. The two old friends stood at Sean's door for a while. Sean was nervous.

"You know," Sean said, "you're the first person I've ever had over."

It was almost like a first date. He hadn't expected anyone and tried to remember if he had left the place decent. It didn't matter.

"Takes a lot of work breaking into your house, huh?" Daniel quipped.

Sean realized that Daniel was calling him out for having installed four different dead bolts with four different keys to get into his unit. He'd had them installed by a contractor soon after moving in.

"You should've heard the voice mail I got from the property manager after she saw it. I told her, 'It's my condo. I own this door.' She said, 'Yeah, but it makes it harder for me to sell units when folks think we're living in a dangerous neighborhood.'"

"I have trouble on my own too. Every noise in the middle of the night is one of those things."

Finally, Sean got the door open and let Daniel in.

There wasn't much to the place. Blink and you missed the tour. Having someone over, it forced him to look through fresh eyes. He saw gaps between the molding and the wall that he had never noticed before. The wall plate for the light switch sat slightly crooked. Grime ringed the sink drain.

The unit was a one bedroom. A tiny thing. Sean had a two-seater couch in the living room but no television. The only thing on these days was the news anyway. In the kitchen, there was an empty fridge and a small, chipped table with two spindle-backed chairs. Sean noticed that Daniel deliberately didn't glance into his bedroom. The look on his face was suddenly one of pity.

"Let me grab us something to drink," Sean said.

A few moments later, he came back from the kitchen with two glasses of tap water and sat beside Daniel on the couch.

Daniel took his glass and gulped it down.

"Sorry," he said, wiping a stray drop from his lips. "I haven't had anything to drink since boarding back in Boston."

Sean hadn't realized that Daniel didn't stop to eat back at the diner. He found Sean and then, suddenly, here they were.

"What'd you wanna talk about?" Sean asked.

"It's weird to say. I'm actually kind of out here on business."

"Oh yeah? What kind?"

"I've been thinking about writing a book," Daniel said. He had trouble looking Sean in the eye when he said it. It felt like he was confessing a dark secret.

"A book?" Sean asked.

There was a lump in his throat. The things he tried so hard to forget were scratching at the windows in his brain. Daniel's DNA was built on STEM and Zara catalogs. Him writing a book was like a dog reciting Shakespeare. It could only be about one thing, Sean knew.

"About what happened?" Sean asked.

Daniel nodded. "I'm sure you realize there's been a lot of people asking about what it was like that day. At first, I didn't want to even think about it, but then the person I was seeing suggested it might be helpful to put some thoughts down on paper. Purge some demons, so to speak."

"You talked to someone? A therapist?"

"Yeah, I did." Daniel was deadly serious.

"Did it help?"

"No. Not at first, anyway. I didn't think so. But the more I went, I found the better I slept."

"And this therapist suggested that you should profit off tragedy by telling all the juicy details?" Sean snapped back.

Daniel didn't look offended even though Sean had said it to deliberately piss him off. "I expected that. That's why I'm here."

"You want my permission to write about the single worst experience of my life?"

"Our lives."

"Fine, go ahead. But don't expect me to stand in line to buy a copy of something I dream about every single time I close my eyes."

Daniel stood, placed the empty glass down on the nearby side table, and gathered his belongings.

"You're right. I shouldn't have come."

He strode over to the one window that overlooked the duplicate apartment building forty feet across the way. "Great view," he sneered sarcastically.

Sean couldn't help but laugh.

"I'm sorry," Daniel said. "For everything." He put his hand on the doorknob.

"Heading home already?"

"No. I'm working my way to California. I have a meeting with a publisher in Los Angeles."

Sean padded his way across the room and met Daniel at the door. "Look, I just had to get that outta my system. Write about whatever you want."

"Thanks. Means more to me than you know."

Daniel flipped the latches on all four deadbolts and opened the door. Together, they stood at the threshold. The buzzing, fluorescent light above cast them both in a pallid and sickly light.

"I really should go."

"You got a draft yet?"

Daniel reached into his bag and pulled out a thick packet of about three hundred sheets of printer paper held together with a binder clip.

Sean took it from him. The weight in his hands was impressive. He'd never felt a raw manuscript before. He thumbed through the pages before focusing on the very first one at the top of the pile. It had just one word on it: Untitled.

"No title?"

"Not yet. Read it. If you think of one, let me know."

"Well, if this writing thing doesn't work out, at least you can always fall back on—you know—being a doctor."

"I burnt out. Needed to get away. It's not about healing anymore. Everything is sickness and death and shielding what this thing really does to people when they get it."

Sean was dumbstruck. One of the critical reasons he'd left town was that people wouldn't stop asking him how he or anyone with that kind of skill could turn their back on it. He understood better than anyone.

"You know," Daniel said, "I lied."

"About what?"

"I don't have any meeting with a publisher. I've been carrying this stack of pages around for weeks. There's no book deal.

"Two months back, I came across this Writer's Digest in a bookstore. Thought never crossed my mind before. Then one night, I started writing—you know, after the therapist— and for three straight weeks, it just poured out of me."

They stood awkwardly. Outside, there was a low rumble of thunder. It shook Sean back to reality. He looked down at the manuscript in his hands and offered a half smile.

"Think Kate would have liked it?"

Daniel looked at him and returned the smile wanly. There was the faint appearance of wetness in his eyes.

"I'd like to think so," he said. "She always did like those scary stories."

"Good," he said.

"Keep sending those Christmas cards."

★★★★★

They said their goodbyes. Daniel left.

The sky was full dark, no stars. After Daniel was gone, Sean locked up and pulled the blinds closed, but left on all the lights. He always went to bed with them on. He placed the manuscript at the bottom of one of his dresser drawers, beneath the darned pairs of socks. *Not yet,* he thought.

At the foot of his bed was a suitcase. It was packed should he need to split in the middle of the night. He fell asleep on top of the covers, fully clothed, hadn't even managed to kick off his shoes. He dreamed terrible dreams. In one, he was standing on the deck of a ship. The beautiful, haunting face of Kate White kept rushing by in an endless tape loop, and she was screaming.

There was a storm coming. He could feel it.

Lightning Source UK Ltd.
Milton Keynes UK
UKHW012145250422
402022UK00003B/691